THE MADNESS
OF MERCURY

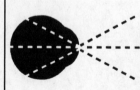

This Large Print Book carries the
Seal of Approval of N.A.V.H.

A ZODIAC MYSTERY

THE MADNESS OF MERCURY

CONNIE DI MARCO

WHEELER PUBLISHING
A part of Gale, Cengage Learning

GALE
CENGAGE Learning®

Farmington Hills, Mich • San Francisco • New York • Waterville, Maine
Meriden, Conn • Mason, Ohio • Chicago

GALE
CENGAGE Learning®

LIBRARY OF CONGRESS CATALOGING-IN-PUBLICATION DATA

Names: Di Marco, Connie, 1945– author.
Title: The madness of Mercury : a zodiac mystery / by Connie di Marco.
Description: Large print edition. | Waterville, Maine : Wheeler Publishing, 2017. | Series: Wheeler Publishing large print cozy mystery
Identifiers: LCCN 2016051248| ISBN 9781410497987 (softcover) | ISBN 1410497984 (softcover)
Subjects: LCSH: Astrologers—Fiction. | Large type books. | GSAFD: Mystery fiction.
Classification: LCC PS3604.I116 M33 2017 | DDC 813/.6—dc23
LC record available at https://lccn.loc.gov/2016051248

Published in 2017 by arrangement with Midnight Ink, an imprint of Llewellyn Publications, Woodbury, MN 55125-2989 USA

Printed in the United States of America
1 2 3 4 5 6 7 21 20 19 18 17

For Marguerite Summers
1922–2016

ACKNOWLEDGMENTS

Many thanks to Paige Wheeler of Creative Media Agency, Inc. for her hard work, good advice, and expertise, and to Terri Bischoff, Sandy Sullivan, Katie Mickschl, Teresa Pojar, Ellen Lawson, Mary Ann Lasher-Dodge, and the entire team at Midnight Ink for welcoming the Zodiac Mysteries to their home.

Special thanks as well to my writers' group and first readers — Kim Fay, Laurie Stevens, Cheryl Brughelli, Don Fedosiuk, and Paula Freedman — for their critiques and encouragement.

I would be remiss if I didn't say thank you to Llewellyn Publications for all the wonderful astrology books they've published over the years. Without that esoteric knowledge, this series would never have been created.

Last, but certainly not least, thanks to my family and my wonderful husband for their tolerance in living with a woman who is constantly thinking about murder.

There are those among us who prey, who hunt under the guise of trust. They kill not just the physical body but the psyche, the dream of the soul. They are the clever ones, the dexterous and silver-tongued. They sway the weak, the old, the gullible, and the infirm. They are the tricksters of the universe and work through enchantment.

They are ruled by Mercury, a god of great cunning, a thief and a prowler. Having no place of his own, Mercury was given rulership of borders, secret passageways, and crossroads where suicides are buried. He alone escorted souls to the underworld because only he could move freely in the world above and the world below. In our time, he leads unwary travelers astray to meet their own twisted shadow in the dark night.

It was a new client whose predicament recalled this mythology to me. My name is

Julia Bonatti — Julia Elizabeth Bonatti — and I'm an astrologer. For too long, I had worked with practical daylight interpretations of the natal chart. For too long, I had happily delineated charts concerned with mundane issues. *What's the best time to plan our trip? When should I invest? I've thought of returning to school, can I afford it?* It was Evandra Gamble and her family and the events surrounding them that indelibly marked me, that caused me to know the dark side of the god.

ONE

Long fingers gripped my wrist with a surprising strength. "She's trying to kill me." A network of veins on Evandra's hand bulged like blue worms burrowing under the dry parchment of her flesh. Evandra Gamble was the elderly aunt of my longtime client, Dorothy Sanger, the very *she* to whom Evandra referred.

I straightened in my chair. "You can't mean that."

"Hah!" Evandra replied. "You think you know her? My charming niece? Believe me, you don't!" Her face shifted. Her watery blue eyes held my gaze. "I am afraid, Julia." Her voice quavered. "Please help me. That's why I needed you to come here today for my reading." Her grip on my wrist tightened.

I sighed inwardly. I've formed a few rules over the course of my practice — number one is that my clients come to *me* for read-

11

ings. For professional reasons, it's important that I work on my own turf. If a client is new, or not referred by someone I know well, I might arrange for a private room at the Mystic Eye, an occult shop in North Beach owned by my friend Gale.

Today, I was breaking that rule. Evandra was on the verge of turning ninety and had suffered a fractured hip. She was on the mend, but mobility was still difficult. Dorothy had asked me to visit the rambling house on Telegraph Hill for her aunt's sake. I complied, imagining my new client's questions would fall in the category of health or decisions over her final wishes. I certainly never expected Evandra to accuse her own flesh and blood of murder.

"Dorothy's devoted to you. She's taken a leave from nursing to stay here with you. Why do you say that?" I replied with disbelief.

Evandra's eyes shifted and grew wary; her expression closed. She sniffed. "I hoped that you of all people would listen and believe me." She released my hand. Her arm was frail, as if muscle had separated from bone. Her thin shoulders and collarbone looked as light and hollow as a bird's. She slumped back against the flowered cushions on the large armchair and closed her eyes.

Evandra's natal Sun and Mercury were under the sway of a Neptune transit. I knew she'd be physically depleted, her normal energy sapped. She was an elderly woman recovering from a fracture, and I was concerned. Neptune's effect on her Mercury, the planet related to mental acuity, could cause confusion, perhaps even delusions. Was the Neptune transit signaling the start of some form of elder senility? I just wasn't certain.

"Please believe me, Evandra. Your thinking is affected during this time."

"You mean you think I'm losing it, don't you?" She glanced at me sharply.

"No. I don't think that. But anyone, at any age, would be affected. Please, please reserve judgment, especially of Dorothy, until this time period is over?" I watched her carefully, not sure how to put my fears into words. "There is another thing I should mention. Illnesses can be extremely difficult to diagnose under this planet's transit." I didn't want to frighten her, but I had to be as honest as possible. "One worry is that you could have an adverse reaction to medication."

She pursed her lips and continued to stare at me, an expression I was sure was designed to engender guilt. My answer hadn't satisfied her. I mentally reviewed my work on her chart. Had I missed anything? Was it my own insecurity? Or was I just being guilted?

"I'll tell you what. I'll have a further look and check your lunar returns for the next couple of months. The lunar return chart describes the current month, based on the Moon's return to its natal position, and I'll see if there's a period of time during this transit that's more threatening."

"My niece is your client. You have her chart, don't you?"

"Yes. Of course."

"Have a look at that too. Please. Before it's too late."

I couldn't respond. The thought that Dorothy would ever harm her aunt was outrageous and unthinkable. The woman *I* knew was a highly regarded and experienced nurse. She had devoted her life to taking care of people. And now she had put her work on hold to care for her aunts — Evandra and her younger sister, Eunice.

Evandra sat forward in her seat. "I need Luis. Can you fetch him, dear? Just pull that tassel over there." She pointed to a length of cord near the canopy bed that undoubtedly connected to a series of bells below.

I rose and passed by the window. Luis was

14

below in the garden, trimming a hedge. He was the sisters' valet, gardener, chauffeur, and all-around gofer. A short man, thickly built, with graying hair, he maintained a gentle and long-suffering demeanor as he was called upon often for any number of odd jobs.

"Damn and blast this hip." Evandra fidgeted in her chair. "I hate being so helpless."

I pushed open the casement window and waved to Luis. He nodded and wiped his brow with a red bandanna, holding up a calloused finger to indicate he'd be upstairs in a moment.

"Old age is not for sissies, Julia." She grimaced in pain. "Why, when I was young, I could party, as they say, with the best of them."

Luis arrived a few moments later and knocked. I hurried to the door and opened it.

"There you are, Luis." Evandra raised her arms. "Help me to the bed." He lifted Evandra's slender form with ease and deposited her gently on the large bed, then covered her with a crocheted quilt. Her complexion had grown pale.

"I'll be working on the back lawn, miss. But you pull the cord if you need help. Miss Dorothy can call me."

"Thank you, Luis. Please tell that niece of mine to stop baking and do something useful around here. For all we know, she's slipping arsenic into those blasted cookies she's always making."

"I will tell her, miss." Luis smiled and winked at me as he shut the door behind him.

Evandra leaned her head back and pulled the quilt up to cover her arms. "I have to rest now, dear. Will you come see me again?"

"I'll stop by again, if you like. Perhaps tomorrow."

"Thank you." She sighed heavily and closed her eyes.

I had been dismissed. I gathered up my notes and charts and stepped softly across the heavily draped bedroom and pulled the solid oak door shut behind me.

The second floor hallway was dim, lined with dark wood wainscoting and lit only by a few wall sconces leading to the top of a curving staircase. A stained-glass window filtered outside light onto the landing. It was only mid-afternoon, but the sky had grown dark, muting the brilliant reds and blues of the window. Heavy Pacific storms were closing in from the north and San Francisco would be buffeted by wind and rain through the holidays.

16

At the foot of the stairs, I called to Dorothy. She didn't answer but a sweet and toasty aroma filled the foyer. I followed the short hallway toward the rear of the house and pushed through the swinging door to the kitchen. At the other end of the room, a wall of windows overlooked the back garden, and beyond that lay a view of the city and the bay to the north. Black clouds, roiling and heavy with rain, were visible beyond the Golden Gate and the Marin headlands. The storm would hit within a few hours.

Dorothy worked at the center island, kneading dough, a full-length white apron tied over her loose slacks and long-sleeved red sweater. She looked up and smiled.

"How did it go with the Dowager Queen?"

I laughed. "Fine . . . I guess."

Dorothy saw the expression on my face. "What's wrong?"

I pulled a stool up to the island, watching Dorothy knead and slap her dough. That's when I broke rule number two: *never talk about a client's reading.*

"I have to ask you something."

Dorothy stopped her work, wiping flour-coated hands on a dishtowel.

"Has there been any hint of senility or psychosis? Medically, I mean."

Dorothy looked puzzled for a moment.

"I've worked with a lot of elderly patients. It certainly happens. They can be perfectly normal their whole life, but with age, do the strangest things."

"Such as?"

"Oh . . ." Dorothy trailed off. "Imagining that someone's stealing their money, or draining their bank accounts. One man I cared for filled his living room with stacks of newspapers floor to ceiling. Don't ask me what that's about, but it does happen. Why? What did she say to you?"

I didn't have the heart to repeat Evandra's fears. I'd known Dorothy for a couple of years, had nursed her through marital problems and a current separation from her husband, and had come to like and respect her. I looked at her open face and the concerned look in her eyes and decided for once to keep my mouth shut — or at least practice the tact that Sagittarians are not famous for. "She seems to have a great level of fear and believes that she's in danger."

"I can't imagine why." Dorothy brushed a strand of hair from her forehead with the back of her hand. "She couldn't be safer. She'll probably potter along for several more years. When she's able to get around, I can go back to work. She has Eunice living here. We have our housekeeper, Alba.

The poor woman has her hands full taking care of this mausoleum. And Gudrun, their companion, also lives in. And I plan to have a nurse stop by every day for a while, maybe a long while. We'll see."

"Tough on you."

"Oh, I'm used to it. It's just harder when it's your own family. If Richard and I were still together . . ." Dorothy trailed off. "He's called a few times lately, but . . ."

I waited, careful to gauge her emotional state. Personally, I was glad Dorothy had separated from her controlling husband. I couldn't exactly say that to her, but I was relieved she was getting back on her feet.

She took a deep breath. "But we're not together." She smiled ruefully. "You're young, Julia. It's hard for you to understand."

I understood all right. Death had taken away my options, but this wasn't the time to remind her. "Not that young."

Dorothy looked at me. "You know, all the time I've known you, I've never asked how old you are."

"Thirty-six."

"See? That's young." She smiled. "I was going to say, if we were still together I suppose I wouldn't feel as free to be staying up here, keeping an eye on everything. And I'm only here till Evandra's up and about. So, everything works out for the best, I suppose."

Dorothy sprinkled some flour from a small glass bowl over the wooden cutting board and returned to kneading the dough. "She's definitely stronger every day, but she can't be on her own. You haven't met Eunice yet, have you? The baby of the family. She's only eighty-seven." Dorothy chuckled. "Gudrun keeps an eye on her too. And then, the renovations."

"I noticed. What's that about?"

"It's the conservatory. Evandra finally agreed to do something about it. There's dry rot around the window frames; most of them need replacing. This is such an old house and I've been worried. My aunts really haven't been up to keeping on top of maintenance and repairs, so I figured this was the best time to have it done. I just hope it'll be finished by the time I'm ready to get back to my own life."

As if in response to Dorothy's explanation, I heard a power saw rev up from a distance at the far end of the house.

"That's them now. We hired an architect to oversee the contractors. Some of the plumbing in the conservatory needs to be replaced too. But the architect's great with these old houses, and his crew can pretty much come and go through the garden at the side of the house without disturbing us very much." Dorothy spread her dough carefully over the board.

An apple and cinnamon mixture was warming on the stove top and my stomach was reminding me I hadn't eaten since breakfast. "What are you making?" I asked.

"Apple pastries, little turnovers. I make them every Christmas. My aunts love them. I thought it might cheer Evandra up, especially . . ." The sound of a gasoline-powered mower drowned out the rest of Dorothy's response. She glanced toward the windows. "Damn. What's he doing?"

"The carpenter?"

"No. Luis." Dorothy walked to the windows and peered out into the garden. "He probably wants to finish the lawn before the rain starts."

A low stone wall formed the perimeter of the back garden, delineating an edge where the ground dropped off to a steep cliff marked with rocky outcroppings. I joined Dorothy at the window and followed her line of sight. The power mower was running, unattended, and butting against the stone wall. A red bandanna hung from the vibrating handlebar of the machine.

Dorothy looked puzzled. "He shouldn't leave that thing like that. Where did he get off to?" She tossed her dishtowel on the table, heaved a sigh, and opened the back door to the garden.

"Luis . . . Luis," she called.

I followed her out the door and joined her on the lawn. The wind was whipping fiercely across the hillside and the sky had grown even darker. In the distance, the sea churned black in the bay. Dorothy's apron billowed like a sail in the wind. She strode purposefully across the grass to the mower and hit the control, silencing the monster. She turned her head to speak to me and hesitated, then turned back and peered over the low wall. Something had caught her eye. She was still for a moment and then took two steps backward.

"What is it, Dorothy?"

Her face had drained of color. "It's Luis. He's down there." Her voice quivered. "I think he's dead."

Two

The rough stones of the perimeter wall stood only knee high. I leaned over carefully, fighting vertigo, and looked down. Luis's body lay on an outcropping of rock perhaps twenty feet below, his sightless eyes staring up at the darkening sky. His leg was bent at an extreme angle and a small pool of blood surrounded his head.

Dorothy was frozen in place, staring at his body. I pulled her back from the edge, resisting the feeling that the ground might collapse under us and send us both careening down the hillside. I grasped her shoulders and led her into the kitchen. She sat heavily on the stool I had just vacated. She'd seen plenty of death in her working life, but none so close to home.

"What the hell happened, Julia?" Dorothy looked more confused than horrified.

"I'll call 911. You stay right here."

■ ■ ■ ■

Several hours later, the paramedics, fire trucks, and police drove back down the hill toward North Beach. Fortunately Gudrun, the sisters' companion, had kept Eunice in her quarters. Evandra, sedated with a pill for pain, slept through the chaos, blissfully unaware of Luis's death. The coroner was noncommittal, except to say that the fall most probably killed the gardener, but it wouldn't be ruled accidental until the autopsy was complete. The real question was how did a man who was familiar with the terrain tumble over a low wall?

"I've told them time and time again to do something about that wall," Dorothy said. "It's just too low, especially now that the rains have washed away some of the hillside and vegetation." Telegraph Hill had been compromised since the mid-1800s, when sailing ships quarried rock from the Bay side of the hill to use as ballast. Several years ago, heavy rains had caused a mudslide, destroying and burying buildings below. The Gamble house was built on solid bedrock — a very desirable thing in earthquake territory, but I had to agree with Dorothy about the low wall.

24

"They need to build that up or replace it with a tall wrought-iron fence. They're elderly ladies — either one of them could have toppled over. My God!" Dorothy cried.

The apple mixture on the stove had hardened to a dry mass. The turnovers were forgotten. I was nibbling on a piece of toast and sipping a cup of strong tea that Dorothy had fixed.

"Julia, thanks for staying with me."

"I couldn't very well leave you with this."

"I'm just heartbroken. We know his family. He's worked for my aunts for more than twenty years."

My heart sank, imagining a family's grief. Sudden, unexpected death. The cruelest blow of all.

"I knew he had some heart trouble, but . . . could he have had an attack and lost his balance?" Dorothy ran her fingers through her thick strawberry-blond hair and slumped into a chair. "I suppose I should put that mower away in the shed before it rains."

"Stay here. I'll take care of it." The storm that had seemed so imminent had mercifully held off, making the job of removing Luis's body from the cliffside easier. Paramedics had pushed the mower several feet away from the spot where we had found it.

Struggling with the ungainly beast in the soft grass, I managed to turn it around and wheel it to the small room attached to the garage. I lifted and pushed the mower over the doorstep into an empty corner. An overhead light bulb illuminated the space. Various gardening tools were attached to one wall, all cleaned and oiled. A container of screwdrivers and small wrenches sat on a rough wooden workbench. Several photos were pinned to the wall above the bench: a wedding snapshot of a smiling young couple, and school photos of a dark-haired boy and girl. Somewhere in the city right now, Luis's family would be receiving the news of his death.

I had visited Dorothy at the house a few times over the last couple of weeks. That's when I'd first met Evandra and had seen Luis, always working. Earlier today, he'd been trimming the boxwood hedges at the front of the house. I'd called out to him while I waited at the front door, and he'd responded with a smile and a wave of his hedge clippers.

His jacket hung on a hook next to the door above an extra pair of well-used work boots. I didn't see the wide-brimmed hat he always wore when he was working outside. I wondered if it had fallen to the bottom of the cliff. I untied the red bandanna from the handle of the mower and hung it next to his jacket. A kitchen mug and a small plate sprinkled with crumbs sat on the workbench. I picked them up and, turning off the light, locked the door behind me. Returning to the kitchen, I dumped the dishes in a tub of hot water in the sink. Dorothy was still seated on the stool, staring into space.

I squeezed her hand. "If you'd like, I can stop by tomorrow."

She looked up. "I'd appreciate that, Julia. I've got to tell my aunts. And I want to reach his family somehow this evening, if it's possible. They'll be devastated." Dorothy quickly wiped her eyes with a corner of her apron. "I'm devastated."

She pushed herself away from the table and stood. I slipped on my jacket as Dorothy followed me through the swinging door to the front hallway. She opened one side of the massive oak entrance and stood watching as I hurried to my car. The sky had grown completely dark. Storm clouds blotted out any possible view of moon or stars. With luck, I'd get home before the rain hit and if I was really lucky, I'd beat the worst of rush-hour traffic.

My apartment is a small flat on the second

floor of a duplex out on the "Avenues," north of Golden Gate Park in an area known as the Outer Richmond. I rarely see my downstairs neighbors, so I feel as if I have the building to myself most of the time. It's fog central and I love it. Many days are bright, sunny, and windy, but so close to the Pacific, the fog rolls in every afternoon like clockwork. Temperatures in San Francisco are always cool and vary so little that it's sometimes difficult to tell February from July, except July can be even colder.

I was overjoyed to reach home. My haven is small, only four rooms, but I have a great rent and a street-level garage to park my car. I'm several blocks from the ocean on one side and in the other direction, a short walk to the Golden Gate straits. Originally this western part of the city was nothing but miles of sand dunes over bedrock with too much fog, the entire area considered undesirable and uninhabitable, ignored until population explosion forced development. Some San Franciscans turn their collective nose up at this part of town because of the wind and the fog, but I can't imagine living anywhere else. My neighborhood may not be Nob Hill or Pacific Heights, but I have the ocean and the sound of foghorns to lull me to sleep at night.

The deluge began just as I pulled up to my building. I hit the garage opener, waited for the door to rise, and drove in. Grabbing my briefcase and purse, I hurried through the door at the back of the garage and climbed the wooden steps to my kitchen. Rummaging for my keys, I managed to get the door unlocked with one hand while holding my case over my head with the other. I flipped on the kitchen light. Wizard, my cat, sat at attention next to his food tray, waiting patiently for my return.

"Wiz." I reached down to scratch his ears. "I know. I'm late. It's been a very rough day." Rainwater dripped off my jacket onto his fur. He meowed and backed away from me, circling around my feet to take up another position close to his bowl. A big hint. "Okay. I get the message." Wizard is completely black and weighs close to twenty pounds. He does his best to converse with me and has a large vocabulary of meows, purrs, and quacks to let me know what's on his mind.

I shrugged out of my jacket and hung it on a hook in the laundry room, kicked off my shoes, and dropped my case and purse on top of the washer. Wizard rubbed his head forcefully against my leg and quacked several times to chide me for being late for dinner and to thank me for finally coming home. Would he still love me if I couldn't operate the can opener? I plunked a fresh can of Fancy Beast into his bowl. He dove in and ignored me to seriously focus on his dinner.

I was famished and the apartment was freezing. I turned the thermostat up and dug a container of split pea soup out of the refrigerator. I'm not much of a cook. My parents died when I was young and I was raised by my grandmother, Gloria, who took care of all that. I was always too much on the go to be fussing in the kitchen. Since then, I've managed to figure out how to make soup. My nod to domesticity.

Gusts of wind and rain were beating against the windows. I closed the drapes in the living room to block out the storm and lit a few candles on the mantel. I got a fire started and by the time I'd devoured my soup, the apartment had warmed. I pulled on a pair of jeans, fuzzy slippers, and a heavy sweater and settled in by the fire, a notepad and my laptop on the coffee table. I needed to catch up with the work that, under normal circumstances, I would have handled today. I also wanted to keep my promise to Evandra by checking her lunar returns for the next couple of months. Images of Luis lying on the rocks below kept flashing before my eyes. I'd known the man only slightly, but I was sure his death would affect the sisters a great deal.

My private clientele keeps me fairly busy, but thanks to Don Forrester, my old friend from college days who works at the *Chronicle,* I met Lester Bartley, an editor who convinced me to do a weekly column of astrological advice. The *AskZodia* feature had become a greater success than anyone anticipated. Don jump-started the column with fake birth dates and outrageous problems, and the newspaper was soon receiving more and more letters and emails every day.

Samantha, Les's editorial assistant, routinely screens emails and letters, weeds out the cranks, and then sends the lot to me. For the ones I don't have time to answer, she returns a form response with a list of ethical local astrologers who might welcome more business. I'm thrilled to have the additional income to tide me over slow times, like now, with the holidays approaching. But I was starting to worry. I was afraid I had created a monster that would eat up my time and interfere with my private clients.

The odd thing is, I never set out to be an astrologer. I have a master's degree in anthropology from San Francisco State. That's where I met Michael, my fiancé. We had both planned on teaching careers and a life together. Those plans were crushed when Michael was struck down in a hit-and-run accident in front of his apartment building. The driver was never found. That was two years ago.

Once the slow acceptance of Michael's death hardened in my mind, I slid into a long depression. Exhaustion dogged my steps. Days and weeks passed in which I stared at the ceiling and the walls of my bedroom until the hard surfaces seemed to breathe like a living thing. I couldn't stand the sympathy I saw in everyone's eyes. What little energy I had, I used to convince everyone I was fine. I only wanted to be left alone to mourn the life I had lost.

One morning I woke and realized the pain wasn't gone, but it had lessened. I was a long way from lighthearted, but I was alive and knew I wanted to live. I cleaned out every drawer, closet, and cubbyhole. I packed the remnants of my former life in a large cardboard box and taped it firmly shut. I gave away all that was superfluous. My Sunset District apartment near the university held too many memories. I gave notice to my landlord and found my cur-

rent digs north of the Park near the foghorns. And, for lack of a better idea, I took
a job at a law firm downtown just to make
ends meet. It was during that time, while
browsing through a bookstore, that I came
across my first astrology book. Something
clicked. I read it avidly. I collected more
books and began to study. I gathered data
and set up charts. I practiced on friends or
anyone who would talk to me. It was the
loneliest time of my life, but everything that
exists now grew out of that cauldron. Astrology offered a lens through which I hoped to
make sense of my own loss. I still study Michael's chart, searching for some sign that
might have saved him. I haven't found any
answers, but it's never far from my mind.

Evandra's chart was on the screen. I
clicked the button that would generate a
lunar return. The current Neptune transit
came into even sharper focus. I didn't like
what I was seeing. Perhaps Evandra wasn't
suffering from senile dementia at all. Perhaps she truly was in danger, although I
found it difficult to believe that Dorothy
could be the culprit.

I jumped when the phone rang. The
display said *private caller.* Had to be Gale.

"Hey."

"What are you up to?"

"Not much. Working on a chart, then I have to get some Zodia questions done."

"Where the hell have you been? You don't call. I don't hear from you. Do I have to email Zodia to get your attention?"

Gale is my closest friend. We met at the Mystic Eye. I was browsing for astrology books while she was busy promoting her new business, now the most popular metaphysical shop in the state. She was right. I had been ignoring her messages. Translated, she was really asking if I was depressed. I haven't dated since Michael's death. The holidays were upon us, my grandmother was away on a cruise, and I was truly an orphan this season.

"I'm fine. Really."

"Okay," she responded hesitantly. "So you can't return a phone call?"

"I'm sorry. You're right. It's been a weird time. My regular clients always disappear during the holidays and the Zodia column's eating up my time. Mercury's retrograde, and it's the last quarter of the moon . . ." I trailed off.

"Oh, of course, that explains it," she replied sarcastically. "But didn't you say you had a couple of new clients lined up this week?"

"Today in fact. But that's . . . uh . . . that

was fine, but it ended rather badly." I filled Gale in on the events of the afternoon at the Gamble house.

"Cripes! Which one is their house?"

"You know it, I'm sure. It's huge, the dark brick one on the left side as you go up toward Coit Tower."

"Ah." Gale was silent for a moment. "What caused the fall?"

"They're thinking he might have had a heart attack, but no final word as yet. Luis was slightly overweight and supposedly had a mild heart condition. What's odd is that he's worked there for years. He was very familiar with the grounds. But the police wouldn't talk to us at all." I sighed. "That's all I know."

"Julia, why didn't you call me? I was right down the hill at the Eye. I could've buzzed up."

"I honestly didn't even think of it. I'm really okay, but I feel just awful for Dorothy. Trying to cope with her two aunts and that house and having that happen. And then she's recently separated from her husband."

"Listen, you do sound kind of down. The reason I called — what are you doing for the holidays?"

"Haven't given it a thought. Gloria's away

and I still haven't done any shopping. Kuan invited me to a Buddhist ceremony. I think he wanted to make sure I wasn't alone." Kuan Lee is my grandmother's close friend, who has lived in the first floor apartment of her house in North Beach for as long as I can remember. He's an herbalist and practices Chinese medicine and acupuncture. He's the closest thing I have to a grandfather and I love him dearly.

"Well, it's up to you. But Cheryl wants to cook a big dinner." Cheryl is our other close friend who manages the Mystic Eye. "I was thinking we could do it at my place, just the three of us, since we're all orphans this year anyway."

That surprised me. Gale usually has a round of posh catered parties to attend over the holidays. "Is that what *you're* up for?"

"Yes. I'm socialed out. I'd love to just be with close friends and not go running all over hell this year."

"Best invitation I've had. What can I bring?"

"Nothing. Just bring yourself. Cheryl wants to do everything. She's having an attackus domesticus. You and I can get pleasantly buzzed and watch her run around the kitchen. It'll be fun."

I laughed. "You're on. I'll give you a call

later this week." We said goodbye and made girlfriend kissy noises through the phone.

Wizard had curled into a fetal position on top of a fuzzy throw close to the fireplace. The wind was buffeting the windows so hard the rain sounded like gravel being thrown against the glass. The logs were blazing and I thanked my stars I could snuggle inside tonight with Wizard and work.

Samantha had forwarded about fifty emails from the newspaper to my private *AskZodia* email address. Since it was a weekly column, there was space for only three or four questions and answers, but now Les was considering running *AskZodia* as a daily feature. I knew I wouldn't be able to handle that kind of volume, but I was sure other astrologers might be open to filling in and perhaps even taking over if I became too busy. I wanted to choose eight emails from this batch, just to make sure I was ahead of my deadlines. To keep the column interesting to as large a group of readers as possible, I like to pick a range of ages and problems.

My first pick was a letter from an older man forced into retirement.

Dear Zodia
I've worked as a bookkeeper in the

corporate world my entire life. I'm 65 and my company forced me to retire. I'm in decent shape financially. I have a good pension and savings, but I don't know what to do with myself. I've tried to find part-time work but no luck. I've never felt so lost and useless. Do you see any kind of work on the horizon for me? My birth date is May 4, 1944 at 10:43 p.m. in Baltimore.

— Discarded

Poor guy. Worked his whole life and now shoved aside. The man's birth chart showed Venus as the oriental planet — that is, the planet rising first before the Sun, a position that can sometimes offer a strong clue to the profession. This man was a natural artist, perhaps a craftsman, with his Mars in Virgo. He was someone with artistic yearnings and capable of patient, detailed work.

Dear Discarded:
Your *true* artistic abilities have never been recognized, much less nourished. A whole new world can open up for you if you pursue some form of craftsmanship to produce beautiful things. Jewelry design, working in precious metals, is just one possibility that comes to mind.

Please take some classes, perhaps at a local university extension and try your hand. I think you'll be amazed at your abilities and imagination. Believe me, you won't look back.

— Zodia

I opened a few more emails and moved a bunch into a folder to consider later. Ones that I felt were not terribly interesting, I set aside to be returned to Sam for her form letter referring the writers to other astrologers. I worked through several more questions and responses and then saved them all. This was hardly a perfect way to practice astrology, but hopefully my quick judgments and answers would be spot on and help someone head in the right direction. I clicked back to the inbox and realized three more emails had arrived while I was working.

I didn't recognize the various senders. I'd set up my *AskZodia* address only for Samantha, but these new emails weren't from her. My private clients use *Julia.Bonatti,* and my friends use *JuliaB.* None of them would even know of my *AskZodia* address. I hesitated. I'm a hopeless non-techie person but rely on my computer for business, so I'm very fearful of viruses. I clicked to open the first email and scrolled down. A jolt of fear shot through me. The message read, *"Thou shalt not suffer a witch to live."*

THREE

The other two emails were along the same Biblical lines: "*In my name shall they cast out devils.* Luke 16:17," and "*Neither shall ye use enchantment nor observe times.* Leviticus 19:26."

A cold knot formed in my stomach. Someone very crazy had figured out my *AskZodia* email address. Someone who wasn't Samantha. I reached for the phone automatically and then realized how late it was. The *Chronicle* office had closed hours ago and I didn't have Sam's home number. I'd have to wait till morning.

My knowledge of Biblical lore is really nonexistent. I had no clue about the context of these quotes; however, the message was clear. Someone considered me a witch and thought my work was the work of the devil. I wondered if the newspaper had received similar missives that Sam hadn't passed on. Crazy letters along these lines might have come in but she hadn't wanted to tell me. I'd ask her tomorrow. She might have thought they would upset me, and she'd be right. But this was different. This was my own personal email.

Should I delete them? Should I save them in a folder? Block them? Had someone sent me a virus? Something very hateful had invaded my home via computer. I finally decided to delete them from my inbox and trash. I shivered involuntarily. What creeped me out was the fact that they came from different senders. I stared at the blank screen. Maybe I'd done that too fast. Maybe I should at least have made a note of the senders' addresses.

I heaved a sigh and closed my laptop. I put Evandra's notes in her folder and straightened up the living room. The fire had turned to embers and Wizard was still curled up on the throw. I made sure the front and back doors were locked and bolted and padded down the hall to bed. I shed my clothes, slid under the covers, and turned on the electric blanket. The rain still drummed heavily outside. Wizard followed me and climbed onto the bed, curling up in a ball next to me. I picked up my new book on eclipses and managed to read a paragraph before I went unconscious, the lamp still lit.

The next morning I woke, groggy, with a crick in my neck. The events of the day before came flooding back. I tried to push the image of Luis's body being raised from the cliffside out of my head. It wasn't working. Groaning, I climbed out of bed and rummaged in the closet for my leopard print flip-flops and my thrift shop Chinese robe and stumbled out to the kitchen, desperate for coffee. I know. I'm an addict and I really don't care. I put the pot on to boil, thinking I should probably break down and buy one of those coffeemakers that can be set up the night before. The problem with that is I'd have to remember to fill it with water and coffee and push the button. A big assumption. Wizard circled my legs and waited patiently while I scooped food into his dish. When the coffee was ready, I filled a mug and added some half and half. I needed caffeine. I had more work to do and a new client coming today.

I peeked out the window above the sink. The rain had stopped, but there'd be more. The temperature had dropped radically during the night and the steam from the boiling kettle had fogged the windows. Wizard climbed onto my lap as soon as I sat down and, stretching his paws, kneaded furiously at my robe as I downed my coffee. The thought of returning to the Gamble house depressed me, but I had promised Dorothy and Evandra I'd come back.

When the caffeine finally hit, I gently urged Wizard off my lap. I pulled my mop of unruly hair up with an elastic band and jumped in the shower. After dressing, I straightened up the apartment and shut the damper in the fireplace to keep the heat from escaping.

The emails from the night before still preyed on my mind. I checked the clock. It wasn't nine yet, but Samantha sometimes arrived at the office early. I dialed her number. She answered on the first ring.

"Julia! Hi. What's up?"

"Listen, Sam, you didn't give my *Ask-Zodia* email address to anyone, did you?"

"No! Of course not. No one at all. Why do you ask?"

"I got a few really strange emails last night."

"Strange? What did they say?"

I repeated the Biblical phrases as best I could. "I didn't write down exactly what they said. I just looked at them and then I deleted them."

"Creepy!" She sighed.

"More than one. All three came from different addresses."

"Did *you* give your address to anyone?"

"No. I only use it for you, for the column."

"I don't know what to say. We have your contact info in the Payroll Department, your home address and phone and your *AskZodia* email, but I don't imagine anyone there would give it out. The emails I send to you are all forwarded from the *AskZodia* address at the *Chronicle*. The only thing I can think of is that someone took the words 'Ask Zodia' and tried different service providers till they found one that worked."

"You screen the emails that come in. Have you seen anything similar before?"

"No. Nothing threatening or strange at all. A lot of them are meandering and don't really have a question. I just send the standard response. You know, 'We receive many more requests than we can possibly answer, but are happy to refer you to . . . blah, blah, blah.' "

"Well, I just wanted you to know. Hopefully the only thing they have is my email address."

"Maybe you should set up a new one for me to use."

"Good idea. I'll do that. I don't want to

use the one I give to my regular clients, though. Do me a favor and don't write it down anywhere, okay?"

"I promise. What's it gonna be?"

"How about *astrochat*. Same service provider. Don't use the word 'Zodia' anywhere."

"I'll remember. So, everything I send you will go to *astrochat* from now on."

"You can tell Les, but no one else, and I'll cancel the *AskZodia* account.

"Maybe you shouldn't do that, Julia. If this becomes more of a problem, the police can trace the emails. It takes a while, but I know they can do that. So maybe it's better to keep it active. Just don't read any of that crazy stuff."

"Easier said than done. But you're right."

"Julia, I'm really sorry. I don't like the idea there could be a leak from our end. Stay in touch, though, and let me know if you get any more."

We hung up and I placed a call to Don at his office next. It was too early to expect him to be there, but I left a message for him to call me as soon as he arrived. I made another cup of coffee and settled back in to work. There were all kinds of freaks in the world. I couldn't let them get to me.

I hoped to squeeze a few more letters in

for the column before my client arrived. I skimmed through and finally chose some others that offered a good range of problems.

Dear Zodia —
I hope you can help me. I was born at 3:15 a.m. on October 3, 1978. My husband was born March 4, 1976. We were married only last year. Over the last few months, his behavior has changed, and the last few weeks, it's much worse. He's threatened suicide and I'm worried sick. What should I do?
— Panicked in Petaluma

I groaned. *Panicked* shouldn't be wasting time writing to Zodia! She needed to find a shrink in a big hurry.

Dear Panicked:
Threats should be taken very seriously. Immediately speak to your doctor or your local hospital about getting help for your husband. Also, talk to anyone at the suicide prevention hotlines. They might be able to give you some guidance. This is a time for intervention. His natal chart shows very adverse aspects to his Sun sign, indicating a lack of

parental support in childhood, possibly even abuse. He's suffering from feelings of worthlessness. He needs immediate help! Following are several names of organizations and 800 numbers where you can get help.

— Zodia

I emailed this to Samantha, asking her to reply privately to the sender immediately. This was one I didn't think needed to appear in the column. I was concerned about some of the letters Zodia was getting. I always respond as best I can given the limitations, but I can't help but worry about some of the people who write to me. I just hoped that *Panicked in Petaluma* wouldn't waste a minute.

I sighed and opened the next letter. Just as I set up the chart, the doorbell rang. From the top of the stairs I called down to the front door. It was Dorothy. I hurried down to let her in.

She was out of breath. "You don't have a client with you, do you? I'm sorry, Julia. I should have called first."

"No, it's fine. I'm working, but I can take a break. How did you manage to get away?"

"Gudrun's there with my aunts now. I really had to see you."

"Sure. Come on up." Was this about Luis? Or something else? I led Dorothy into the office. She sat in my client chair without taking off her coat.

"I'm really sorry to barge in like this."

"No worries. What's on your mind?"

"It's Richard, Julia. He wants to get back together," she blurted out.

I nodded noncommittally, but inwardly my brain was short-circuiting.

"Can you look at our progressed composite chart again? Maybe things would be different now?" Dorothy's face was flushed. I knew that in her heart of hearts she'd very much wanted her marriage to be a success. It was after much arguing, stress, and accusations about financial matters that Richard had announced he was not happy and moved out. Dorothy was heartbroken.

I knew from the charts that Richard was controlling and had a heavy effect on her. She hadn't been on terribly firm ground during all the marital upheaval, but when Richard left, she'd fallen apart. Privately, it incensed me that Richard wanted to come back just when she was getting stronger. My heart was heavy, but there was nothing for it but to pull up the charts and have another look.

"Okay." I smiled to soften what I knew I

would have to say. "Here's your progressed chart, and here's Richard's." I turned the computer monitor so she could see the charts. Offering clients a view of the aspects I'm describing often helps them gain a little emotional distance.

Progressed charts are based on a theory that the first day of life is indicative of the first year of life. In other words, the thirtieth year of life is foreshadowed by the thirtieth day of life. To find out what's currently happening in a relationship, one very good method is to create progressed charts for the two individuals, and then set up a composite chart. A composite is a new chart using the midpoints of both individuals' charts calculated for the city in which they live. I clicked on the toolbar and mentally thanked the gods for computer programs. How would I have ever managed before all this technology?

"Things have eased a little between you two right now, since the separation. I'm afraid, though, that there could be more difficulties to come." I really didn't like the transits that were about to hit.

Dorothy tried her best not to show her disappointment. "Richard says he's sorry he was so stubborn. He really wants to do things differently."

I nodded. *Julia, be careful what you say.* "The stresses between the two of you are not going to change. Now, I'm not saying they can't be worked on, as we've talked about in the past, but the same energies still apply. I can see from this that there's an easing of the hostilities, but, frankly" — I looked up at Dorothy — "my advice would be to just wait a bit. Wait until after the holidays before you make a firm decision."

"Christmas is less than a week away. You mean after Christmas?"

"Yes. That's a good way to time it. Just wait until then. Right now the Moon is close to Venus in this progressed composite, and that's very nice, but it's somewhat temporary — it's not everything. Keep talking to each other and review what's gone on before. Maybe make a list of the things that upset you so much and discuss them with Richard, or together with your counselor."

"Yes, he's agreed to go to counseling with me now," Dorothy breathed. "Isn't that wonderful, Julia?"

Oh please. Too bad he wouldn't agree to that months ago! "Yes, it is. It means he's serious about working on the relationship, and perhaps dealing with his control issues."

My concern has to be primarily for my client, so I needed to stay as nonjudgmental as possible about her choices, but I truly had my doubts that Richard Sanger could change that much. And as difficult as Richard could be, Dorothy could be just as stubborn. Either one of them might do fine on their own, but this was a case of each exacerbating the worst traits in the other. Dorothy's natal Mercury formed hard aspects with Saturn and with Pluto; Mercury indicates how we think, how we perceive, how we communicate, so Dorothy's placements led her to bend reality and refuse to see things as they really were. We all do that to some extent when we want something very badly, but in Dorothy's case, I feared she could become even more single-minded and obsessive. She had chosen a person who would bring her own worst failings to the fore.

I had become very fond of her. I wanted to see her have a chance at happiness. I certainly knew how rare a thing it is to find a wonderful, loving mate. I'd lost my chance, but it wasn't too late for Dorothy. I definitely didn't want to see her rush back into a situation that had made her miserable for the past few years, especially a situation that might not improve.

"There are correspondences between your charts indicating lifetime connections, but it takes more than that to make a relationship fulfilling," I continued. "I'm not saying don't consider this. It's your decision. I'm just saying wait until this current Moon progression has passed, and then see how you feel. There's no need to jump at anything. You're doing great, and you're on firmer ground now."

Dorothy took a deep breath and nodded. "You're right. I need to not feel desperate. And I need to slow down and take my time with this." She rose from her chair. "Thanks, Julia. I guess I needed you to talk me down."

"No worries. We all need that sometimes." I walked her to the door and we hugged. "Any more news about Luis?"

Dorothy sighed. "I spoke to his family last night. Just awful. Evandra and Eunice are so upset."

"I'm so sorry."

"What do I owe you for today?"

"Nothing."

"But . . ."

"Shush. No. Put your wallet away."

"Thanks, Julia. I'm sorry I have to rush off so quickly. Are you still coming by today? Evandra's been asking for you to visit."

"Yes, definitely, if I'm not running too late."

After Dorothy left, I filled a bowl with the

last of the pea soup and stuck it in the microwave. Then I dropped two kitty treats on Wizard's tray. He lunged at them, quacked, and walked away. I finished my meal and went back to answering a few more letters.

Between Dorothy's wanting to reconcile with her husband and *Panicked in Petaluma,* I felt discouraged. I know astrology works and I know sometimes I can actually point people in the right direction, particularly when a question of timing is involved, but I often wonder if my clients actually listen and take what I say to heart. Other times I wonder if I'm deluding myself that I have anything pertinent to say anyway.

The phone rang and I grabbed it, assuming it was Don returning my call. The voice was male, low and gravelly. *"A soothsayer shall be put to death and they shall stone them with stones."*

FOUR

My heart was banging against my rib cage. A wave of anger washed over me. "Who is this?" I shouted. I heard a chuckle on the other end.

"Lose my number, you whack job!" I slammed the phone back in its cradle, but not before the caller clicked off. I was so furious my face was burning and my hands shook. They — whoever they were — had my home number. But not my cell. Not yet. I dashed an email off to Samantha. I was sure now that my address and phone number hadn't been secure at the newspaper.

The phone rang again. I grabbed it on the first ring, certain it was another anonymous caller.

"What!"

"Hey! What's wrong?" It was Don.

"Oh. Sorry," I replied sheepishly. "I thought you were . . ."

"Were what? Or maybe I should say 'who'?

You left me a message earlier?"

"Have you talked to Sam?"

"Not yet. She left me a message to call her, but I figured I'd get back to you first."

I brought Don up to date about my emails and anonymous caller. I felt better already just hearing his voice. Don is the backbone of the newspaper's research department and able to lay his fingers on every ounce of trivia in the city and elsewhere. He's a one-man walking encyclopedia. I knew he'd have some good advice.

"That's bad, Julia," he said when I'd finished. "I'll have a chat with Les and Sam and see what they can find out. You think your info's been leaked from here?"

"Has to be. I can see where these creeps might guess at my *AskZodia* email address, but how else would they have my landline at home? Don . . ." I hesitated. "It's just hit me. That means they know my name and my home address."

Don sighed heavily. "Jeez, I'm sorry, Julia. Why in the hell are there so many crazies in the world?"

I shivered, thinking of the dark thoughts behind the Biblical quotations. I doubted anyone would be able to stone me to death outside my apartment on a city street, but I didn't want to take any chances.

"I'll see what we can do at our end. If we find out who accessed your info, they're done for, believe me. Les'll fire 'em on the spot, which is a lot less than I'll do if I get my hands on them. One thing though, Julia. Don't delete any of those emails. If this gets any crazier, they can be traced. The police have a department for that, and you can go to the District Attorney about it. And keep a log of these calls too. That could be important. Just the date and time they come in. The phone company won't give you any info, but you can file a complaint if they find they're coming from the same phone line, okay?"

"How depressing. Like I don't have enough to do. I'm going to turn off the phone in a little while when my client arrives, but I'll talk to you later."

"Stay in touch, all right?"

Don and I hung up. The living room clock chimed once at the half hour. I'd have to get moving. Darlene, my new client, was due soon. I made a small pot of coffee and heated water for tea in case she wasn't a coffee drinker. Then I lit a cone of incense and placed it in the small niche in the belly of my big bronze Buddha. He sits on the hallway table and guards my apartment. I made sure there was a fresh tape in the recorder in case my client preferred something portable instead of digital. I straightened up the desk, checked that a box of tissues was close by, and placed my big amethyst crystal in front of the monitor. Amethyst reminds me to be humble and helps me avoid the bad habit of wanting to be right.

Darlene was thirty-five and had recently gone through a breakup with a boyfriend. She was considering a geographical move. When I checked her chart for the location she had chosen, I wasn't happy. She needed to focus on a new career path, not a new location, and I hoped she'd be open to my advice. I'm always a little nervous with a new client. Once into our session, I'd be better able to gauge her reaction and judge how carefully I needed to tread.

I brushed my hair and pulled it back with a clip, then slapped on a little makeup to look presentable. I live in jeans but always try to wear slacks or a skirt when meeting clients. I placed Darlene's folder in the center of the desk and booted up the computer. All was in readiness. While I waited, I reviewed her chart one more time, and double-checked the timing on a couple of transits. I glanced at the clock. Another quarter of an hour had gone by. Either my new client was running late or she had cold feet and might be a no-show, which sometimes happens.

The phone rang. I hesitated for a second or so, fearful it might be another threatening call. It could also be my client. I grabbed it on the third ring.

"Julia?"

"Yes. Is this Darlene?"

"I drove by your apartment, but I was afraid to stop."

"What? Why?"

"Have you looked out your window?"

"No! What's wrong?" Carrying the phone, I ran the length of the apartment to the living room windows that overlook the sidewalk from the second floor. Thirty or so people, carrying signs, had formed a walking circle around the entrance to my building. From my perspective I couldn't read the signs.

"Hold on," I told Darlene. I opened one of the windows and leaned out. Cold air blew into the room, rustling the drapes.

"Hey! What do you think you're doing?" I shouted.

Several heads looked up and a woman screamed, "There she is!" Others joined in. In unison, a chant began: *"Witch! Witch! Burn the witch!"*

Stunned, I continued to hang out the window staring at the group that was marching, as if on a picket line, in front of my stairway. I was frozen in place. Then I remembered my client was still on the phone. I slammed the window shut.

"Darlene, I have no idea what's going on."

"I'm so disappointed. I really wanted to see you."

"Where are you now?"

"Parked around the corner."

"Do you know the Mystic Eye in North Beach?"

"Oh, sure. I've been there a few times. It's on Broadway, right?"

"That's the place." I took a deep breath to calm my nerves. "Can you meet me there in twenty minutes? They have private reading rooms that I use sometimes. I'm really sorry. I have no idea what's going on."

"I'll head down there now. Are you sure you'll be all right?"

"I'll be fine. When you get there, park in the alley behind the store where it says private parking. I'll explain to them." I clicked off the phone, muttering obscenities. It rang immediately and I jumped involuntarily. My nerves were on edge.

"Julia! What the hell is going on? I've called the cops." It was Ann, my next-door neighbor, a young nurse in her twenties who worked the night shift.

"I don't know," I wailed, "but thanks for calling it in. These people have chased away my new client, so now I have to go meet her in North Beach. This is unbelievable."

"Don't worry. I'll give 'em hell and talk to the cops when they get here."

I thanked her and hung up. I ran up and down the hallway searching for Wizard and finally found him curled in a ball in the big armchair in the living room, fast asleep and totally unconcerned. I breathed a sigh of relief. I didn't know who these people were, but I hated to think what they'd do to a black cat. I slid the metal kitty door in place and made sure it was securely fastened, then checked my front door. It was locked but I put the bolt on for good measure. I rummaged in the hallway closet and grabbed a coat with a hood. Hurrying into the office, I shoved Darlene's folder into my case with the laptop and the tape recorder. I grabbed Evandra's folder as well, and then, locking the kitchen door behind me, escaped by the back stairs.

My duplex is protected from the street by a locked door. There's no way, or at least no easy way, to gain entrance to the side or back of the building. In the garage down-

61

stairs, I climbed into my car and pulled my hood up. I wasn't afraid of these people as much as I was afraid they'd do something to my cat or my Geo. In fact, I have a bad temper and I didn't trust myself not to physically attack a few of them. I was boiling mad, but right now my client was my first priority.

I hit the button to lock the car doors, and then the garage door opener, and I gunned the engine. As soon as I thought I could clear the door, I backed out quickly, sending several marchers skittering away. I envisioned running over a few but the prospect of jail time stopped me.

Several in the group, who, I might add, looked like perfectly normal people, stared at me as my Geo moved past them. One woman, her face twisted in a grimace, called out, "There she is! That's her. There's the witch." Several people moved closer, surrounding my car. One man started pounding on the passenger window and tried to pull the door open. I leaned on the horn and revved the engine. Once I was sure the garage door had locked, I put my car in gear, gunned the motor, and took off for North Beach.

FIVE

I emerged from the Broadway tunnel, the Mystic Eye on the opposite side of the street. Cheryl was on the sidewalk waving her arms and talking to two patrolmen. I couldn't make a U-turn. The street was jammed with traffic. I'd either get killed or get a zillion-dollar moving violation if I got caught. I turned right at Columbus and drove around the block, struggling through traffic and the pedestrians milling around the outdoor Chinese markets. When I reached Broadway, I crossed over, cut down the alleyway, and pulled up next to Cheryl's VW. Parked next to it was a small dark sedan. Likely Darlene's. I grabbed my case and purse, locked the car, and hurried down the alleyway to the front of the store. Cheryl waved as I approached. Her face was flushed. "Julia, some woman just went in asking for you."

"Sorry to barge in like this. Can I use one

of the private rooms? I'll explain later."

"Sure. Go right ahead." Cheryl turned back to the two patrolmen, one of whom was taking notes. I was curious, but I couldn't take the time to ask what was going on. I had a more than sneaking suspicion that the Mystic Eye had shared my fate and become a target of the same crazies. I pushed through the door.

Inside, the Eye was an oasis in a storm. Deep red draperies framed the glass front windows and thick carpeting masked street sounds. Cubbyholes formed by floor-to-ceiling bookshelves carved out the larger spaces, creating reading nooks with stools. A fragrant incense evoking cinnamon and sandalwood filled the air. Water tinkled through small fountains next to well-lit display cases that held jewelry and delicate glassware. Plaster gargoyles looked down from high on the walls, and center tables displayed the newest acquisitions.

I spotted a woman with bright carrot-red hair and a prominent nose. This was my client — her coloring and features shouted Aries rising. She wore a long skirt and boots with a dark tweed blazer. She was leafing through a book on one of the front tables.

"Darlene?"

Her face lit up when she heard her name.

"Julia?" She replaced the book on the table. "I'm so glad you're here. What was that stuff all about?"

"I honestly have no idea, but I'd be willing to bet those same people were here too. The manager here is outside now, talking to the police. She's my friend so I know I'll find out more later. But enough of that. You've gone through too much trouble already. Let's grab a private room and have our session."

Darlene meekly followed me toward the back of the store and through a doorway that opened into the short hallway. I pushed back the curtain at the first door on the left, turned on the lamp, and hung my coat over the chair. The tiny reading room was almost completely filled by a small round table and two chairs, but it would do just fine for our appointment.

"Please, have a seat," I said.

Darlene nodded and took off her jacket. I set up my laptop and tape recorder. I took a deep breath and did my best to push all the recent upsets out of my head.

Darlene fidgeted, turning a ring round and round on her finger. "I have to tell you. I'm a little nervous today."

"Don't worry." I smiled. "Lots of people feel that way the first time. Let's demystify the process, okay?"

Darlene nodded.

I turned the laptop so she could visualize the placements as I pointed them out. "First, let's start with the breakup."

Darlene groaned. "It's been awful."

I nodded sympathetically. "They generally are, no matter the circumstances. Here's the thing. Saturn, by transit, reached your seventh house cusp, the house of partnerships. Your seventh house has the sign of Libra on the cusp, the sign associated with relationship. Saturn is a constricting but stabilizing force. Wherever Saturn touches, we're forced into a deeper level of maturity. We're compelled to take a hard look at the reality and not the fantasy."

"I blame myself. I think I made too many demands."

I watched her face carefully. I could read the sadness, and the fact that she'd tortured herself with guilt. "I really doubt that, Darlene. Your chart has a heavy western influence. That means most of your planets are on the right-hand side of the chart. You're an extremely compassionate person who's easily able to put herself in another's shoes. I think it's highly unlikely you were selfish or demanding. In fact, you probably bent over backward. Your former boyfriend was a great guy, eccentric, fun-loving; I can see that from his chart. But, he's not terribly ambitious. He couldn't adjust to your level, at least right now, or maybe ever. You're ready for something solid in your life, and the Saturn transit made it blindingly obvious this relationship would not serve you in the future."

Darlene's eyes had filled with tears. She pulled a tissue out of her purse. "You're right on the money there. We tried to patch it up a couple of times, but it was just so frustrating for both of us. It just wasn't working."

I nodded. "And now, Saturn is exactly opposite your seventh house Moon."

"What does *that* mean?"

"Loneliness. You feel terribly isolated right now. But this will pass. The Moon represents our emotions, our deepest needs. With Saturn in opposition to your natal Moon, none of your needs are being met. I always think of a Saturn-Moon transit as a reality sandwich. It's forcing you to take a hard look at your desires, your needs, and make more realistic choices."

"I really want to move. I can't tell you how badly I want to get away from the city, from everything that reminds me of him. I'm always afraid I'll run into him somewhere and I just . . ." She wiped her eyes with the tissue. "I just can't stand being alone anymore."

I shook my head. "Here's what I think, Darlene. Not right now."

She frowned. "You're kidding. You can't mean that!"

"I have to be honest. I just don't think it would be a good thing to do, at least not right now. Not with this transit to your Moon. The Moon describes our sense of belonging, our home — both our physical home, represented by the fourth house of your chart, and our emotional home, the place where we feel safe and nurtured. I have to tell you that relocations or house moves made under adverse transits to the Moon generally turn out to be unsatisfying. If you packed up and went to Boise right now, you'd be taking the Saturn-Moon transit with you. You'd probably rent an apartment that you would find extremely 'Saturnian.' "

"In English, please." She smiled for the first time.

"You'd find yourself in a space that would be limited, cramped, too small, dark, dirty, depressing. It's amazing but true, I've seen it many times, not just with Saturn, but with other transits as well. I had a client once who moved under a Uranus square to her natal Moon. As she passed her first check across the landlord's desk, he told her he intended to tear the building down in six months. She grabbed her check back and ran. She then rented another place, moved in, and found out that half the wiring was faulty and the landlord refused to fix it. Uranus, by the way, rules electricity. She had to pay for the repairs herself and then fight with the landlord over reimbursement. It's uncanny, but I've seen things like that often."

I realized as I spoke that I hadn't checked my own transits lately. Was this a case of the shoemaker's children or what? I'd been so busy with other people's charts, I hadn't even taken a good look at my own. Uranus was in the sign opposite my Moon. When I wasn't paying attention, had it snuck up on me? I needed to have a look.

Darlene's words brought me back to the present. "It's just so hard right now. I feel I have to revise my life and I don't know how to get started. I've put so much into this relationship over the past few years, and I just feel like I've wasted my time. I'm so depressed right now, I can't think straight."

"It is a depressing time. I won't deny that, but you're not crazy. You're not neurotic. I can only stress that this won't last much longer. Look at it as necessary down time. When you come out of it, you'll be better able to revamp your life and get realistic about *your* needs. The kind of work you want, the partnership you want. Let's talk about career direction. What kind of work are you doing now?"

"Sales. I work for a radio station. That was another conflict my boyfriend and I had. He thought I should be happy with my job. I make good money. But I just see it as a dead end."

"This will sound complicated, but it's really fairly straightforward. The ruler of your sixth house — this is the house of the work you do on a daily basis — is placed in your ninth house of publicity. Your ninth house ruler, the Sun, is in your natal tenth house, close to your Midheaven. The tenth house is all about career and public standing. This is a very big issue for you. Frankly, I don't think you'd be happy staying in sales, no matter how much money you made. What was your degree in?"

Darlene laughed. "Communications . . . broadcasting."

"Well, there you have it. That's perfect for the ninth house, not to mention travel and publicity. That's what you should be doing.

You're young, you're very attractive, well-spoken — why shouldn't you be doing the evening news? Or if you'd rather work behind the scenes, perhaps you could do research for special broadcasts or documentaries or something along those lines?"

"Julia, that's so weird. When I was little, that's what I used to play at. Being one of those women on TV who delivers the news. It seems silly now, but I remember thinking how confident they looked."

"Here's my advice: don't leave the city. It's smaller than, say, New York or Los Angeles, so it might be easier to get a start here. Forget the boyfriend. You didn't do anything wrong. Find a headhunter and start figuring out how those women got to do the news."

Darlene took a deep breath. "You've given me a lot of think about. And I do feel better than when I walked in. Thanks."

"You're more than welcome. It's been delightful for me too. I'm just sorry you had a scare this morning."

"Who were those people?"

"I haven't the foggiest. Obviously some kind of religious cult, but who's behind it, I don't know."

"What are you going to do about it?"

"Not sure yet. But I'll figure it out. Next

time you see me, my home will be a place of peace and serenity." I really had to check that Uranus transit as soon as possible. Here I was, doling out advice about the sense of home while mine was being turned upside down. How dire could this get?

SIX

I walked Darlene to the door at the back of the shop and waved to her as she climbed into her car. Inside the store, not a customer was in sight. The police were gone and Cheryl was at the counter ripping open boxes of books. I pulled up a stool and started working on the next box.

"Thanks for today. Sorry I had to barge in unexpectedly."

"Not a problem. As you can see, we're not exactly crowded."

A petite blond with tons of energy, Cheryl had stumbled into the Eye six months ago when she saw a *Help Wanted* sign in the window. She'd just left her cheating husband and hadn't worked since college. When asked for a résumé, she burst into tears. Gale, for all her exterior toughness, is a true softie. She led Cheryl into the back room of the shop, made some coffee, and listened to her tale. Gale needed someone to manage the shop, and Cheryl needed friends and a new home. Gale hired her on the spot.

"I'm just lucky my client was willing to meet me here," I said. "She would have been perfectly justified in telling me to forget it. Were they here too?"

Cheryl glanced at me sharply. "What do you mean, 'too'?" Her voice rose a few octaves, as it always does when she's upset or nervous. It makes her sound like she's on helium.

"They were at my apartment this morning, outside on the sidewalk marching around. That's why I rushed here to meet my client." I neglected to mention the choice threats that had been hurled at me. "What happened here?"

Cheryl groaned. "Pretty much the same thing. They scared off my customers. I'm sure we have Reverend Roy and the Prophet's Tabernacle to thank."

"Prophet's Tabernacle? Why does that ring a bell?"

"Don't tell me you haven't heard of him? Look at this!" Cheryl handed me a flyer advertising daily services every evening at six o'clock. The page was peppered with Biblical quotations and at the center was a photo of a man in long robes, his arms outstretched as if welcoming his flock. He wore a saintly expression. His hair was combed back into a high pompadour. "While those freaks were picketing the Eye, they were passing these out to everyone on the street."

"What do they want? Where did this guy come from?"

"Crawled out of the swamps of Louisiana apparently. He's supposed to be a real ordained minister, but it looks more like revival stuff to me. He's here, he says" — Cheryl's voice dropped to a mocking tone — "because San Francisco is a hotbed of blasphemy and devil worship." She slammed a pile of books on the counter. "He's on television. He's got that ridiculous show, *Prophet TV.* They should call it Profit TV, as in 'send me money.' " She took a deep breath. "He's raising hell all over town. His followers call themselves the Army of the Prophet and they target anyone who speaks out against them. He's after the gays, the strip clubs, abortion clinics, occult book-shops like ours, psychics, you name it." Cheryl hesitated when she saw the expression on my face. "What is it?"

"A few days ago, the paper printed one of my Zodia responses. A woman wrote because she was worried her mother was planning to sign over her property to some religious group. I just remembered. Could it be the same group?"

"What did you write to her?"

"Just the obvious, I guess. Advice to have this church checked out, find a lawyer to deal with the situation. My thought was that the mother was martyring herself. I think I spouted off a bit about scams and false prophets. It wouldn't be the first time my big mouth got me in hot water. I can go back and check my emails."

"Well, now you know why they're after you. But you're not the only one, believe me. I've got a call in to Gale. She'll have a fit! The cops chased those psychos off today, but they'll be back."

"Cheryl, this is the twenty-first century. It's San Francisco. Who would listen to this guy?"

"Every nut job from Sonoma County to Daly City and beyond, apparently. He's got a big following. They hold meetings at the old theater on Mason Street, and they fill the house if you can believe it." Her voice was rising. She was still upset.

I filled Cheryl in on the details of the emails and the threatening phone call. "I'm sure my personal information was leaked from the newspaper. How else could they know where I live and my home phone number? I don't advertise. My clientele is strictly word of mouth, and I always know who's referred whom."

"What do they have to say at the paper?"

"They've promised to investigate. But the horse is out of the barn, or whatever the expression is, if they know where I live."

"I hate bigots." Cheryl slammed another pile of books down on the counter.

I smiled. "I think that's an oxymoron. But if you're going to hate any group, why not bigots?" I finished unpacking the last box and dusted off my hands.

"What are you doing now?" Cheryl asked.

"I figured I'd stop up the hill to see Dorothy."

"Oh," Cheryl gasped. "I'm so sorry. I totally spaced. Gale called this morning and told me what happened. I was just so caught up with the chaos here, it slipped my mind. Are you sure you want to go back?"

"I think Dorothy could use the company, and her aunt is a new client. I was checking the aunt's lunar returns and I promised I'd see her today. But do you need me here? I'd be glad to help out."

"No, that's okay. We're hardly busy, as you can see. The police promised to check a couple more times before their shift ends. Frankly, it was weird, now that I think of it." Cheryl stared off into space. "They didn't seem all that . . . sympathetic. They just looked at me like I was speaking a foreign language. They didn't even want to make a report, but I insisted." She sighed. "Gale'll be here later anyway. I'll be fine."

"Okay." I leaned over and gave her a hug. "I'll be close by and I have my cell if you need me." I left by the back door and climbed into my car. I pulled slowly out of the alleyway onto Broadway. I wondered if I should file a police report myself? The Army of the Prophet had to be behind the disturbance at my apartment, but I had no real proof, no one I could name. I remembered Ann's promise to talk to the police. Hopefully she had.

SEVEN

My engine coughed as I downshifted and climbed Filbert Street to the Gamble house. I've always loved the view from Coit Tower at the top of Telegraph Hill. It's definitely the most breathtaking in the city. My grandmother loved it too, and one of our favorite things to do when I was a kid was to hike to the top. The hill was named for the wooden semaphore, the arms of which once signaled city merchants, giving them cargo details of ships entering the Golden Gate. Merchants could then predict upcoming local prices. A decade later, with the advent of the electrical telegraph, the structure was obsolete. The wooden armature was torn down, but the name given to the hill remained.

I pulled to the right as far as I could and then executed a U-turn, parking in front of the house, making sure to curb my wheels as the street signs constantly admonish us. The sky was a dark steely gray, promising another winter downpour, while the temperature hung in the low forties. Ivy branches, bereft of leaves, twined over the dark, brick-fronted façade. Through frosted windows, I could see the front room lit by several lamps. A figure moved near a tall Christmas tree. I scrambled out, lugging my case, and pulled my hood up against the wind. I hurried across the street and knocked. A few second later, Dorothy swung the door open. Her face was wreathed in smiles. "Julia, come on in."

"Is this a good time? I should have called first."

"It's fine. We've been expecting you. Evandra will be delighted."

A tall man appeared behind Dorothy in the open doorway. He was heavyset with dark, graying hair and wore a long-sleeved shirt under a sweater vest. He reached around Dorothy to grasp my hand. "Hello. You must be Julia. I'm Richard. Richard Sanger." His grip was strong. "Come in. I've heard so much about you, I feel like I know you."

I smiled in response. I'd heard a lot about him as well but wasn't about to bring up any details. I was taken aback he was there, but I tried to cover my surprise for Dorothy's sake. We'd just discussed Richard that morning and, estranged though they were, here he was in the flesh. Was he just visiting? Or had Dorothy not listened to a thing I'd said?

As I stepped inside, I caught Dorothy's eye and looked at her quizzically. She smiled, and as Richard headed for the living room, she leaned closer and whispered, "He stopped by to see me and to make sure I don't need anything. Don't worry. I'm taking it slow."

"That's good," I whispered back for lack of a better response. A knot had formed in my stomach.

"Grab a seat in the living room, Julia. Would you like some tea or coffee?"

"Tea sounds great. Anything that's hot."

"I've got some in a pot right now. I'll bring it in."

I stepped into the living room and shed my coat, dropping it with my bag on the nearest chair. A ten-foot-tall Christmas tree stood in front of the center window.

"It's beautiful. Where did you find such a big one?"

Richard, balanced on a stepladder, replied. "I had it delivered. Isn't it a beauty? Really fresh too. I figured I better — Dorothy certainly never would have thought of it."

Criticism already, I thought. He was placing

tiny white lights around the circumference of the tree. Starting at the top, he had worked his way halfway down. He stretched as far as he could, then climbed down and moved the ladder to another position.

Dorothy returned with a tray loaded with a teapot and cups and saucers. "I should warn you. Evandra's been in a state since . . . well, since Luis . . ." She trailed off and poured the tea. She placed a cup on the table for me. "Would you like cream or sugar?"

"No thanks. Just straight."

"I'm so worried about her. I found her in the hallway last night wandering up and down and talking to herself. Almost as if she were hallucinating. Maybe you were right about the . . . what was it, a Neptune transit?" Dorothy sat heavily in the armchair across from me and reached over to pour another cup for herself. "She's very upset. Eunice too. I've been doing everything possible to keep them both calm."

Richard had finished stringing the lights and now was unpacking boxes of antique ornaments. He turned to Dorothy. "These are really old. Don't we have some better decorations?"

"They love those antique ornaments, Richard." She smiled, but I caught a flicker of defensiveness in her eyes. Her voice took on a sharper tone. "I just haven't had a chance to go shopping for anything, much less ornaments."

Richard started to retort, then thought better of it.

I took a last sip of tea. "I'll leave you to the decorations. I'll just go up and say hello to Evandra." If they were going to argue, I didn't want to be a witness. I grabbed my case and climbed the stairs to the dark wood-lined hallway. I walked to the end and knocked on Evandra's door.

The door opened immediately and I was face to face with a woman at least six feet tall, large-boned, and heavy in the hips. This had to be Gudrun, their live-in companion. Her hair was dyed a dark red and pulled back in a severe bun. She wore a skirt and a double-breasted navy blazer that would have been more appropriate at a boys' school. She spoke with a strong guttural accent.

"Yaass?" she inquired.

"Hello. I'm Julia. I'm here to see Evandra."

"Julia, my dear, come in. I'm so happy you came today," Evandra called out from behind the heavy door. "Let her in. Let her in right away, Gudrun."

Gudrun sniffed but stood back to let me

enter. The scent of lavender permeated the room. Evandra was ensconced in her cushioned armchair and another elderly woman sat opposite on a delicate loveseat, her feet barely reaching the floor. In the light from the window, Evandra's complexion had a gray tone I hadn't noticed the day before. A tea tray sat on a small low table in front of the loveseat.

"You're having tea. Is this a bad time?"

"Not at all, my dear. You haven't met my sister Eunice yet, I don't think." Evandra waved a thin hand, indicating that I should draw nearer. "Sit here, close to me."

Eunice wore a delicate flowered gown, a pale pink shawl wrapped around her shoulders. "I understand you're an astrologer," she twittered. "You seem like such a nice young woman. Isn't that rather dangerous?" Her delicate voice belied her frank statement.

"Dangerous?" I felt I had missed something.

"The Reverend tells us that studying the occult is devil's work."

Oh no, could it be?

"Do shut up, Eunice," Evandra snapped. "Don't insult Julia. Your Reverend, I'm sure, is full of the proverbial horse pucky."

"Is not!" Eunice retorted, her cheeks

blushing suddenly. "He knows about these things."

Evandra turned to me. "Eunice has become enchanted with a local snake oil salesman and has Gudrun driving her to these disgusting revival meetings."

I glanced at Eunice. She looked crestfallen. "They are *services,* and they are very inspiring. The Reverend says I can even join the congregation at Prophet's Paradise anytime I want."

"Prophet's Paradise?" I asked.

"Yes, that's the Reverend's nature community up north." She turned back to her sister. "If you're going to be so judgmental, Evandra, I just might do that," she sniffed.

"You're welcome to, dear. I won't have any of that nonsense in this house, so just keep your mouth shut about it."

Eunice's collar held several tiny jeweled pins. She noticed my look. "Yes, they're bees, my dear. The most important life form on the planet, you know."

"Eunice! She doesn't want to hear about that," Evandra hissed.

"But she must. It's terribly important." Eunice looked imploringly at me. "You know, dear Albert said that if the bees disappear, we won't last very long."

I wasn't sure which Albert she was referring to. I felt as if I had stepped back in time. Did she mean Victoria and Albert?

Evandra saw my expression. "She means Einstein. Eunice, please, we have company now. Let's not talk nonsense."

"But it's not nonsense." Eunice turned to me. "I have studied, you see. I was at Berkeley. They did allow women in those days, even though Father wouldn't hear of my working in the field. It wasn't considered proper for a young lady in my social position." She shot a scathing look at her sister. "That's why I wear them." She brushed her fingers lightly over her collar. "To honor them. To let them know how important they are. To help them survive."

Evandra turned her head slightly. "Gudrun, would you please run down and bring us another cup and a fresh pot so we can visit with Julia?" Gudrun had been standing at attention by the door, as if I would be required to leave very soon. She nodded sullenly.

"I can go. There's no need to have Gudrun . . ."

"No dear, stay here with me for a bit."

Gudrun turned and left the room, shutting the door quietly behind her.

"I heard you weren't doing so well today." I addressed Evandra.

"So strange. Dorothy told me I was wandering last night, but I really don't remember. I'm fine now, just very tired. I really don't need the doctor." She hesitated and glanced at her sister. "Eunice, could we have a few minutes alone?"

Eunice pursed her lips, obviously unhappy to be asked to leave. "I'll speak with you later, Julia." Carrying her tea cup, she tripped daintily out of the room. As soon as the door shut behind her, Evandra gripped my hand.

"You heard about Luis, didn't you?"

"Yes. I was here."

"Well! I told you, didn't I? You didn't believe me," she said in a quavering voice.

I wasn't following Evandra's logic. "What didn't I believe?"

"That it was meant for me. He was murdered. I know it."

"I've heard Luis had a heart condition and might have fallen."

"Hah! I don't believe that for a minute. I may be old, but I'm not stupid."

"What do you think happened?"

"Why, she did it."

"Dorothy?"

"Of course. That's why she's staying here with us." Evandra leaned forward as if someone were eavesdropping. "She doesn't give a hoot about me, but once my sister and I are gone, she inherits everything. She's the last of the family, so she'll get this house, the investments, everything. That's how the trust was set up."

Dorothy had never mentioned this to me, but it made sense. Who else would inherit? "Evandra, I'm sorry. I don't mean to dismiss your fears, but it can't be possible. I was with Dorothy in the kitchen when it happened." I felt I had to inject some reality into this conversation.

"I don't know how she did it, but she did it. She did something to him. For all we know, he may have been dead before he hit that rock."

I hardly knew what to say. "I've known Dorothy for some time. She's been my client, and it's . . . it's very difficult to believe she could be capable of such a thing."

The old lady nodded her head wisely and a crafty look came into her eyes. "Happens more often than you would suspect, my dear. You see, we're the last of the Gambles, my sister and I. Everyone has passed over, so, as I said, it will all go to Dorothy once we're gone. She's the last living heir. The trust was set up by my grandfather. We draw an annuity, and there are some real estate holdings in the city as well. In the normal course of events, the bulk of it would have gone to the next *male* heir, with generous allowances for anyone else, but since there is no male heir, and Dorothy's past child-bearing years, it will all go to her."

"I see." I thought for a moment. "I know Dorothy's parents are dead, but I think she once mentioned there was an Australian branch."

"No. Although we hoped there was, for many years. You see, my grandfather, Elisha Gamble, was born in the late '60s."

I raised my eyebrows.

"The late 1860s, dear," Evandra continued. "He made his fortune in the silver mines. He had one sister, Lily, who died under mysterious circumstances. But that's another story I'll tell you some other time. Elisha had one son, Lysander, who was my father. And my mother's name was Evangeline."

I'm fascinated by family history. I'm more fascinated by people who go to the trouble to remember or explore that lineage. "That's how you were named!" I exclaimed.

"Exactly. Evangeline and Lysander. They combined their names and called me Evandra. A very unusual name for the time, or any time for that matter."

Gudrun returned, carrying a small tray

with an extra cup and a fresh pot of tea. She deposited the tray on the table wordlessly and took a seat across the room, watching her charge carefully.

Evandra took a sip of her tea. "That will be all, Gudrun," she announced.

Gudrun, expressionless, appeared not to have heard.

"Thank you, Gudrun. You may leave us now." Evandra spoke louder.

With a glare in my direction, Gudrun rose. *"Sehr gut,"* she said as the door closed behind her.

"Dreadfully depressing woman. I don't know where Dorothy found her."

I had to agree but stifled a giggle. "So what did Dorothy mean when she referred to an Australian branch of the family?"

"Oh, she's talking through her hat." The old lady waved a speckled hand dismissively. "You see, I was born in 1926. My sister, Eunice, two years later. We had a little brother Jonathan, who was five years younger than I, and of course, Elspeth, the baby. My father, God rest his soul, was not an evil man, but he was very very strict, and particularly harsh with Jonathan. My mother couldn't seem to convince him to spare the rod."

"He beat your brother."

"Yes. It was very sad. But it was a different time. Today, it would be considered child abuse and the authorities would be called in." Evandra sighed, recalling the past. "Jonathan ran away when I was twenty years old. We believe he went to Australia right after the war ended. After my father died, my mother hired someone to try to locate Jonathan, but she had no luck. We never heard from him and could find no trace. For all we know, he could have died there. We hoped that if he knew our father was dead, he might return. My mother spent a great deal of effort and money trying to locate him, but it all came to nothing. Poor dear, she never recovered. It broke her heart. She lived another twenty years, but nothing could ease her pain over the loss of her little boy."

"How terribly sad. And did you or Eunice ever marry?"

"No, dear. Neither one of us. I was far too wild and independent. Somehow, as strict as my father was, he let me have my way. I think he understood I was just as ornery as he was and would never back down. I would have done exactly what I wanted, no matter what. Eunice was a different creature. Scared of her own shadow. Never could stand up to him." Evandra smiled, a mischievous look in her eye. "I was a member of the Rosicrucian Society and even had a short dalliance in Europe with Aleister Crowley and the Temple of the Golden Dawn."

"Really? That must have been quite shocking for your family."

"Oh, they never knew the half of it. My father trotted every drooling marital prospect he could find through our parlor, but I had no intention of settling down to panty girdles and bridge parties." Evandra reached her hand to a small, silver-framed photograph on the table next to her armchair. "Here we all were in happier days." She passed the photograph to me. A smiling woman in a huge hat and long dress stood in a garden with an infant in her arms. Evandra, the oldest child, stood close to her mother clinging to her hand. A younger girl and a small boy stood in front of their mother. The two girls wore long white dresses.

"This was taken here, in the formal garden. Our house has quite a history, you know. Lilly Hitchcock Coit, whose fortune as you must know built Coit Tower, stayed here often. My father thought she was a trollop, living in Paris and coming back to San Francisco to become what you girls today would call a firemen's groupie. And Rudolf Valentino actually danced the tango here one night before he was driven out of the city by a jealous husband. Before my time, but my mother told me all about it."

"Valentino? In San Francisco?"

"Oh, yes. He wasn't a famous movie star then, just a dancer. He performed at the Cliff House in those days. They used to say he moved like a cat."

"That's fascinating. So Dorothy is Elspeth's daughter?"

"Yes." Evandra glanced lovingly at the framed photograph in her hand. "Elspeth's just a baby here. Our family was very fond of old-fashioned names, you see. Elspeth was ten years younger than I and sadly the first to pass over. She married a man named Marshall. That's Dorothy's maiden name, of course. My mother was rather a snob and considered Elspeth's husband a commoner. That caused another rift in our little family, so we were not able to stay particularly close. But I managed to stay in touch with her since they stayed in San Francisco." Evandra's hand shook slightly as she replaced the silver frame on the table. She leaned forward in her armchair. "Now tell me, Julia. Am I in danger?"

I wasn't sure how to approach this. I took

93

a deep breath and dove in. "I've rechecked everything again and looked at your lunar returns for this month and the next couple of months. There's a four-day period this month that's particularly intense. And as I told you, the most difficult transit at the present time is the Neptune opposition to your Sun and Mercury. Very soon, this will be exact."

"Is that a bad thing?"

"No. It's not a happy, exciting time, but it's not the worst thing. As long as you're aware of the pitfalls. We feel these pressures most keenly as the planets approach a sensitive point and become exact. Its effect on your Sun sign is depleting your energy and causing depression. Its effect on your Mercury can lead to mental confusion and an inability to sort out reality."

Evandra shook her head. "I just don't understand. And now Dorothy tells me I was wandering . . . am I going crazy?"

I bit my tongue. I wasn't qualified to diagnose dementia, if that's what was affecting Evandra. "I don't believe so. You *are* feeling extremely fearful right now, and not up to your usual energy level. The fact that your Mercury is affected by this transit could lead to a certain amount of paranoia. I have to say that I think you're misguided as to Dorothy's motives, but it's also possible that someone is deliberately working to delude you, to pull the wool over your eyes. Deception isn't a rule, but it is *possible* under a Neptune transit. That's what makes it difficult. Think of it as fog. It's terribly hard to know what is real and what is not."

"What about right now?"

"This month, this coming week or so, until perhaps the holiday, is the most sensitive time for you. My main caveat is that you must be very careful about any medications you take. Neptune is associated with pharmaceuticals and drugs of all sorts. If you feel something isn't right, then call your doctor, and do not continue. And particularly when your Sun sign is affected, the physical body is very vulnerable. A medication that normally would be fine could have a much more powerful effect during this time period. Listen to your body. If it doesn't feel right, it isn't, at least until this transit is over."

Evandra's eyes had filled with tears. "I'm just grateful you don't think I'm losing my mind."

"Be patient. You'll see. When this transit is over, everything will become very clear."

"Julia, I know I'm in danger. I saw her

last night."

My face betrayed my confusion. "Her?"

"Lily. Listen very carefully, dear." Evandra leaned closer and whispered, "I told you about Lily, my grandfather's sister."

I nodded.

"Well, it was very different in the late 1800s, you know. A woman couldn't make her own decisions. Lily wanted to marry a man she loved, a man of dubious prospects, but Elisha, my grandfather, refused. He'd arranged a marriage to one of his older business partners. Lily became very depressed and died."

"How did she die?"

Evandra pursed her lips. "No one would ever say. It was all rather mysterious, but I suspect it was a suicide and the family didn't want anyone to know."

"And this is who you think you saw last night?"

Evandra hesitated and took a deep breath. "There's a legend. It's said that when she appears, someone in the family is in danger. She appeared to my father just before he was killed by a runaway horse. I've seen her before — that's how I know. She always wears blue, her favorite color, and when she's present, you can smell gardenias." Evandra gripped my wrist. "Julia, I saw her

96

and smelled gardenias the night my mother died."

I shivered involuntarily.

"That's how I know I'm in danger. Or someone is. Someone in the family. And I think it's me."

"Under a Neptune transit, one can have strange dreams, strange otherworldly experiences," I explained. "And it's not uncommon for the veil to be lifted, to perceive other dimensions. But it's also possible that you're suffering from fear and paranoia."

"Is that what you really think?"

"I'll keep an open mind, believe me," I said. "I wouldn't rule either out. Sometimes both take place. Anyone at any age can have adverse reactions during this time, reactions they wouldn't normally have. Just be aware of that."

"That silly doctor probably wants to give me more medication." Evandra sniffed. "Well, I'll take your advice and not take it."

"You can take a prescribed medication, I didn't mean that." I groaned inwardly. I was sure her medical doctor would not like to hear about her astrologer's advice. "You can take what the doctor gives you, but if for any reason it doesn't feel right, or you think it's hitting you too hard, then call the doctor immediately and stop taking it. Don't take any chances."

"Will you come visit again? Or perhaps you could stay a few nights if you like. I'd feel so much better if you were here in the house."

"Richard seems to be spending time here with Dorothy. Doesn't that make you feel better?"

"Oh, yes. It does. I like him very much. I don't think Dorothy would dare to do anything funny with Richard around. You know, he's a very good cook. He makes me mint tea and little cookies with caraway seeds that I just love! He's promised to cook a great big turkey for our Christmas dinner." Evandra smiled, and in spite of her pallor, I saw a sparkle in her eyes that hinted at the child she had once been. She leaned back against the cushions and breathed deeply, closing her eyes for a long moment. I watched her carefully and finally decided she must have dozed off.

But just as I started to rise from the chair, her hand reached out and grabbed my wrist. "There's something I want to do. Will you help me?"

"Of course . . . if I can. What is it?"

"I want to hold a séance."

EIGHT

"Is she crazy?" Dorothy shouted, brushing an unruly curl from her forehead with the back of her hand. "A séance, no less!" She resumed chopping vegetables at the counter. "I'm running a madhouse. Eunice has Gudrun driving her to those ridiculous Prophet meetings, and now a séance!"

"I heard about Eunice's activities," I said. Although I'm always suspicious of do-gooders and preachers — just my natural cynicism, I guess — in light of my recent experience with the followers of the Reverend Roy, my antennae were sounding a red alert. "Do you think that's a good idea?"

Dorothy stopped chopping and paused with her knife in mid-air. "I hadn't given it a lot of thought. Why do you ask?"

For once, I decided on discretion and kept my big mouth shut. "It's a long story. I'll fill you in some other time. I'm just distrustful of those types of groups."

Dorothy wiped her knife off on a paper towel. "Julia, do you know how hard it is to care for elderly people? I've been a nurse my whole life, in some very difficult circumstances, believe me, but it's nothing compared to trying to take care of a family member. This beats it all. A séance no less!"

"I don't think she's crazy or suffering from dementia. Dorothy, listen to me. It's not that I'm a believer; I just try to keep an open mind. But one thing is true — she's having a Neptune transit. Physically she's completely exhausted and perhaps even suffering from too much medication, or not the right kind of medication, or even an allergy. Could she be allergic to something you're not aware of?"

Dorothy heaved a sigh. "Anything's possible. But not that I know of. I keep a good eye on her, you know," she stated defensively.

"And she's genuinely afraid."

Dorothy looked up and gave me a piercing glance. "Afraid of me?"

I wasn't about to tell her the details of what Evandra had shared with me, and ethically, I had no right to talk about a client's reading. Although, I remembered, that hadn't stopped me yesterday when I'd asked if Evandra was showing any hints of dementia.

Dorothy sighed. "You know, she won't let me give her any medications. She has them locked in her armoire and will only take them when Alba, our housekeeper, or Gudrun is here." She shook her head. "Maybe I'm too close. Maybe she is getting senile. I do need to talk to the doctor."

"Luis's death has undoubtedly affected her," I said. "Right now she's afraid of everything and everybody. And the truth is, if she were fifty years younger, she could still be having the same reaction."

Dorothy didn't respond, just continued her work. I watched as she deftly swept the vegetables into a pan and sautéed them. "What should I do, Julia? What do you think?"

"I think Evandra's got a bee in her bonnet and she's not going to be happy until she has her séance. Other than that, I can't say." I shrugged.

"Hmph! I guess she thinks she's going to communicate with Lily's ghost. Has she told you about that?

I nodded reluctantly.

"And when is this séance supposed to take place?"

"She says it has to be the night of the 21st,

two evenings from now. Apparently that was Lily's birthday."

"Where does one go to arrange such a thing, anyway?"

"I'm not really sure. I know some people from the Eye who are trustworthy. I can arrange for them to come here. I can't say I believe in this, but at least the people I know aren't charlatans and won't charge her for more than their time. Let me give it some thought and work on it. As long as it's okay with you."

Dorothy shook her head. "Fine. Whatever. Maybe Lily will come through and knock some sense into her head. Anything to keep the peace."

I returned to the front parlor. The tree was now completely decorated and dripping with antique ornaments. I wandered to the far end of the room, where multi-paned beveled glass doors overlooked a sunken formal garden on the side of the house. Balustrades outlined the perimeter, dotted with yew trees and marble statuary. In the center, low hedges of boxwood formed a maze-like pattern surrounding rose bushes, now bare and stunted. Stone benches stood at the end of the garden. I recognized the location from the photograph Evandra had shown me. Beautiful, but there was a desolate sadness to its formality. It recalled a bygone era. I heard a step behind me and jumped.

"Sorry, didn't mean to scare you." I hadn't heard Richard enter the room. "How is Evandra?"

"Rather frail right now."

He nodded ruefully. "I hope we're able to cheer her up. I don't think this house has seen a real Christmas and home cooking for many decades. It's such a waste to keep this rambling old place going for two little old ladies. I've tried to talk to Dorothy about that."

I stared at him. "What are you suggesting? That her aunts be put in a home?"

"Well, that would make more sense, wouldn't it? No need to pay for live-in help and the upkeep on this place. Costs a small fortune, not to mention the taxes and insurance."

I felt my cheeks grow hot, and I struggled to keep my voice neutral. "Well, fortunately for them, they're in a position to afford just that, and they seem perfectly capable of making their own decisions. And after all, it is still their house."

He'd put my back up, no doubt about it. Here he was, an estranged husband, a man who'd walked out on Dorothy, venturing his opinion about what should be done about two elderly aunts who weren't even his own blood relatives.

"True. That's true," Richard said. "I guess I'm just very practical about money matters." He smiled disarmingly. *Practical on how to get your hands on it,* I thought. "Dorothy's got something delicious going. Can you stay for dinner?" he added.

"Can't tonight, but thanks. I'll just say good night to Dorothy."

Richard nodded and climbed the stepladder, placing an old-fashioned angel at the top of the tree. I slipped on my jacket and grabbed my purse just as Dorothy entered the room.

"You're not staying?" She looked at me quizzically.

"Thanks, no. Richard invited me for dinner, but I can't manage it tonight. I have to get some errands done."

"Well, let me know if you're able to arrange something for the séance. I'm just happy you're willing to humor Evandra."

"She's having a tough time and I can't say I blame her. Neptune transits are not fun."

Dorothy followed me to the door. "Thanks again, Julia. Stop by any time." She enveloped me in a big hug. I could smell pastry dough on her skin. As I stepped outside, she followed and pulled the front door closed behind her. She moved closer, whispering. "Look, I know you think I'm jumping the gun, letting Richard visit like this, but he's such a big help."

"I'm just an astrologer, not a psychologist or a relationship expert. I'd like nothing better than to see you be happy, believe me. And Richard does seem very . . ." I struggled for the right word. "Solicitous of you."

"Oh, he is, he's a changed man," Dorothy gushed.

I couldn't help but wonder just how much Richard knew of Dorothy's potential inheritance. She watched from the doorway as I climbed into my car. I leaned over to the passenger side and waved to her as I headed down the hill.

NINE

I drove down Montgomery from North Beach and cut up to Union Square, joining the line of cars waiting to enter the underground public parking. After a five-minute wait, I finally pulled in, went down two levels, and parked. I took the elevator up to street level and joined the crowds of holiday shoppers.

My business is generally slow around the holidays, although it always picks up after the New Year. With the recent bad weather and a retrograde Mercury, it was particularly slow this time around. I had only one more client to see that week, so I was especially grateful for the income from the Zodia column. It irked me no end that the Army of the Prophet was raining on my parade. On top of everything, I hadn't done any shopping and needed to find some presents.

I always keep a few bottles of wine and

small boxes of truffles on hand in case a neighbor drops by with a present. And I send winter solstice cards to all my clients, offering them a discount in the first month of the new year, but my personal shopping list is small. My grandmother wouldn't be back from her cruise until mid-January, but I wanted to shop for her now. Gale and Cheryl and I had agreed we'd keep it simple and inexpensive but creative. Also, I'd have to find something for Kuan. He never expects a present, but he's more family than friend and I always enjoy looking for gifts for him. I'd secretly checked out his small library, the part written in English at least, and felt sure I could find a book on a subject he might like. That was my entire list.

I hurried across Geary and turned around to look up at the tree in the middle of the square. It was magnificent, hung with huge glistening balls and sparkling with thousands of tiny lights. I love the holiday season — the cold weather, the smells, the lights and decorations. I guess I celebrate the solstice more than anything. The Romans called the darkest time of the year Saturnalia, and that's how I think of the holidays. A time to drape evergreens over the mantel, light the Yule log, enjoy good food, and burn candles against the darkness. When January rolls around and all the decorations are put away, winter seems so much more bleak.

I don't have very clear memories of my parents, but I do remember lights on a Christmas tree. I remember my mother's perfume and her auburn hair, the same color as mine; my father's dark eyes and being lifted onto his shoulders. The smell of pine brings those images to me in a rush, and I've been known to stick my head between the branches of pine trees just to inhale that sappy aroma.

On a side street near the Square, I found a small jewelry store and bought a garnet necklace for my grandmother. At Macy's I purchased a soft plum-colored shawl that matched the necklace perfectly. Next I took the elevator to the ladies department to search for the sweater that I knew Cheryl wanted. She had shown me a picture of it in the latest catalogue and asked me what I thought. It was cream colored with tiny pearls splashed across the front. I roamed through every rack and counter on the floor and had no luck. In desperation I tracked down a saleswoman who remembered the item, but thought it was sold out and suggested I try to order online. I was frustrated and disappointed. I kicked myself for not starting sooner, because now I wouldn't have enough time to find what Cheryl really wanted.

I browsed through the large bookstore on the corner, hoping to spot something that Kuan might appreciate but probably not buy for himself. I discovered a reference book of Native American medicinal herbs. Perfect gift and something I thought he'd truly enjoy. The next person on my list was Gale, and she was always a problem. She had everything and could afford to buy anything she wanted. I needed something unexpected and unique, but not expensive. I didn't have a clue, but maybe I'd find something in my travels.

As I stood in line at the checkout counter of the bookstore, an uncomfortable feeling stole over me. Was I being watched? I turned slowly and surveyed the customers in line behind me. No one looked suspicious. No one turned away suddenly. Just holiday shoppers focused on their own business. As I turned back, my eye caught someone standing at a table close by, separated by a metal bar from the line of shoppers. A man — dark hair, black jacket — seemingly immersed in a book he was holding in his hands. No shopping bags in sight. Something about him . . . I mentally shook myself, pushing the thought out of my mind. I was being paranoid. Nerves were getting the better of me.

When I reached the street, the wind had picked up. Shoppers were doing their best to hang on to their packages and hats and scarves. I pulled up the hood on my coat and, protecting my few finds, headed back to the square. I climbed the steps to the top of Union Square and took cover inside the small coffee shop. The aroma of freshly ground beans filled the space. I ordered a cappuccino and carried it gingerly to a stool near the window where I could watch the skaters on the ice rink under the tree. Maybe this was picking at old wounds. Maybe I just wanted to remember a happier time.

The windows were completely fogged. I rubbed the condensation away with the sleeve of my coat and peeked out. The top of the seventy-foot tree and its huge bulbs swayed back and forth in the chilly gusts. Michael and I used to skate here. He was hopeless on his rented skates and wouldn't believe me when I told him it wasn't his ankles, his skates were too large. We'd manage a few passes around the rink before we'd collapse, laughing, on the ice. For a split second I saw his smile and felt the warmth of his hands, remembering how safe I felt when he put his arms around me. An aching so acute swept over me, I didn't trust myself not to burst into tears. What is it about the holiday season that brings our missing pieces into such sharp focus? Loss and pain may be there at other times, but somehow it doesn't hurt quite so acutely. Maybe stopping here wasn't such a good idea. I needed to quit feeling sorry for myself. Michael would have been disgusted with me. I was pathetic. I snuffled and rummaged in my purse for a tissue, blowing my nose and wiping my eyes, hoping anyone watching would think I was down with the flu. Suck it up, Julia.

Bundling up against the cold, I retraced my steps and approached the garage entrance. Two people, a man and a woman doing their best to stay warm under the overhang of the garage, were handing out flyers. One stepped in front of me, blocking my path, and shoved a flyer at me. Annoyed, I grabbed it and walked briskly into the garage. I glanced down at an announcement of services at the Prophet's Tabernacle. I sighed, and crumpling the paper up, I tossed it in a nearby trash can.

I took the elevator down to the lowest level, where I'd parked, then stepped out and glanced around. In contrast to the crowds of people on the streets, not a soul was in sight. I felt a frisson of fear. Why was it so deserted? My nerves were just on edge, I decided. I was imagining threats where there were none. I took a deep breath and hurried to my car, unlocked the door, and threw my bags onto the passenger seat. Before I turned the key in the ignition, I glanced in the rearview mirror.

A face in a ski mask stared back at me, the eyes bright in the ambient lighting. A gasp caught in my throat. My heart raced as a gloved hand pulled my head back and covered my mouth. I felt the sharp prick of a knife point at my neck. I froze. I couldn't move. I couldn't speak.

"Forget about the Prophet. Make sure you keep your big mouth shut or my next visit won't be so nice," he growled. He pulled the knife away, let go of my jaw, and jumped out of the car.

I struggled to breathe. I was shaking, but I somehow managed to start the car and pull out.

Where did he go? I thought I saw a shadow near the entrance to the stairway. I drove in that direction, but when I got there, I saw nothing. I circled the parking level and then the next two levels above, my tires squealing on the cement, but spotted no one who could possibly be my assailant.

The shock was hitting me now. My hands were shaking and I was running on adrenaline. I pulled into an empty spot and hit the brakes. The tears came then. Tears of fright and anger and frustration. Who were these people? What did they want? And why me?

When the sobs subsided, I blew my nose and wiped my eyes. I must have been followed. But from where? From my apartment? From the Gamble house? My instincts in the bookstore were correct. I'd have to pay better attention from now on.

Once out of the downtown area, traffic was light. I debated if there was anything I could do. My attacker would be long gone. I knew what this was about, but the police would never believe it or be able to do anything about it. Reporting it would be a waste of time. I refused to let these bullies get to me, and that's what they were — dangerous bullies.

I stopped at a discount store on Geary to pick up wrapping paper, ribbons, a few candles, and a wreath with a red bow. I was determined to live my life as normally as possible. Screw the Prophet. I may not have been in the swing of the holiday season, but I hoped that if I went through the motions,

I'd catch the spirit or it would catch me. Either way was fine.

My cell rang as I climbed back into the car. I recognized the number of the Mystic Eye. It was Cheryl. "Is everything all right?" I asked.

"It's fine. Just wanted to get hold of you to see if you could make a meeting at the Eye tomorrow night?"

"Sure. How come? Other people being hassled?"

"You could say that. Gale's talking to her lawyer, but she wants to get everyone who's associated with the Eye together, all our readers and friends, to hear their ideas before she does anything."

"I'll be there." We rang off.

The wind buffeted the car in short angry gusts as I drove the length of California Street. I turned down 30th Avenue, relieved to see an empty sidewalk. The weather had undoubtedly helped. No crowd was at my doorstep. I pulled into the garage, made sure the door was shut and locked, and trudged up the back stairs with my loot.

The adrenaline had left my system and I realized I was starving. I dug some leftover chicken from the refrigerator and wrapped it up in a flour tortilla with tons of mayonnaise and salt. It was almost ten o'clock. Ann's shift at the hospital ended at eleven. She'd be home soon, but I didn't want to bother her this late at night. I'd catch up with her in the morning. I devoured my chicken wrap as Wizard trotted into the kitchen, yawning, and waited by his bowl. I rubbed the top of his head, grateful we were both safe in the house, and dished some food into his bowl. He quacked back at me. When he finished eating, he jumped on my lap. I held him close and rubbed his fur. "Don't worry, Wiz. I'll keep you safe. It's just you and me now. I won't let anything bad happen to either one of us."

The message light was blinking. I listened to three heavy-breathing hangups. Lovely. A message from Don, asking me to call him at home. And at the end, a message from Ermie, my apartment manager, telling me to give her a call as soon as possible. I didn't like the sound of that. I checked the clock again. I wasn't sure what time parents went to bed, but hopefully if I called Don back now, I wouldn't be waking anyone up.

He answered on the first ring. "I think I know who's behind your nasty emails."

"I think I do too, and they staged a march around my building today on top of everything else." I decided not to tell Don about

115

the man in the ski mask. He'd hound me until I made a police report, even though both of us would know it wouldn't do any good.

"Did you call the cops?"

"My neighbor did, but my client was afraid to ring my bell. I had to rush to the Eye to meet her."

"Oh, no. I'm sorry, Julia."

"When I got there, a similar bunch had been picketing the shop and passing out leaflets. Scared the customers away. Gale's called a meeting. I think she plans to look into getting a restraining order against them."

"Well, at this point you may know more than me, but this Prophet guy and his followers have targeted other people. I did a little research. He started his so-called ministry about five years ago. He has a nonprofit organization based in Louisiana and has applied for the same tax status in California. And his legal name is Royal Earl Potter."

"What kind of a minister preaches hate?"

"That's just it, Julia. He doesn't. He preaches 'love' and 'compassion,' if you can believe that. He's well connected to local charities and politicians, runs a soup kitchen for the homeless, set up some shelters. He has a big following. He carries on about sin a lot, but hey, what else would you expect, he's a preacher."

"So it all depends on how he defines sin," I replied sarcastically. I love California and I love the tolerance of people in San Francisco. The city certainly has its share of oddballs, but most people live and let live.

"You be extra careful. This guy's either a con or a megalomaniac. He may or may not believe what he preaches, but I think he'll use anything to gain a power base. He's appealing to elements of the population that feel disenfranchised. And they could turn violent. I'll keep digging and see what I can turn up. By the way, don't delete any emails, and like I told you, keep a log of the calls."

"I'll be damned if they're going to intimidate me." *Brave words,* I thought. "My problem is that I can't have clients coming here and dealing with this. It'll wreck my business."

"I hear that. Just be careful. Call me if you have any more trouble. I'm only fifteen minutes away."

"Thanks, Don. Really. That means a lot."

I hung up. I was angry now, really angry, the more I thought about the monster hiding in my car. I grabbed a large pad of paper and forced myself to replay the three hangups, making evil faces at the machine each time I heard heavy breathing. I listened to the last message from Ermie more carefully. She was letting me know that my downstairs neighbors had complained to her. Now I regretted not checking my machine during the day and getting back to her. Hopefully she wouldn't think I'd been deliberately avoiding her.

After noting the time of each of the hangups, I kicked off my shoes and headed to the kitchen. I poured myself a generous glass of wine, turned up the heater, and arranged my new candles on the fireplace mantel while debating whether to hang my wreath at the front door or inside the house. I opted for hanging it over the fireplace, where the smell of pine would permeate the apartment. I hauled down the large picture over the mantel, slid it into the hallway closet, and hooked the wreath on the same nail. It worked perfectly. I propped my feet on the ottoman as Wizard ambled over and climbed on my lap, purring contentedly. I was too tired and shaken to even think about lighting a fire. I finished my wine and, picking Wizard up, headed down the hall to the bedroom.

The phone rang as I passed by the office. I tensed. Then I thought perhaps Ann was home and trying to reach me. I looked at the display and saw Gale's cell number. I grabbed it immediately.

"Thank God you're there." She sounded very shaky.

"What's wrong?"

"I'm at the Eye. Something very strange just happened. I heard a knock at the back door. I thought it might be you."

"Are you alone?"

"Yes. I closed up and sent Cheryl home. When I opened the door . . . oh God, Julia. Someone left a dead cat on the doorstep."

I cringed. "I'll be right there."

"I'm sorry. You don't need to come. I wrapped it up and put it in plastic in the dumpster. It looked like its neck had been broken."

"Don't argue. I'll be there in twenty minutes. Less than that."

TEN

I drove the length of California Street as fast as I could, slowing at each red light. Once I was sure no other cars were crossing, I ran through several intersections. Gale might be safe for now, but someone definitely wanted to send a message. When I reached the Eye, the shop was closed but the display lights were on in the front windows. I pulled down the alleyway and parked next to Gale's car, then tapped on the door. "Gale, it's me."

She opened the door immediately. The storeroom was dark. A stack of empty boxes and packing materials stood against the wall. Inside, the only light was a small desk lamp in the office.

Gale is tall and self-assured, with a regal bearing. Tonight she was completely shaken. She hugged her arms, more from fright than from cold. "I feel bad now that I've called you. I was just so freaked out. I recognized the cat — it was the little gray one that hangs out behind the apartment building next door. I think it's a stray. Everyone around here feeds it, even the restaurant people, and it's such a friendly little thing. Some sick bastard probably gave it some food and then snapped its neck. God, I think I'm going to be sick."

"Shouldn't you call the cops?"

"And tell them what? I found a dead cat? Please. Like they'd listen. Even if they thought someone had killed it, what could they do?"

"It shows a pattern of harassment. Might be worth making a report."

She sighed. "Yeah. You're probably right. I just wasn't thinking straight. I was so upset." She collapsed in the chair behind her desk.

I shrugged out of my coat. "Why are you here so late?"

"We just got a huge shipment of books and supplies in. Cheryl's been working late every night, so I sent her home. I'd just finished stacking the boxes in the store-room" — she shivered involuntarily — "when this . . ." She stopped in midsentence.

"What?"

"What's that on your neck?" She came

close and touched the spot on my neck where the attacker's knife had left a small mark. "What happened, Julia?"

I recounted the incident in the parking garage.

"Dear God. We've got to call the police."

"No."

"What? Why? You were physically attacked and threatened!"

"I know, but it's not going to do a damn thing except waste my time. Just like the cat. You know I'm right."

"I'll have to tell Cheryl. If they did this to you, we're all in danger."

"Maybe not. Maybe just me."

"Why do you say that?"

"My column reaches a lot of people. I'm more of a threat. And I'm wondering if the Prophet's image isn't a lot of crap. Don told me he preaches love and compassion and good works and all that stuff, but that doesn't jive with what we're all experiencing. Gale, there's a much bigger game here. I'm just not sure yet what it is."

"Whatever he's preaching, it doesn't look like any version of love and compassion to me," Gale said bitterly. "Look, let's get out of here. Have you eaten? Why don't we go up the block and grab some food? Actually, a drink sounds even better."

"Okay."

"Get your coat. We can leave the cars here and walk. I'll just get my purse."

I headed to the front door and checked that the locks were all in place. The drapes separating the display windows from the shop were drawn for privacy. Gale left the desk lamp on in the office and walked out to the front counter. As she reached under the counter for her purse, we heard glass breaking.

For a split second, I thought she'd knocked something over. Then I saw a flash of flame through the doorway to the back storeroom.

I screamed. Gale straightened quickly, looking confused. I ran back to the office and grabbed my coat. The empty boxes and packing materials had caught fire in an explosive flash. The smoke alarm started to ring, filling the shop with earsplitting sound. Using my coat like a blanket, I dropped it over the center of the flaming pile. It wasn't enough, but I had to do something before the entire storeroom went up, if not the entire building. My coat was heavy enough to cut off the oxygen from the center of the fire, but not large enough to contain it all.

Gale shouted behind me, "Julia, get out of the way." She was holding a large red fire extinguisher. She pulled the metal ring and aimed it at the pile of cardboard and paper that continued to blaze around my coat. "There's another one in the office. Grab it!" she shouted.

I ran back. I found a fire extinguisher in the closet as large as the one Gale held and rushed back. She'd managed to extinguish most of the blaze, but some hot spots were still visible. I aimed the chemical at the edges of the fire, moving toward the center until I was sure the danger had passed. Once the blaze had been extinguished, we stood there, breathless.

Gale turned to me. "Are you hurt? Any burns?"

I shook my head. "Don't think so. My coat's gone, but that's no great loss."

"If you hadn't been here, Julia . . ." Gale wiped her face and dropped the extinguisher to the floor. I'm calling the police and the fire department." She turned and headed for the office.

I hit the main light switch for the rear storeroom and looked around. Most of the stock was undamaged and still neatly stacked on shelves. With the exception of the boxes recently emptied, very little loose material was in evidence. The smoke alarm continued to scream. The noise was earsplitting. Without a full-sized ladder I had no way to turn it off. I rummaged through the shelves and finally spotted a small fan. I plugged it in and unlocked the back door, hoping to clear the air in the room. In a moment of caution, I picked up a hunk of wood left over from past shelving work and, holding it like a baseball bat, opened the back door. If anyone was still around intending to harm us, I had a weapon and I would use it.

I stepped outside and looked around cautiously. Not a soul. The only light came from the storeroom behind me and the back doors of the restaurants on Columbus. I stepped back inside and aimed the fan at the doorway. After a few minutes, the alarm subsided. By then, I heard approaching sirens.

Gale met the police and firefighters on the sidewalk. Traffic was in chaos — the fire trucks blocked Broadway. A black-and-white pulled up behind them and an officer climbed out and began to direct traffic around the fire trucks. A crowd had already gathered on the sidewalk. Everyone was talking excitedly and shouting questions. Some of them were in nightclothes and wrapped in blankets, frightened residents of the apartments above the shop.

Gale's voice was raised. "They tried to firebomb my shop!"

"Ma'am, let's go inside. We'll need to check the damage."

I pulled open the front door and held it for the firefighters. They formed a single line behind Gale, who led them to the rear.

An additional man in plain clothes had joined the group. "Did you see who did this?" he asked me.

"No. My friend and I were just getting ready to leave by the back door when it happened. They smashed the glass window and the next thing we knew, we heard a whoosh and saw the flames."

Gale chimed in. "I didn't see who did this, but I *know* who's behind it. We filed a police report for harassment earlier today. It's those freaks from the Prophet's Tabernacle, that's who's responsible."

"Ma'am . . ." They were obviously trying to calm her down.

Gale is intimidating even when she's not angry. Right now, she was very angry. "Don't ma'am me! I want you to do something about it. I want you to roust them out of that temple or whatever the hell they call it up on Mason and arrest them."

"We can check that out and question those people, but odds are the place is locked up for the night." The detective turned to me. "Unless you saw someone, or have some evidence . . ." He trailed off.

"No. I didn't see them. I was inside and a damn good thing too!" Gale's voice was rising. "If we hadn't been here, that entire stock room would have gone up in a few minutes, and half the city block as well. This is a major crime. Arson is a felony, isn't it? People could have died here. I'm calling my lawyer and I'm going to the DA if you won't do anything."

One of the firemen spoke. "That's your privilege, ma'am, but I assure you, we'll document everything, we'll collect evidence, we'll check for fingerprints and anything we can find."

The detective stepped forward. "You're absolutely right. It's very serious and we're not minimizing this. I just find it hard to believe you're accusing the Reverend Roy. Do you have any evidence? Have they threatened you?"

"Trust me. I know that sick son of a bitch is behind this."

"Now, ma'am . . ."

"I told you not to ma'am me, didn't I?"

I walked over to Gale's side and put an arm around her. She needed to calm down. She was on the verge of tears. "Oh, Julia,

I'm so glad you're here." Her voice broke.

"Let them do what they can do tonight. You can talk to the lawyer tomorrow." I gave the detective a dirty look for even attempting to defend the Army of the Prophet.

Gale took a deep breath and did her best to calm down. "Fine. Do your thing. I want the name of your supervisor in the department and I'll be on the phone to him or her first thing tomorrow."

The detective stepped closer and reached into his pocket. "Here's my card. I'll write my captain's name on the back and his number." He scribbled for a few moments and replaced his pen in his pocket. "I'll have a patrol car come by and keep watch a few times tonight, just to keep an eye on things. Do you have someone who can secure that back window for you?"

"Yes. I have a handyman. I can try to reach him."

"I'll stop in tomorrow if you'll be here and we can talk some more. There might be something you remember that you're not recalling right now."

In the back room, someone had unplugged the small fan. Shards of glass littered the threshold and the floor. A firefighter stood by while another took photos of the debris and a charred section of the wall and floor.

I smelled gasoline and another pungent odor I couldn't identify. I stepped gingerly around the scene, tiny pieces of glass crunching under my feet.

Gale joined me in the rear storeroom. Her jaw was clenched. "Julia, if I hadn't had those fire extinguishers, I don't know what would have happened. This old building is a tinderbox. People were asleep upstairs. Thank heavens you were here and we managed to put it out."

"Have you called Cheryl yet?"

"No. And I'm not going to. Let her get some rest. I'll catch her early tomorrow before she comes in. Look, I'm sorry I panicked earlier. I just had to call somebody."

"Don't you dare apologize. I'd be furious if you hadn't called. If you can find some plywood and a drill and some screws, I can cover up that opening."

"Can you? You handy girl! That would be great. I'd hate to call Edwin this late. I know he'd come, he's wonderful, but I don't want to drag him out of bed." Gale turned in a circle, surveying the room. "I think there's a few small pieces of plywood around. I'll find everything for you."

It was another hour and a half before the

firefighters left. Two patrolmen had turned up who stayed with us until everything was secured. Once that was done, we all left by the rear entrance.

"Follow me home," Gale said. "I can give you one of my coats."

"I'll be fine. Don't worry."

She reached over and squeezed my hand. "But your coat's ruined."

"I have plenty of clothes. No great loss. But I think I should follow *you* home."

"What? You think someone might attack me?"

"I don't know what to think. If they're capable of endangering us and so many others, they're capable of anything. I just want to make sure no one's watching us to see where you live. They already know where to find me, but you're still an unknown. They haven't put your face or your home address together. And I don't want them to. Don't argue."

The patrolmen watched from their black-and-white while we climbed into our cars. We pulled out onto Broadway and I followed Gale up the hill to Hyde Street and her Russian Hill condo. I pulled over to the curb and watched while she entered the circular drive. The night doorman approached and opened her door. Gale stepped out and waved to me. I waited until she was safely inside her building, grateful she lived in a secure place. I doubted whoever threw that bomb had hung around to wait for the police, and I was fairly certain we hadn't been followed.

ELEVEN

The following morning, the smell of smoke and gasoline still lingered in my nostrils and my hair. My head was pounding and some low level of noise had interrupted my sleep. Wizard jumped on the bed and howled at me. I lifted my head and stared at him groggily. "Wiz." He meowed loudly again. "What's the matter?"

Then I heard it. Far away. Chanting. I jumped out of bed and rushed down the hall to the living room windows. Shouts carried up from below, most of it coming from my neighbors across the street. Today, fifty people — I counted — were marching in a circle and chanting something I couldn't make out. They carried a large effigy of a witch on a broomstick draped in black cloth with a crazy Halloween hat on its head.

I peeked sideways from the edge of the drape and spotted Ann standing on her front steps next door, a slender figure in her bathrobe. Her hair hung in ringlets around her face. She must have been woken from a dead sleep. She pulled her robe closer and craned her neck to look up at my window. She held a fist up to her ear to indicate she'd call me.

I was so focused on the commotion below I almost didn't notice, but a flash of light caught my eye. A man in dark clothing with binoculars stood on the next street, 31st Avenue, on the other side of the tennis court that connects the streets and provides a clear line of sight. The watcher had an unobstructed view of the proceedings. The light reflecting from the lens of his binoculars had given him away. Otherwise, I might not have noticed him. Something about his body language implied a focus and control of the situation. It was nothing I could put my finger on, but I was certain this man was in charge of orchestrating the chaos below my windows. Was he the man in the ski mask who'd been waiting in my car? There was no way to know. I'd only seen that person's eyes. I couldn't possibly identify him even if he was right in front of me.

A moment later, the phone rang. "Can you believe they're back?" It was Ann. "They've painted something on the sidewalk, but I couldn't get a good look."

"Hang on." Holding the phone to my ear, I peeked through the living room drapes, trying not to be seen while I watched the circus below.

"Julia, I've called the police and I'm sure other people have too. I'm so sorry this is happening to you. You don't deserve this."

I moved away from the window. "Thanks, Ann, I —"

I heard a crash. The window exploded and a large rock rolled across the carpet inches from where I stood. Shards of glass littered the living room. Wizard leaped from his chair at the sound and skittered down the hallway to the bedroom.

Ann shouted, "What was that?"

"A rock just came through my window. I'll call you back." I was furious. I slammed down the phone and ran to the bedroom. I pulled on my jeans and a sweater and opened the back door. I hauled the end of a fifty foot garden hose to the kitchen sink and attached it to the faucet. Then I lugged the other end of the hose, uncoiling it as I dragged it to the living room. I opened an unbroken window a few inches and wedged the end of the hose against the windowsill. I ran back to the kitchen and turned the water on full blast. The force of the pressure was causing water to spew wildly over the street and sidewalk. I hurried back to the living room and grabbed the end of the hose. I aimed it directly at the followers of the Prophet, particularly the man carrying the effigy of a witch.

I managed to give one or two a good soaking before the rest scattered out of range of my hose. I only wished I'd had boiling oil to dump on them. Best I could hope for was that a few of them might catch pneumonia in the cold. I was just starting to have some fun when a cruiser pulled around the corner from Clement Street. But that didn't slow me down — the high pressure stream of water could still reach a few standing in the street.

The cruiser pulled into the driveway of the building next door. Two patrolmen climbed out, an older man and a rookie. The man in charge looked up at the window and shouted. "Lady, turn that thing off. Now!"

I glared at him and then aimed the hose at a particularly loud woman. At that moment, I didn't care what the police thought.

"Ma'am. Now!"

I managed to soak a few more before I slammed the window on the hose and walked calmly back to the kitchen to turn the faucet off.

Down on the sidewalk, I saw one of the officers talking to a man and a woman they'd cornered, pointing to the front of my building. I couldn't hear what they were saying, but a minute later the doorbell rang. As I opened my door, I realized I was at a definite disadvantage. My teeth weren't brushed and my hair was sticking up all over my head. I smelled of burned soot from the fire the night before. In an effort to stay in control, I demanded, "Are you going to arrest those freaks?"

The officer shook his head. "Look, they're gathering without a permit. They're disturbing the peace. We can issue citations and charge them with defacing city property, namely your sidewalk, and they'll have to appear before a judge."

"What? My sidewalk? That's it? They can harass me and my neighbors and that's all you can do? They threw a rock through my window!"

"Did you see the person who threw the rock?"

"No, I didn't, but that's not the point. They're all guilty of harassment."

"Those are misdemeanor charges. They can be forced to pay for any damage. Have they threatened you in any way?"

"These are the same people who've been threatening me with phone calls and emails and hangups. Those maniacs are from the Prophet's Tabernacle. They were here yesterday doing the very same thing. My neighbor filed a complaint. I'd call that harassment and threats, wouldn't you?"

"What did you say?" He cocked his head.

"You heard me. They call themselves the Army of the Prophet."

The older patrolman's face hardened. "Maybe you've offended the Reverend in some way."

A chill ran through me. Then I saw red. "I frankly don't give a crap if the *Reverend* is offended, and if I can personally find a way to offend him further, believe me, I will. I thought your job was to 'protect and serve,' not keep order for a fascist masquerading as a man of God." By now I was shouting.

The officer's face grew stonier. His lips were a thin line. He was doing his best to control his temper. I had already given up that battle. "We'll file a report today, but by all rights, they could charge *you* with assault."

"With a garden hose? After what they've done? I don't *think* so."

"Wouldn't amount to much, but could cause you some trouble."

Was he threatening me? I took a deep breath and tried to bring it down a notch. "They're breaking the law, disturbing the peace — for me, for my neighbors. I need you to arrest them, or whatever it is you do. Just put a stop to this. Surely I have a right to peace and quiet in my home. I don't bother anyone. I don't deserve this." I was still furious and sounded on the verge of hysterics.

The younger patrolman, who'd remained outside until now, climbed the stairs to join us. His other partner heaved a sigh. His whole attitude seemed to convey that this was a minor neighborhood squabble.

The younger man turned to the senior officer. "They say they're doing God's work."

"God, my ass," I shouted. "I'll go after them with more than a garden hose if I see them again. They've made threats implying that I'm a witch and I should burn at the stake. Doesn't that qualify as a death threat?"

The two men looked at each other quizzically and turned back to me. "We're not really sure," the younger man replied.

"That's very reassuring. Thank you very much," I replied sarcastically.

The older man turned away dismissively

and headed down the stairs. The younger officer started to follow, then hesitated and turned back to me. "Look . . . I'm really sorry. We've been told to lay off the Prophet and any of his followers."

"What? Lay off them? Who's giving the orders?"

The man's face was sympathetic, but he remained silent and shrugged. "If they come back or bother you again, please call us."

I mentally rolled my eyes. Fat lot of good that would do me. I slammed the door behind them and pounded back up the stairs, so furious I was mumbling to myself. I grabbed the phone and dialed Ann's number. She answered on the first ring. "Julia, why don't you come over and have some coffee. I can't get back to sleep now anyway."

"I'll be there in a minute." I hung up, pulled off my sweater and nightie, put on a bra, put my sweater back on over my jeans, and brushed my teeth. Satisfied I wouldn't frighten my neighbor, I grabbed my keys, made sure Wizard was locked in, and headed for Ann's house. I double-checked that my front door was locked behind me. I wasn't in a very trusting mood. For all I knew, I could return to find strange people in my living room. When I reached the sidewalk, I circled around the painted words. In red dripping letters, it read, *"Burn Witch Burn."*

TWELVE

Ann's house is a tiny cottage, the kind that was constructed as quick housing after the 1906 quake and is now dwarfed by taller buildings. I knocked and peeked through the glass in the front door. Ann was in the doorway of her kitchen. She waved and headed toward the front door.

"Come on in, Julia. Grab a chair." Still in her bathrobe, she almost looked like a high school student. But she was a lot more put together than I was at the moment. She poured me a generous mug of coffee and placed a container of half-and-half on the table. I added some to my coffee. I needed caffeine very badly.

Ann sat across the table from me. "Did you notice their armbands?"

"I didn't get a close look, but I saw there was something bright blue."

"It's a cross outlined against a rising sun. They call themselves the Army of the

Prophet."

"I know. Last night they tried to firebomb the Mystic Eye."

"Oh, no!" Ann exclaimed. "When the hell are the police going to do something about them?"

"I've just been told they have orders to lay off the Prophet."

"You're kidding!"

"I wish I were." I took a large sip of coffee. "What happened after I left yesterday?"

"The cops took their time getting here. I called them first and then went out and yelled at those nuts. One of the guys from that big house at the end of the block tried to chase them away, but they just ignored us. Then a little while after you left, they dispersed. They were gone by the time the patrol car arrived. The police didn't want to make a report. I guess we know why now. I insisted, though. More importantly, why are they bothering *you*?"

I hesitated. "I . . . uh . . . you know the *AskZodia* column in the paper?"

"Yeah. I love that column!" Ann gasped. "Don't tell me you're Zodia?"

I nodded. "In one of my responses I had a few choice things to say about false prophets and people who martyr themselves. I'm sure that's what did it. Apparently Reverend Roy believes that psychics and astrologers, among others — we're all lumped together — are doing the work of the devil and should be driven out."

"Others being feminists, gays, planned parenthood clinics, liberals and the like, right?" Ann asked sarcastically. "These are the kind of people who murder abortion doctors. What are you gonna do?"

"I don't know." I sighed. "My grandmother's away. I think I might just stay at her house. If I'm not around and they know it, the neighborhood could get some peace. Not to mention my clients."

"Oh, speaking of clients . . . can we set something up soon?" Anne smiled conspiratorially.

"Sure. I'd love to. Something going on?"

"I hope so. I met a new guy and I'd like you to check him out."

I laughed. "Okay. I love romance! You've got my cell number. When you get his information, just give me a call and we'll figure out a time."

"And you have *my* cell. If you need any help, call me, okay? Promise?"

"I will. Thanks."

I trotted down Ann's stairs and then climbed my own, locking the front door behind me. I passed the door to my office and noticed the blinking light on the answering machine. I hit the button. Three more hangups. I heaved a sigh and pulled out the pad of paper to add them to my log. I jumped when the phone rang. I grabbed it immediately, sure it was another harassing call.

"Julia?"

"Yes." It was Ermie, my apartment manager. I cringed when I remembered that I'd failed to return her call the day before.

"Please tell me what's going on at the building? I've been getting calls from your downstairs neighbors."

My neighbors are a childless forty-something couple. They're very quiet, never bother me, and are generally out almost every day. They're perfectly pleasant people, if a bit uptight, and we've probably never spoken more than six words to each other.

"I wish I knew," I said. I wasn't about to tell Ermie I was the author of *AskZodia* — I was afraid she'd think I'd brought the trouble on myself. "I'm sorry, I really am. And I have no idea what's going on. The neighbor next door called the police on them yesterday and today. We believe they're members of that cult, the Prophet's Tabernacle."

"You mean that bible thumper with the

pompadour? The *Prophet TV* guy?"

"That's him. Look, Ermie, I don't know what to do. I've filed a police report."

"I don't understand why they're bothering you."

"Apparently the Reverend Roy, or at least some of his followers, have decided I'm a sinner because I'm practicing astrology. By the way, don't worry about the sidewalk. I'll clean the paint off today."

"Paint? Did they get paint on the house?"

"No. Just the sidewalk. Really sick stuff."

"Well, dear, I hate to be hard on you, you're a good tenant, but I can't have this kind of thing going on around the building. I personally don't care if you're running a business out of your apartment. I've looked the other way, but if these people have some beef with you because you're an astrologer, you might want to think about looking for an office somewhere."

My heart sank. "These crazies are attacking me. *I* haven't done anything, Ermie."

"I'm not saying you have, Julia, but I can't have this going on. You have to realize, I'm not the owner. I haven't said anything to her about your seeing clients in your apartment, but it's not covered by your lease and she'd be within her rights to evict you. Technically you're in violation. I'm going to have to tell her about this, and if anything more serious happens, well . . . maybe you should look for another place."

"I see." I almost burst into tears. I loved my apartment and my neighborhood. My rent was probably one-third what I'd have to pay if I were forced to move, plus I didn't have to pay for office space. I love being close to the sea. I love watching the fog roll in over the tops of the pine trees in Lincoln Park. It was my neighborhood now. I even had a little backyard with grass for Wizard. I couldn't move, not to mention the expense.

As if she could read my mind, Ermie spoke. "If you don't get a handle on this nonsense, you'll be paying an awful lot more for a rental in the area, you know that."

"Ermie, look — I'll stay somewhere else until this is sorted out. You have my cell number. Please call me right away if you have any further problem. If I'm not at home and the Prophet's followers know that, maybe they'll find someone else to harass. I'll handle this. I promise. I'll find out who's behind it and put a stop to it." I had no idea how I was going to keep my word, but it was all I could think to say.

"I certainly hope so." With that, Ermie rang off.

I stifled a sob. I couldn't really blame her. It was her job to take care of the building and in her eyes, I was the cause of all the upset. Now I might be homeless. Well, not exactly homeless. I could always live at Gloria's and see clients at the Eye, but it wasn't an ideal situation for anyone. It wasn't what I wanted.

THIRTEEN

I found a small roll of bubble wrap in the closet, cut two large pieces, and taped them carefully over the hole in the window. It would keep the apartment insulated until I could get the pane replaced. Then I swept up the glass, dumped it in the trash, and hauled out my vacuum to pick up the smaller shards. When I finished, I pulled on a pair of my grubbiest jeans and a sweatshirt, grabbed my keys, and headed down to the garage. I found a hardware store on Geary and bought a pair of heavy duty rubber gloves, a wire brush, and a large can of paint remover. I was still fuming. I parked across the street to keep my car safe from chemical splatter.

After tying my hair back, I pulled on the rubber gloves and lugged the heavy-duty hose from the backyard to the door of the side entrance, attaching it to the spigot closer to the front of the house. Then I carefully poured paint remover over the hateful words on the sidewalk. I let it sit for a few minutes and when the paint started to bubble, I scrubbed the concrete with the wire brush, careful not to kneel in the chemical and scald my knees. It took some doing since the concrete was porous, but eventually the words started to disappear. I hosed off what I could and repeated the process two more times until there was only a faint hint of pink on the gray concrete. Anger fueled me. Who did these people think they were that they could threaten me and interfere with my business and my life?

By the time I finished, my jeans were soaked and I was chilled to the bone. I rinsed off the wire brush, rewrapped the hose in the backyard, and dumped the empty paint remover can and the rubber gloves in the trash. On my way up the front stairs, I checked the mailbox. Two bills, several flyers, and a free newsletter. I left them on the desk to open later and checked the answering machine in the office again. No more calls. I breathed a sigh of relief. The only bright spot was that my cell number was safe — so far. Don knew my cell and Samantha had the number too, but I'd never listed it on the contact form for the newspaper.

I stripped off my clothes and dumped them in the washer with soap and fabric softener. Then I climbed in the shower and let the hot water warm me. I dressed in fresh jeans and a heavy sweater and searched through the coats in the hallway closet. I found a double-breasted tweed jacket with a hood to replace my coat destroyed in the fire. Next I packed an overnight bag. I collected Wizard's food, dishes, and litter container and loaded all that in an empty box. I recorded a new outgoing message on my machine, saying that I would be unavailable until after the holidays and would return calls then.

The washer had finished its cycle. I dumped my wet clothes in the dryer and then wrote a note to my downstairs neighbors, apologizing for the upset and leaving my cell number in case they needed to reach me. I didn't know what else I could do to calm the situation down.

When Wizard saw his dishes and things being packed up he knew he was about to be transported — probably his least favorite thing in the whole world. I searched the entire apartment and finally found him hiding behind a garment bag in the bedroom closet. I managed to coax him out and wrestle him into the cat carrier. He hates being in the carrier and howls a lot, but I wasn't about to leave him unattended in the apartment.

I looked around, sad that I was leaving my fresh wreath above the mantel. Was my apartment safe? Would anyone try to break in? I double-checked that all the windows and doors were locked, especially the window over the kitchen sink. That was the only vulnerable window in the whole apartment. It would take an extremely limber person, but it might be possible to balance on the railing of the tiny landing and push that window up. I had to trust that the lock would be good enough to prevent that. I packed up my Christmas finds in a giant department store bag, with wrapping paper and ribbons and, making two trips, lugged everything, including Wizard, across the street to my car. I sat in the driver's seat for a moment and looked up at my windows, imagining a protective bubble over my apartment until I could return again. I started the car.

Wizard immediately began to howl. I shushed him, clicked on the radio, and drove toward town.

FOURTEEN

I pulled up in front of the street level garage
of my grandmother's house in Castle Alley.
Parking in North Beach is next to impossible and any other option would involve
circling the entire area for an hour. I lugged
Wizard's stuff — which far outweighed my
laptop and overnight bag — up the stairs
and unlocked the front door. No cats travel
light.

If Kuan is free, he peeks out to say hello
when he hears my car. A *Do Not Disturb* sign
in English and Cantonese hung on his door.
He was with a client.

I made two trips up the interior stairway
to Gloria's kitchen, depositing my overnight
bag in the room that was once my bedroom
and now is a sitting room and workroom. I
wasn't worried about needing clothes. I had
underwear, jeans, a couple of sweaters, and
a skirt; enough for a few days. My grandmother is a retired seamstress and once had

her own shop. Now she keeps closets full of samples in my size. There's no event that wouldn't be covered from the wardrobe she keeps on hand for herself and for me.

I organized Wizard's stuff, filling his cat box with litter and his bowls with dry food and water. The apartment felt chilly, so I checked the thermostat in the hallway and turned it up to warm the place. Then I set up my laptop on Gloria's worktable and resolved to get some work done.

In spite of the harassment the column had engendered, or rather my opinionated big mouth had caused, I was still happy to be working for the newspaper. I decided not to check my *AskZodia* email at all — I had no further need of Biblical quotations, thank you very much. Samantha had sent another twenty letters to my new email address and, breach of security or not, I was still obligated to prepare Zodia's responses.

I opened each email and quickly read through all of them. I dragged the ones that offered a range of different generational issues into an archive. The rest, as usual, I returned to Sam, asking her to send a form response.

I thought back to the reply I'd written a week or so prior, and which the newspaper had printed a few days ago. I clicked into my folder where each week's letters were saved and scrolled down the list until I found it.

Dear Zodia:
I've never written to an astrologer before or asked for help of this sort, but I'm at my wit's end and don't know what to do. My mother has become involved with some sort of religious group that seems to have taken over her life. She's at meetings day and night and now wants to live with them. It's called Prophet's Paradise. I'm so worried about her, especially since she must transfer the title to her home to the church in order to move into the community. My birthday is August 15, 1955. My mother's birthday is January 10, 1930.
— Desperate in San Leandro

Dear Desperate:
I don't blame you for being worried. I'd be extremely suspicious as well. Your mother's chart shows that Neptune is transiting her Ascendant and Mercury, and her progressed Moon has entered her 9th house. Renewed interest in spiritual matters makes perfect sense, but with Neptune close to her Ascendant

and Mercury, she may be attracted to movements that require sacrifice and subservience. Perhaps you should investigate this so-called Prophet's Paradise yourself. Frankly, it sounds an awful lot like a criminal scam designed to defraud the unwary. Beware of false prophets! Another alternative would be to seek legal help to have yourself appointed as her guardian, so she would not lose her home.

— Zodia

Well, there it was. Undoubtedly the statement that had painted a bull's-eye on my rear end, although it might have happened anyway simply because of my column. There was nothing I could do about it now. And, more to the point, why was this supposed do-gooder requiring his followers to sign over their real estate? I opened a browser and found the Prophet's website.

Very slick. Pictures of soup kitchens, summer camps for kids, religious retreats for adults, artful photos of adoring congregations. Testimonials from devoted members and upstanding citizens. Lots of talk about God's love and not much of real substance.

A new idea popped into my head. A sweet revenge. They'd tried to intimidate me, I was sure, because of this response. On an impulse I forwarded the email to Sam with a note asking her to reprint it again as soon as possible in the Zodia column. As far as I was concerned, the paper could run the damn response in every column. Let's see what the Army of the Prophet made of that. Keep my mouth shut? I don't think so!

It was time to have a belated look at my own chart. Sure enough, Uranus had moved into exact opposition to my fourth house Moon. Both the fourth house and the Moon are intimately connected with the concept of home. Mars had moved into position squaring the opposition yesterday, the first day the zealots had arrived on my doorstep. I groaned. I knew this was coming, but never in my wildest dreams had I thought it would manifest in this form. Mars would be stationary on that degree for a few more days. Uranus wouldn't move on for another week. I quickly checked to make sure that neither the Sun, Moon, nor any eclipses would be hitting sensitive points in my chart during this intense time. Whatever happened, the worst would be over soon, and with luck I'd survive the coming week without an eviction notice.

Wizard meowed and climbed onto my lap, burrowing his face into my sweater. I scratched his ears. They were cold. Come to think of it, I was cold. I picked Wiz up and checked the thermostat again. It read seventy-two but felt twenty degrees colder. I turned it up to eighty-five to jump-start it. Wizard hopped out of my arms and ran back to the daybed, snuggling under my jacket.

"I don't blame you, big guy," I said. "Don't worry. I'll get the place warmed up."

I went down the stairs to the kitchen and put a kettle on to make some tea. I needed to find food too. My grandmother is a fabulous cook. Now that she lived alone, she couldn't stop cooking larger portions. I was sure the freezer was stocked with many small meals, enough to last for weeks in case of a dire earthquake emergency. I also suspected she would trot downstairs to Kuan's apartment regularly to bring food to him. I was too hungry to wait for something to defrost, so I found a can of soup in the pantry, dumped it in a bowl, and heated it in the microwave. It helped to warm me, but by the time I finished and rinsed the bowl, I realized the heater still hadn't kicked on. Something was definitely wrong.

I walked downstairs to the front door and peeked through the beveled glass window. Kuan's door stands at a ninety-degree angle to Gloria's. The sign was gone; it was safe to knock. Kuan answered the door almost immediately. He's is in his seventies, wiry and energetic with beautiful posture. That day he wore an outfit of black cotton pants and a plain long-sleeved shirt without a collar.

"Julia, how are you? I heard you arrive."

"I'm fine, but the furnace doesn't seem to be working. How's yours?"

"It's warm and toasty in here. You might want to call a repairman, see what's wrong. You're welcome to stay here if you like."

"You have patients coming today?"

"Just one later, at five o'clock."

"In that case, don't worry about it. I don't want to disturb you. Keep your fingers crossed the furnace hasn't died. I'll turn on the kitchen oven for now and call someone." I kissed his cheek. "Thanks anyway. I'll see you later." Gloria was nothing if not organized. I pulled her Rolodex out of the desk drawer and found a card for Prager Heating & Cooling. A woman answered. I could hear the sound of screaming children in the background.

"Jerry's out on a call right now. He's in Daly City, but maybe I can reach him and have him stop by later."

"That would be great." I gave her Gloria's

address and my cell number, stressing that I'd be waiting all afternoon. I resigned myself to working on the kitchen table and turned the gas oven up to four hundred degrees. I know that's not the best idea, but I was desperate. I reheated the mug of tea and used it to warm my fingers.

I debated again whether to sign on to my *AskZodia* email, and this time decided to do it. As soon as it opened, a new email popped up. With a feeling of dread, I opened it, hoping no one had sent me a computer virus.

"If my people which are called by my name shall humble themselves and pray, and seek my face, and turn from their wicked ways, then will I hear from heaven and will forgive their sin . . ."

I closed the browser. I didn't need to read any more, but I was delighted to learn my sins could be forgiven. I picked up the phone and dialed Samantha.

"Hey, it's me."

"Julia! Les has been calling everyone into his office for the third degree. Everyone who had access to our files here and in Payroll. He's really upset about this."

"Good. I hope he gets to the bottom of it. I've got some more responses to send back to you, by the way. Did you get the one I asked you to reprint?"

159

"Yes, I did."

"Can you do that?"

"Sure, why not? If that's why you're being harassed, then all the more reason people should read it."

"Good. Thank you."

"Julia, I just love the Zodia column. And it's such a success. I read the letters that come in before I send them to you. And then I read your responses every week. I really hope you don't let this scare you away."

"A few kooks aren't gonna shut me up. Don't worry." I heard the doorbell ring. "I gotta go. We'll talk later." I pushed my laptop away and walked down the stairs to the front door. A thirty-something chubby man in baggy jeans with a round apple-cheeked face stood on the threshold.

"Jerry?"

"That's me. Jerry Prager. What's the trouble?"

"Well, I don't know. The furnace doesn't seem to give off any heat from the vents."

"I'll have a look. Where is it? The garage?"

"Yes. Wait a sec, I'll get the keys." I ran upstairs and rummaged through Gloria's desk until I found a set, then walked down the outside stairs to where Jerry waited. I turned the lock and heaved the old-fashioned wooden garage door open. Jerry followed me into the darkened space. He pulled out a flashlight and examined the furnace.

"Well, at least this baby is a lot newer than your house. Must be from the early sixties. A wonder it's lasted so long."

"What do you see?"

"Your furnace is cracked."

"Cracked?"

"Yup. Gotta shut your gas off."

"What? You're kidding. That's the only thing that's keeping any heat at all in the house." It doesn't snow in San Francisco, at least that I've ever heard, but in winter, the freezing winds off the Pacific and the Alaskan currents hitting the west coast keep the weather cold and damp.

"Sorry, lady. It's required. And these old houses don't have a separate shut off for just the furnace, so if you have a gas stove, you won't be able to use it. It's real dangerous. You can check with the gas company if you don't believe me. You've gotta replace this one."

I groaned. Not only couldn't I go home, but I couldn't let Gloria come back to a freezing house, not after her cruise. She'd end up with pneumonia. "How soon could you replace it?"

"Well . . ." Jerry pulled off his baseball cap. I could see a premature bald spot and pink skin on the top of his head. He scratched the bald spot and replaced the cap. "Best I can do . . . is three days from now, maybe two. I've got one helper down with the flu, another furnace replacement on the schedule, and I've gotta order a new one delivered from the factory. Even if I could do it sooner, I doubt I could get you one till then anyway." He shone his flashlight at Kuan's furnace. "I see the downstairs apartment had a new one put in. Maybe a few years ago? Now that's a real beauty. I could get you one of those."

"Okay. How much?"

Jerry scratched his bald spot once more and quoted me a price. I gasped. I'd have to put it on a credit card. I knew Gloria would insist on refunding me the money when she returned. I wasn't worried about that, just about how much room I had on my one big credit card.

"Hang on. I'll get a work order out of my truck."

I shivered while I waited for Jerry to rummage in the front seat of his cab. After a few minutes, he returned with a form in triplicate and lots of fine print. I signed on the bottom line, committed to the delivery and installation of an honest to goodness working furnace, and if Jerry thought it was a real beauty, that was good enough for me.

After he turned off the gas to Gloria's apartment, we shook hands and he climbed into his truck and pulled away from the curb. I closed the garage door and locked it, dropping the keys back in my pocket. When I reached the kitchen, I saw that Wizard had moved onto my vacated seat cushion for warmth. What warmth there was wouldn't last long without the oven. The Uranus transit had even interfered with my second home.

I checked Wizard's bowls and made sure he was set for the afternoon. I grabbed my purse and coat and rubbed his ears. "I'll be back very soon, Wiz. You'll be fine. You have a fur coat. I don't." I headed down the stairs and locked the front door behind me. As I turned around, Kuan's door opened.

"What's the verdict?"

"Furnace has to be replaced. Gloria's gas is shut off."

"I thought so. Same thing happened to mine a while back. Offer's still good."

"Thanks, I appreciate that, but I'll be fine."

"Are you going back to your apartment now?"

I hesitated. I didn't want to tell Kuan about the crazy picketers or the trouble with my landlady or any of the rest of it. "Don't think so. I'll probably come back here." I sensed that he knew I was withholding something, but I didn't have time to explain the entire situation, and he didn't push it.

He nodded. "How soon can they get one put in?"

"Three days."

"If you're busy, let me know. I'll make sure I'm here to let them in."

"Thank you! I'll be back and forth while Gloria's gone, but don't worry if you don't see me." I gave him a kiss on the cheek. In response, he held his hand up, palm facing me, separating his middle and ring fingers in the *Live Long and Prosper* sign.

"How do you do that? I never can."

Kuan smiled and shut his door.

FIFTEEN

If Evandra wanted a séance tomorrow night, I needed to get in touch with someone who could set that up. The only person I could think of was Nikolai, a psychic and past-life regression hypnotist I'd met through the Mystic Eye. I had his address and phone number and I could call him, but I felt I'd stand a better chance of having him say yes if I asked in person. Evandra had been very firm that the séance take place on the evening of December 21st, Lily's birthday. That was tomorrow, and I had no idea if Nikolai would agree to do it. I didn't know if he was even in town.

Nikolai lives in a converted garage in the Inner Sunset. His living quarters are upstairs, but most of the time he can be found working in his "studio" on the lower level. When I pulled into the driveway leading to his space, I saw three cars, in addition to his, parked there. He had company. I left my Geo behind the last car, closest to the street, and walked up the driveway to the side door of the garage. An outside stairway led to his apartment, but if Nikolai was at work, I'd find him here at ground level.

I knocked loudly. Inside, someone yelled "Cut." There were footsteps and suddenly the door was flung open. Nikolai filled the doorway. He's over six feet and very portly. He sports a full gray beard and long gray hair. Today he was dressed in a voluminous, deep maroon robe.

I took two steps back and looked up. "What the hell? Are you channeling Rasputin?"

"Julia! Vat delight. Haf you finally realized your great lust for me?" Nikolai's booming voice could be heard two houses away.

"Oh, stop it."

"I knew you would someday. Dat's vy you knocked. Today's my lucky day. Come in."

"I'm not interrupting?" Behind Nikolai I could see some commotion with a camera and a tripod.

"No . . . just exorcism. For my community access cable show."

"How many entities do you have in that garage?"

Nikolai responded with a belly laugh.

"Come in and meet them all. They don't bite."

I mentally shook my head. Astrology makes sense to me. There's an order and a logic to it. But exorcism? I wasn't sure if I believed in such a thing, the driving out of evil spirits who possessed people, but Nikolai's show had gained in popularity to such an extent that it was about to be aired on a local TV channel, not just community access. Nikolai's subjects were always very young, attractive women with theatrical ambitions. It was truly amazing how many aspiring actresses in San Francisco were possessed by evil entities.

Nikolai indicated a small thin man with large glasses. "Dis is Chuck, our technical vizard." I shook hands with Chuck, who was a good foot shorter than I, with dark greasy hair and thick glasses that slid down his nose.

"And dis is Lydia, my charming subject." Lydia rose from the velvet draped bier on which she had been reclining.

"Hi." Lydia didn't look particularly happy to be interrupted. She was wearing a long gypsy skirt in bright colors and a tight, low-cut tank top. She turned to Nikolai and pouted. "I thought I was your only subject today."

"You are, my dear, you are. Julia and I are colleagues. Vee take a little break, okay?"

Lydia sighed and moved to a makeup table set up in the far corner, where she began to add to her rouge and eyeliner. Nikolai winked at me and led me to two armchairs at the back of the space. Indicating I should sit on one of the chairs, he took the other, after placing a hard cushion over the frayed upholstery and metal spring peeking through.

"Vhat's up, Julia?"

"I have a client who wants to hold a séance." I hadn't sorted out my feelings about the plan. I guess I'm not a particular believer in communications with those who have passed over, and perhaps this makes me uncool to some people, but I was determined to keep an open mind. "Are you up for it?"

"Are you kidding?" Nikolai beamed. "I'd luf to! Vhen?" Rumor had it that he'd once worked in a top-secret Soviet psychic program; remote viewing, to be exact. No one knew exactly how the rumor had started, but when questioned, Nikolai would become very serious and refuse to talk. I'd learned to stay away from that subject.

"My client wants to hold this tomorrow night, the 21st. That's if you possibly can. She's elderly. Her niece, who is also my client, is a nurse, and she's been staying with her aunt to take care of her after she fractured her hip."

"Ve need medium."

"Oh!" Who knew?

Nikolai pulled on his beard and thought a moment. "Zora would be good. You know her?"

"Sure. In fact, there's a meeting at the Eye tonight. She'll probably be there. Are you coming?"

"I vould luf to, but I'm tied up. I heard vhat happened there. Terrible." Nikolai shook his head in dismay.

"It was. We were lucky we were able to put the fire out."

"Vere you hurt?"

"No, I'm fine. Gale and I were just scared to death."

Nikolai nodded in response.

"You should know going in that Dorothy, the niece, is not happy about this at all."

"Not a problem. She vill luf me when she meets me. Now vhat about other people? Vee need a group, you know."

"I can be there. There's Dorothy, her husband Richard, the two aunts Evandra and Eunice, and perhaps Gudrun, their companion. Oh, and there's Alba, their housekeeper.

169

"Let's see, dat vill be seven. Should be fine. I call Zora dis afternoon."

"You really think she'll be up for this? I can talk to her tonight."

"Sure she will. Holidays are so slow, as you vell know. Zora vould be essential. I pick her up and bring her. Must be good-sized table and enough chairs."

"Oh, my client's house is huge, and there's more than enough furniture."

"Write down address for me. How's eight-thirty? Vee get rolling at nine."

I jotted down the address to the Gamble house on the large pad that Nikolai passed over to me. He rubbed his hands together and smiled. "I'm delighted, Julia. Tank you. Haven't done vone of dese for a while."

"I should tell you there's a family legend about a —"

"No! Not a word." Nikolai held up a hand. "Less I know is better."

I put my coat on as Nikolai walked me to the door. I said goodbye to Chuck and Lydia, who both ignored me. Chuck was busy adjusting his camera, and Lydia stayed focused on touching up her makeup. Nikolai gave me an all-enveloping bear hug and lifted me over the threshold. I felt my back crack as he let me go.

"You vay too tense, Julia. You should stop

by see me more often." He smiled and gave me a knowing wink.

"Not a chance. I have to look out for my virtue."

Nikolai let out another huge belly laugh and waved goodbye. I hurried back to my car. I had to admit my back and shoulders felt a lot better.

As I reached into my coat pocket to retrieve my keys, I spotted a folded piece of paper tucked under the windshield wiper. I lifted it out. It was a flyer advertising services at the Prophet's Tabernacle. These people were everywhere. I walked back up the driveway and discovered the same flyer stuck under the windshield wipers of the other cars.

Visiting Nikolai had lifted my spirits, but suddenly my buoyant mood collapsed. The upheaval of the past three days came flooding back and I felt a wave of anger that I had been uprooted from my nest by crazy people. I returned to my car and climbed in, then looked more carefully at the flyer. The lettering was in large bold Gothic type. It said, *"Do not turn to mediums or wizards. Do not seek them out, to be defiled by them. I am the Lord your God. Leviticus 19:31."*

The Tabernacle held a service every evening at six o'clock on Mason Street. If I hurried, I could make it. Perhaps it was time to observe the enemy in its own camp.

SIXTEEN

I fought afternoon traffic along 19th Avenue through the Sunset and cut over to Geary to head back downtown. I drove up to Mason. It was ten minutes to six, still within prime tow-away time, four to six p.m. I didn't dare take a chance. I could see a tow truck a block away with a meter reader in attendance, lying in wait for anyone foolish enough to jump the gun. I pulled into a lot near the corner, hoping I had enough cash on me to bail my car out when I returned.

I walked the block and a half back to the theater. A large sign on the marquee announced the new home of the Prophet's Tabernacle. Inside, the street-level lobby was overheated and noisy, full of the Reverend's worshippers. Large posters the size of movie ads dominated the walls, showing Reverend Roy in various poses, preaching to his flock, his arms outstretched, welcoming them to his Tabernacle. Enlarged photos displayed pictures of the Prophet's Paradise in Mendocino County. Happy children played by a swimming pool, while elderly residents tended a vegetable garden. A long table held a coffee urn and plates of homemade cookies and brownies. Next to that was a basket for voluntary donations. Two women stood on either side of the entryway, smiling, welcoming followers and newcomers. It had all the earmarks of a neighborhood church social.

I eased inside and pulled my collar up. From a corner, I scanned the room, hoping to see someone I recognized from the crowd of demonstrators outside my apartment. I shivered when I thought of the man who'd held a knife to my throat and the man who'd stood with binoculars at the other side of the tennis courts. That second man could have been a curious neighbor, but my instincts told me he'd been in charge of orchestrating the commotion outside my apartment. Even if he was here tonight, though, I wouldn't know. He'd been too far away for me to get a good look at his features.

None of the faces in the lobby were familiar. Some men in jackets and jeans looked as if they did manual labor. They had hard faces and calloused hands. A few were accompanied by wives or girlfriends. There were white, Asian, Hispanic, and African-American faces among the crowd. I heard Spanish and Russian spoken in muted conversations. I didn't see a lot of designer labels in the room.

The lights flashed, as if at a play's intermission, and everyone ditched their paper coffee cups and napkins and moved toward the stairs leading to the lower level of the theater. I joined the throng, curious to see what the attraction was all about. In the auditorium itself, the house lights were lit, allowing everyone to find a seat. I followed the crowd and snagged a seat halfway down one side, next to the aisle. I left my coat on in case I needed to make a quick getaway.

A few minutes later, the house lights dimmed and piped-in music with a gospel flavor filled the space. It grew in volume and reached a crescendo as the rear doors were flung open and the choir entered, picking up the thread of the music, humming and singing. The choir numbered at least fifty. They wore purple robes and slowly marched and sang their way down the center aisle, finally climbing to the stage. The piped-in music diminished and the choir went into its full routine. The congregation clapped in rhythm and sang along.

The music increased in tempo. The singers formed a semicircle around the upstage area, swaying in unison. Many people stood in the aisles, others held their arms up, waving them in time to the music. As the gospel choir reached fever pitch, a man in white robes, carrying a Bible, entered from the wings. He was taller than any other person on stage, well over six feet. His hair was bright red, naturally curly and slicked back, rising in the front. His face was gaunt, with a strong jaw and full, sensuous lips. Energy like an electrical charge, almost sexual, pulsed from the stage and swept over the audience.

"Welcome." He spoke one word and the entire theater was at full attention. Holding out his arms, he said, "Jesus." The choir picked up the name, singing it in harmony. The room vibrated. "Jesus loves you."

The crowd shouted in response. "Amen."

"Jesus loves you. He doesn't care if you're poor. He doesn't care if you're needy. He doesn't care if you're old or sick or homeless." The man's voice rose. "He doesn't care if you've sinned." The choir echoed his words at intervals. "He only cares that you'll come to him and kneel down and seek his forgiveness. He has sent me to care for his flock. To care for you."

The power of the man was fascinating. I couldn't tear my eyes away. He swayed the room with his words, with his voice. I felt a martial energy. He had to have a fire sign rising. Aries perhaps, no, Leo. Definitely Leo. Mercury must be prominent in his chart to give him the ability to move the crowd to this extent. I wanted to know his birth information. In spite of myself, I was impressed. I fought the impulse to be part of the energy in the room. To someone less cynical than I, less sophisticated, more in need, Reverend Roy would have enormous influence. He spoke of Jesus's love and compassion, of the need to care for each other. It all sounded just wonderful, but what darkness lay beneath? What was his real agenda?

I'm not a joiner. I don't understand the need to belong to a group. I do understand the need to be close to loved ones, but identifying with any group and being swept away by religious fervor is not in my makeup. I consider myself a spiritual person and believe in a force for good in the universe. I have great respect for anyone's faith, but I do tend to be skeptical of those who say they are God's messenger.

As Reverend Roy spoke, the choir hummed in the background. His voice rose stronger and faster, each sentence punctuated by an *"Amen"* from the congregation and the choir. I once attended a Buddhist ceremony where everyone chanted in unison for a long period; it felt to me as if the building would rise off its foundation from the power of the sound. But the Prophet's show beat it all. It was super-charged and produced very cleverly, yet it rested on the energy of one man with an intense talent.

"We all render unto Caesar that which is Caesar's due, my brothers and sisters. But there comes a time when we must render unto God that which is His. And may God help those who impede that rendering. God may stay His hand in wreaking vengeance upon them, but as an instrument of God, my brothers and sisters, I will not stay mine!" His eyes burned across the sea of faces and looked directly at me. I was sure of it. I couldn't tear my eyes away. That's when I heard it — the Reverend shouted, "The Bible says, *'For without are dogs and sorcerers, and whoremongers . . . and whosoever maketh a lie. Do not listen, for the Lord shall smote them and punish them.'* "

This man was most certainly behind it all. He had compelled his followers to go forth and punish anyone who would speak against him.

I glanced around the auditorium. Many people were standing, some lay prostrate in the aisles, and others rose to get a better view. I did the same. Across the room, closer to the stage, I saw a tall figure, a woman. She was standing, her hands raised at every "Amen," her face slack in an ecstasy of fervor. I stared. I realized with a shock the woman was Gudrun.

SEVENTEEN

Bundling my coat around me, I moved quickly up the aisle, pushing through the padded doors to the darkened entryway. I was certain Gudrun had not seen me, focused as she was on the Reverend. I climbed the stairs and took a deep breath when I hit the sidewalk. I needed to talk to someone. I was shaken by what I'd witnessed. This was powerful stuff. Impressive, but very dangerous if misused. I kept going until I hit Market Street and then called Don at his office.

"Where are you?" he asked.

"On Mason, heading toward Market."

"You just caught me. I'm working late on a project tonight and just about to grab some dinner. I'll meet you halfway. There's a deli at the corner of Taylor and Turk."

Relief washed over me hearing Don's familiar voice. I wasn't sure what I found more upsetting: the fact that I'd been targeted by the Reverend Roy's followers, or the realization of the kind of control one man had over a crowd. And Gudrun! Who very kindly drove Eunice to services. But it was the other way around — *she* was instrumental in proselytizing Eunice. Was Dorothy aware? And if Evandra had suspicions about Luis's death, could Gudrun be involved?

I hurried along Market, and when I entered the deli, I spotted Don at a padded booth on the side. He held up his hand to get my attention.

I slid across the vinyl banquette. "I'm not sure I'm hungry."

"Too late. I ordered for both of us. Now tell me, what's going on? You didn't sound quite right on the phone." Don is a huge guy, tall, close to three hundred pounds, a techno-geek with thick glasses and a razor-sharp mind, and he has the kindest eyes I've ever seen. He's always reminded me of a large, unkempt teddy bear, although I'd never in a million years tell him that.

While in college, I'd shared my small apartment in the Sunset, near the university, with a woman named Denise. Denise and Don were an item in those days, and Don was crazy about her. After college, Denise left to join a vegetable-growing commune near the Oregon border. Don was heartbroken and took to hanging out at the apartment at all hours looking for support and sympathy. He eventually got over the heartbreak and now is happily married to his high school sweetheart. They have a three-year-old boy who looks like Don cloned himself.

His concern made me feel better, even though nothing had changed. Just the fact that I had good friends who were willing to watch my back was comforting.

I shrugged. "I don't know how to explain . . . I went to a Prophet service."

"Hmm." Don sat silently and stared at me. "And? Are you now ready to join his flock?"

"Don, it was frightening. He held them in the palm of his hand. I've never felt anything quite like it. The *control* he had over that crowd. I mean the service itself was well orchestrated. Piped-in music, virtually choreographed, gospel singers, well-put-together — but there was a dark energy. I can't put my finger on it. His eyes burned. I felt as if he stared straight at me and knew I was there and I was his enemy. It was frightening."

"Now you're letting your imagination run away with you."

The waitress arrived and placed a heaping hot pastrami with cheese on a huge roll in front of me. Don's dish was a platter with two of the same.

"Eat up, Julia. You're too skinny."

I couldn't imagine getting that huge sandwich inside of me, but when I lifted up the top bun and smeared dark mustard over the inside, my stomach growled. I was starving. I took a bite. It was fantastic. Warm cheese dribbled down my chin and I hastily wiped it off.

"You don't know what you're messing with, Julia. Local politicians love this guy. Haven't you seen the pictures we've run in the paper? And I told you what I think. He'd do anything to build a power base. So you're right to be frightened — where've you been?"

"In my own little world, I guess. Where the hell did he come from?

"Bayou country. Louisiana."

"That much I know."

"Started preaching when he was just a kid at one of those revival tent things. Said it was his calling. Clever guy. He did the same thing down south. Built up his church preaching a similar kind of message, opened soup kitchens, housing for the destitute and elderly, the whole ball of wax. Had a few local politicians on his side too. Very charismatic. People just loved him there."

"So why here of all places? All I've heard is that he thinks San Francisco is debauched."

"From what I can gather, the church and its retreat got some bad publicity. Some woman came forward with a story she had been held against her will and beaten, but she couldn't actually prove it. No one backed up her story, so she dropped the charges. Now God has spoken to him and he's decided he's needed in San Francisco.

"Let me guess: San Francisco is a 'hotbed of blasphemy and devil worship'?"

"They're big believers in Satan."

I shivered. "Great! And I'm a tool of Satan, I suppose."

"He's got his church in the city and a compound north of here, up around Lakeport, I think it is. Same kinda set-up. Summer camp for kids, a homeless shelter, a retirement village. Everybody loves this guy — his congregation, cops, social workers, politicians, society people. You wouldn't believe it. Lots of people have the impression his followers are poor, but that's not the case at all. Plus, he donates piles of money to good causes and charities."

Don polished off his first pastrami sandwich and started on the second. "He gets invited to all the biggest events, photo ops with senators and the mayor. Everybody likes what he has to say. Personally, I think the guy's a whack job. I've watched him on TV and there's definitely something off."

"So why is everyone so supportive?"

"One very good reason. He controls a lot of people. And believe me, he can get out the vote. If he wiggles his little finger, three or four thousand people will demonstrate, march, vote for the candidate he suggests. No politician is going to cross his path. Frankly, I've never seen anything like it. The scary thing is how fast it's all happened."

"And what about the people he judges to be driven by Satan?"

"Yeah, I know. Crazy, huh?" Don shoveled a steaming pile of pastrami that had slipped out of the bun into his mouth and wiped a spot of mustard from his fingers. "But all the psychics, astrologers, numerologists, and past-life readers in the city — even the gays, with all their political power — don't amount to a hill of beans when politicians are worried about their constituents. Besides, if some members of his congregation take it upon themselves to harass some poor unsuspecting astrologer, well . . . he didn't tell them to do it, they did it on their own.

He's not responsible. Look," Don contin- ued, "everybody's sick of crime, prostitu- tion, drugs. So what if he says his mission is to rid San Francisco of sin and the follow- ers of the devil."

"I'd take LaVey any day of the week," I replied. Don was well versed in the folklore of Anton LaVey, a San Francisco character who, before he passed to the other side, lived around the corner from me in a small house painted entirely black. He was infa- mous for his Friday night Sabbats. "At least he didn't bother his neighbors."

"Unless you count the time the lion got loose in his house and ripped out the plumbing." Don chucked. "He and his fam- ily had to barricade themselves in the bathroom till the neighbors heard them screaming and called the cops and the animal control people from the zoo."

"Look, Don, I have to go home sometime. I can't live like this and I don't want to give up my apartment. But I can't have prayer vigils and riots on the sidewalk when my clients arrive. My manager is grumbling about evicting me. But I am not going to hide out forever."

"Can the cops do anything?"

"I heard they've been told to lay off the Prophet and his followers. If they grab one or two demonstrators, they can charge them with some municipal code about requiring a permit. If I had the money to fight them, I could hire a lawyer and get a restraining order, but I don't, for all the good that would do. I'd have to have the cops camped out on my doorstep every day and we know that's not possible."

"Julia, believe me, this kind of stuff scares me too. He's managed to gain an enormous power base in a very short time. The mayor, the police chief, the city council. They all think the sun rises and sets in his you know what. He's also become quite a mover and shaker in real estate circles. I've kept digging, as promised. He has a company, Revelations LLC, and within the last year it's become the owner of hundreds of properties. If he's in bed with the real estate developers and the politicians, there's no telling how powerful he might become." Don paused to take another bite of his pastrami. "I think there are people who don't buy into the con, but I guarantee you, they're afraid to speak out against him. There are rumors that he destroys people — either financially through litigation, or by any means necessary. I'm just sorry you've been hit with this. Let me know if there's anything I can do for you."

"Actually, there is something. I'd like to find out his birth date, and if possible, the time. Maybe I can find a chink in his armor." I shuddered. I still couldn't shake off the feeling that had come over me in the theater. "Those people were transported, Don. It's a cult, not a church."

"Be forewarned. I'm inclined to believe some of the rumors floating around. There's nothing I know for a fact, but he'd be vicious to have as an enemy."

"I may have already made him one. With my column." I thought about the attack in the parking garage, which I still had no intention of telling Don about — I'd never hear the end of it. "And by the way, I asked Samantha to run that same letter and response again, the one to the woman who was worried about her mother's involvement with the church. *Desperate in San Leandro.*"

"Whoa." Don shook his head. "What are you trying to do?"

"I'm sending a message that I'm not afraid of him. I just don't understand who would follow this guy."

Don shook his head. "Some are desperate. Some, unhappy. Some just want to be led."

EIGHTEEN

By the time I reached the Eye for Gale's meeting, a *Closed* sign hung on the front door. The windows were lit, and displays of recent books, haphazardly but artistically arranged, were surrounded by Wiccan objects, magic mirrors, and dark plaster gargoyles. In one window, Tarot cards were splayed across a velvet shawl, their intricate designs promising entry to mysterious and magical worlds.

Cheryl had drawn the heavy interior drapes so that our meeting would be hidden from street view. I knocked at the front door and she opened it a moment later for me. As the invitees arrived one by one, I helped her clear the central area. We hauled folding chairs from the storeroom and set them up in a loose semicircle. Fortunately, none of the damage from the firebomb had affected the front of the shop. Cheryl had arranged a large urn for coffee and a tray of small sandwiches and cookies. Everyone was milling about, chatting, checking out the latest book displays and munching on the offerings.

I was doing my best to maintain a positive attitude, but I couldn't escape the feeling that we were tilting at windmills, outmanned and outgunned. Eventually I counted twenty-five attendees, plus Gale, Cheryl, and myself. Everyone practiced one of the occult arts professionally. I recognized at least two other astrologers. One was a woman I knew only slightly, but whose work I respected. I'd referred clients to her at times, and she to me. The other astrologer was a man who practiced outside the city and dealt mostly in the business and stock market area. All were people who knew Gale, knew her shop, offered their talents occasionally for psychic fairs, or benefitted from her connections for their clientele.

Zora the medium was at the refreshment table, helping herself to liberal amounts of food. I hoped that Nikolai had had a chance to arrange her services for the following evening's séance. Zora is a plus-sized woman, fond of wearing several draping layers of clothing, lots of jewelry, and multiple rings on her fingers. She has a brusque, street-tough personality that I've always found intimidating, but Cheryl has assured me she's very reliable and has excellent references from her clientele. I started to head in her direction to speak with her, but before I could do so, the meeting was called to order.

"Okay, everyone, let's get started." Gale stepped to the center of the circle of chairs. "First, I want information from anyone who's been harassed or threatened in any way, and whose business has been interrupted because of this . . . Army of the Prophet. You can talk openly tonight, or, if you prefer, send me an email with all the details."

A tall woman with short, wispy silver hair raised her hand. "I don't know what good this will do. I came out of curiosity, but what can we really do?"

Gale nodded. "I've talked to my lawyer, and he feels I have a pretty good claim for intentional interference with economic something or other. At any rate, it's enough to obtain a restraining order, and probably most of you could claim this too. If you've been intimidated by this group, it's something you can do individually, or else we can organize a class action together."

"I haven't been bothered, but I'm worried. This makes my stomach go in knots," a man in a business suit piped up.

"It just means they haven't identified you yet, but they probably will soon," Gale responded.

A young woman in jeans and high-top sneakers raised her hand. "Why are they doing this? What do they want?"

"They claim they're driving sin from the city." Gale laughed. "As if such a thing were possible. But we're not the sinners."

Eric, a past-life reader, addressed the young woman. "I'm sure there's more behind it, undoubtedly an economic motive that doesn't bear investigation, but that's the banner they're flying. We just happen to be a few of the scapegoats."

"Has anyone seen last Sunday's paper?" The man in the business suit spoke up again. "There's a picture of this Roy character with the mayor at some society fund-raiser. He really gets around."

Gale spoke. "The reason I want to hear from everyone who's here, and everyone who couldn't make it, is that we may have a better chance as a group."

A tall woman with a mane of curly blond hair spoke up. "I don't particularly want to be identified with a 'group.' My clients are very private and their business is personal. It's important that I remain incognito, at least in the sense that I don't advertise. My clients hear about me through word of mouth."

Gale turned to her. "Marguerite, I'm sure that's true for everyone here. All of you are discreet with your clients' business. But if you're identified, you've been tagged, so to speak. Now some of you" — Gale nodded in my direction and glanced at a few others — "I already know have had bad experiences and lost some income. But send me a detailed email anyway, so I can organize the info and pass it on to my attorney. It may or may not make sense to obtain a restraining order as a group. I just don't know yet. But please let me know if, and again that's an 'if,' you'd like to be included in such a group. If not, please let me know that too. I completely understand."

A plump woman with gray hair, who was dressed entirely in black, raised her hand. "A lawsuit may be a very good idea at the practical level, but how about using our occult powers to stop this man?"

Marguerite sat up and stared at the plump woman. "What are you talking about, Yvonne?"

"Well . . ." Yvonne hesitated. "I'm Wiccan — I know this method could work. I'm proud to say I was part of the gathering in

California in 1971 to end the Vietnam war. Occult powers were also used with great success to prevent Hitler from invading England in World War II."

Eric nodded. "Yes, I've heard of that."

"It was on August 1st, 1940. Lammas Day, which is a very old pagan holiday. It was called 'Operation Cone of Power.' " Yvonne turned to address the group. "A cone of power is a field of psychic energy raised for a particular purpose. On that day, hundreds of witches from covens through-out southern England gathered in the New Forest to stop the Germans."

Gale frowned. "I've never heard of this. What did they do?"

"Well, the coven and all its members dance in a circle, chanting and drumming. As the energy increases, the cone rises. When it reaches its apex, the energy is sent out to cast a spell. Some people say they can actually see the energy as a shimmering light. Wiccans believe that it stopped the Spanish Armada in 1588 and defeated Napoleon in 1700."

Gale shrugged. "Well, it's as good an idea as any I've heard."

Cheryl stood up. "All that being said, it's very important that we have a central clearinghouse for all our information, both on this Roy character and for any actions taken against you. And after tonight, we should all stay in touch with one another. I'll keep the information confidential — you don't have to worry. It's terribly important that as a society we band together. I can't stress that enough."

"I agree," several people answered, and all in the group nodded.

"Anything you hear would be greatly appreciated. I want to know anything we can find out about this guy, especially his past history. We know he's operated in the South, but he seems to have come out of nowhere and hit the city like a lightning bolt. What are his connections here? That kind of stuff. If you hear anything, then please pass it on."

There was a general consensus that the meeting had concluded. People stood up, chatting with one another and milling about, most heading back to the snack trays. The noise level started to rise.

I spotted Zora at the edge of the crowd. She had loaded a plastic plate with five or six tiny sandwiches and a few cookies. She was eating daintily, picking up the sandwiches with the tips of her long nails, her rings flashing. She swiped at a crumb in the corner of her mouth with a red nail. Tonight her ensemble was topped with a fringed shawl in a luscious fabric. She waved a finger in my direction and I headed over.

She polished off the last hors d'oeuvre on her plate and wiped her mouth. "You know, I have to say this — I'm not so sure about that cone of power thing. A good idea, but keeping everyone focused and on the same page psychically *is* very difficult. I think a candle burning ritual might be more applicable. What do you think? Have you had any experience with candle rituals?"

I hoped she wasn't trying to sell me her services. "No. I've never tried anything like that."

"Very efficacious, my dear. You see, when one concentrates, channels are opened to the deep mind. It is possible to exert your will, but it's also likely that you will receive important information about whatever problem is at hand. But that's not what you wanted to talk to me about, is it?"

"Actually, no. Have you already spoken with Nikolai?"

"Yes, and I'm very excited about this and flattered that Nikolai thought of me."

"He said he'd arrange to pick you up. He has my client's address."

"Nikolai's perfect for a séance. He'll give it just the right touch — very theatrical — but most importantly, he's very talented."

Zora thought for a moment, raising a tiny cookie to her mouth. "Why tomorrow night, if I may ask?"

"December 21st was the birthday of the person my client would like to contact."

"Very good reasoning. That is, assuming the spirit is willing."

NINETEEN

I waited until everyone had gone and helped
Gale and Cheryl return the folding chairs
to the storeroom and clean up the tables.

"Julia, there's so much food left over. Why
don't you take some home, and you too,
Cheryl."

Cheryl replied, "Don't mind if I do." She
produced some large plastic containers from
the office and we filled them to capacity. At
least now I wouldn't have to worry about
food for the next day or two while I camped
out at Gloria's house. I stayed while Gale
and Cheryl went through the movements of
closing the shop for the night, and we three
left together, retrieving our cars from the
parking area behind the Eye.

As Gale closed and locked the shop's back
door, I eyed my handiwork of the previous
evening. Gale spoke as if she knew my
thoughts: "I'm having Edwin come by
tomorrow to remove the plywood and put

in some sort of reinforced glass that can't be broken the same way, or maybe just a solid panel. The metal bars are still good, and hopefully that'll deter any more back-alley attacks from those cowards."

Cheryl watched silently. "I feel terrible I wasn't here when it happened. When I think . . ." She trailed off.

Gale reached over and squeezed her hand. "It's okay, sweetie. Fortunately Julia was here too, otherwise . . . I don't know. I doubt I could have done it alone, and then the whole building could have gone and the people in the apartments upstairs . . . I had nightmares last night when I was finally able to get to sleep."

We said good night to each other and one by one pulled out of the alleyway onto Broadway. I headed across Columbus back to my grandmother's house. When I arrived, I found Wizard curled up in a ball, depositing cat hairs on my heavy knitted sweater. I bundled him up in my arms and carried him downstairs to the living room. I found my grandmother's space heater in the hallway closet, closed the doors to the kitchen and the hallway, and plugged it into an outlet in the dining room. I turned it up full blast. The house felt even colder than before, if that was possible, but I really had no choice but to make the best of it. Since the gas starter in the fireplace wasn't working, I opened the damper and managed to get a fire going with a few wood logs I piled in. Between the heater and fireplace, I thought the two rooms should stay warm enough to be comfortable.

The spirit of the season had still not bitten me, which was a good thing if it kept me from spending more money, but I decided I'd better wrap my few presents while I had the time and the space to do it. I pulled out the roll of Christmas wrapping paper from the bag I'd packed and found scissors and Scotch tape in the hallway desk. I placed my grandmother's plum shawl in a small box with tissue and her garnet necklace in the box from the jewelry store. It wouldn't be possible to disguise the fact that Kuan's present was a book — it was way too large — so I just wrapped it as it was, adding ribbons and labels, and then placed the gifts on the hallway table. I still needed to find a present for Gale, the girl who has everything, and I planned to check Macy's again for the ivory sweater with pearls for Cheryl. There wasn't time to order online, and if I had no luck, I'd find her something else. Christmas was only five days away. I didn't know if I'd be able to return home by then, or if I'd even have a home at the rate things were going, but at least here, my little finds were safe until the holiday arrived.

I pulled the drapes closed to keep as much warmth in as possible. I found sheets, blankets, and pillows in the linen closet and made up a bed on the sofa. I threw another log on the fire for insurance and put on my T-shirt and thermal leggings. Grabbing my laptop, I curled up under the covers of my makeshift bed.

I decided to compare Evandra's chart against Dorothy's and Richard's. I wanted to know why she was so convinced Dorothy was trying to hurt her. After several minutes of study, I was no further along, but I did notice that Richard's natal Neptune exactly connected with Evandra's Moon and Ascendant. Given Evandra's transits, it wasn't a connection I liked. It could represent a deep spiritual tie, but could he possibly be deceiving her? Or was he psychically or even physically draining for her in some way?

What was more interesting was that the difficult aspects in the Dorothy-Richard composite chart made negative connections to Evandra's natal chart. It was as if the combination of their energies affected the elderly woman far more than either one of them as individuals.

Wizard joined me and snuggled in the space between my knees and the back of the sofa. I couldn't think about these people any longer. I closed my laptop and grabbed my book on eclipses from the coffee table. Before I could work my way to the end of the first chapter, my eyes closed. The book slipped out of my hand to the floor. I started, then resettled myself, drifting off to sleep watching the fire while Wizard snored softly amid the mass of blankets.

TWENTY

My cell phone woke me the next morning. I fumbled for it on the coffee table and squinted, unable to read the caller's number.

"Hello," I mumbled. I could see my breath in the air. The fire had gone out during the night and the open damper had sucked the rest of the warm air out of the room. The little space heater was still working its heart out to little avail.

"Julia, it's Dorothy. I'm so sorry to bother you. I'm just at my wit's end."

"What's going on?"

"I really need help. Richard's not here and I can't reach him. I found Evandra outside in the garden in the middle of the night. She was in her nightgown. She could have fallen or caught pneumonia. The doctor's on his way, and I have that architect and designer and their crew coming in. Damn this house. It's so big and the walls are so thick, I didn't hear a thing. I hate to ask, but is there any way you could come by? Gudrun's with her now, but Alba's busy and Eunice might need help. I need to go out to pick up some groceries."

"Sure. I'm actually at my grandmother's at the bottom of the hill. Just give me a few minutes to pull myself together."

"Bless your heart. I'm sorry to have to ask."

"Not a problem. See you in a bit."

I untangled myself from the blankets and padded over to the fireplace. A tiny amount of warmth still emanated from the hearth, even though the fire was completely out. I grabbed the poker and shoved the damper closed. I pushed back the drapes in the living room and dining room. Frost had even formed on the inside of the windows overnight. That furnace couldn't arrive soon enough. Two more days.

I dished a little food out for Wizard, gave him some fresh water, and headed for the shower. I turned the faucets on full blast and then remembered the hot water heater was gas powered. No hot water. What could I do? I could heat some water on the stove to wash. No, I couldn't. No stove. This is ridiculous, I thought. I felt helpless. This was worse than camping out, an activity I completely loathe. Such a city slicker I am. What's next? Coffee! No stove. Maybe Gloria had an electric coffeepot. I rummaged in the pantry and the big cabinets under the counters but didn't see one. I was sure she had one; I just didn't know where she was hiding it. I was panicking. The microwave. Why didn't I think of the microwave? How quickly civilization unravels. I downed some coffee and, once restored, washed my face and brushed my teeth in cold water. I threw on my jeans, a warm sweater, and socks and sneakers. I picked up the living room, leaving a warm blanket on the sofa for Wizard. On the way out, I tucked a note under Kuan's door asking him to check on Wizard when he had a chance, then headed to the Gamble house on Telegraph Hill.

TWENTY-ONE

Barren ivy branches, like determined fingers, clung to the house as if claiming it for the earth. Blank windows faced the street like sightless eyes in the gray early light. I rang the bell next to the double doors and Dorothy opened them a moment later. Her hair was pinned back. Dark circles were visible under her eyes, and freckles stood out against her pale skin.

"Thanks for coming, Julia. I'm completely wiped out. There's coffee in the kitchen though."

"Sounds great."

We went through the swinging door. Dorothy poured a generous mug for me and placed a small pitcher with cream next to it.

"So tell me . . . what exactly happened last night?"

"Something woke me. I don't know what. But thank God I did wake up. I don't know what it was, Julia, but I had this urge to check on both of them. Eunice was sound asleep in her room. I could hear Gudrun snoring in the room at the end of the hall. I cracked the door to Evandra's room. It was completely dark, but somehow I knew she wasn't there. I hit the light switch and the bed was empty. I just panicked. I ran up and down the hallways, checked all the rooms upstairs and down, and couldn't find her. I didn't know what to do. Then I was standing in the front parlor and something caught my eye at the side windows — her nightgown. I didn't know what it was at first, but there was Evandra. Outside, in the formal garden at the side of the house. I went out through the conservatory and found her wandering around, talking to the statues like a lunatic. She didn't really recognize me and she didn't make much sense, but I was able to get her back in the house. I don't know what to do. I can't have her wandering around. It's just not safe."

"Can you have a lock installed on her door and make sure she can't open the windows all the way?"

"I guess I'll have to. But I hate to do that. She'd be a prisoner in her own home. I can't ask Gudrun to give up her bed and spend the night with my aunt. What else can I do?"

"Maybe leave your bedroom door open? Or get one of those monitors they sell for babies, so you can hear her if she wakes."

"That's a good idea. I didn't think of that. I'll have to find one. It took me a long time to get her settled, but I finally did. I fell asleep in the chair next to her bed — I was afraid to leave her. But I really didn't sleep very well after that. She terrified me. I've never seen her like that. I don't know what was wrong with her."

"Like the other night when you found her wandering?"

"No. This was different. She seemed to be in a much worse state."

I couldn't help but wonder once again how much of Evandra's behavior was due to the Neptune transit. Its effect on her Mercury could certainly cause confusion and muddled thinking, even delusions or paranoia in an extreme case, but this was even more serious. Her life was at risk in this house if she wasn't watched every minute.

When I told Dorothy how I'd spent the night, she insisted I stay at the Gamble house. "You'll freeze without any kind of heat."

"It was fine until I woke up and realized I couldn't take a shower. By the way, would you mind if I used yours?"

"Not at all. I'll have Alba make up a bedroom for you. Stay here, at least until the furnace is installed, and frankly as long as you like. I could use the moral support."

"I have Wizard with me. In a pinch he can stay downstairs with Kuan, but it's not ideal."

"Bring him here. He can have the run of the house."

"I think I'll take you up on that offer. One morning without heat and hot water and I'm dying."

"Do whatever you want. This old place has plenty of rooms and bathrooms. I tell you, Julia, when Richard's here I don't mind, but when it's just my aunts and Gudrun, this place gives me the creeps."

"What exactly is it that scares you?"

"Oh, I guess it's just an old house. It creaks and groans. But last night really freaked me out. To hear Evandra talking and laughing, all by herself, outside . . . She was, I don't know . . . I know old people can become senile, even suffer from forms of dementia, but it was more than that. She was hallucinating. She was talking to people who weren't there. It was all I could do to get her in the house and into her bed. She seemed dehydrated and her heart rate was fast. I've been worried sick." Dorothy looked at me, a pleading look in her eyes. "I'm glad to have you here, believe me. At least I have Gudrun every day, but between you and me . . ." She leaned closer and whispered, "that Austrian sourpuss isn't fit company."

"I have to talk to you about Gudrun."

"What about her?"

"Dorothy . . ." I hesitated. "She's heavily involved with the Prophet's Tabernacle. I saw her at one of their services. I think she's been influencing Eunice, and not in a good way."

"Really?" Dorothy frowned. "But what can I do? I don't want to have to find someone else right now. I don't like Gudrun either, but she does a good job. Besides, Eunice wouldn't do anything crazy. I'm sure she wouldn't."

I wasn't so sure about that, but this wasn't the time to pressure Dorothy about it. "You have huge circles under your eyes. Go lie down. I'll take care of the architect and the doctor when they arrive. I plan to stop down at the Eye later, but I'll be back with Wizard and my things if you're sure that's okay."

"It's fine. I'll go shopping a little later. Help yourself to anything you need in the kitchen." Dorothy headed upstairs to her room.

A few seconds later, Gudrun entered the kitchen. The timing was such, I wondered if she had been listening at the door. She carried a large breakfast tray.

I held out my hands. "I'll take care of that, Gudrun. Don't wake Dorothy. She's gone to take a nap."

Gudrun handed me the tray, turned quickly, and left the room without a word. Dorothy's description of her was apt. I carried the tray to the sink, rinsed out the pot, and washed all the plates and cups and placed them in the dish strainer. As soon as I finished, the front doorbell rang.

I pushed through the kitchen door and headed for the front of the house. Gudrun was on the telephone in the hallway. She was speaking in a low tone, her hand over the mouthpiece. When she heard my step, she turned, startled, and replaced the receiver. Then she hurried up the stairway without looking back. Something about her behavior sent a chill up my spine. I wanted to call her back and demand to know who she was talking to, even though I had no authority in this situation. I'd have to remember to mention her behavior to Dorothy.

The doorbell rang again. I opened one side of the heavy door. A tall man in an argyle sweater and a long dark coat stood on the threshold. Behind him, like a Sherpa, was a woman carrying a load of blueprints and two briefcases.

"You must be the architect."

"Hello. Yes, I am. Is Dorothy at home?"

"She's resting now, but she told me to let you in. Just go right through to the conservatory. I'll be in the kitchen, so let me know if you need anything."

"Thanks. We'll be fine. Two of our workmen are here today but I'll let them in from the side yard. You won't have to worry about them."

I retreated to the kitchen and looked around to see if there was anything I could do to help out. I opened the refrigerator. Two covered casserole dishes took up most of the space. Dorothy had already prepared dinner.

The doorbell rang again. I shut the refrigerator and headed back to the front hallway. This time I found a man standing outside with his back to the door, surveying the street and surrounding houses.

"Yes?" I asked, quite sure he wasn't the doctor Dorothy had described.

The man slowly turned and met my eyes,

and I recognized one of the detectives from three days before. The day we'd discovered Luis's body.

"I remember you . . . you're Detective . . ." My mind went blank.

"Rinetti," he volunteered. "May I come in?"

"Please do." I opened the door wider and he stepped into the foyer. He scanned the walls and stairway as he spoke. "Is Mrs. Dorothy Sanger available?"

"Dorothy's resting right now. Is there anything I can help you with?"

"Yes. I'd like to have a look at the gardener's quarters if you don't mind."

"Well, Luis didn't really have 'quarters.' He didn't live in. He just used a small outbuilding next to the garages."

"I see. Would it be possible to have a look at that space?"

I hesitated, not sure what Dorothy would think if I gave my permission, but I couldn't imagine why she would have any objection. "I don't think that's a problem. I hate to wake Dorothy — she's been having such a rough time with her aunt. Follow me, and I'll get the key." I retraced my steps to the kitchen and pulled the key to Luis's shed from the hook by the kitchen door. "Here it is. You might as well go out the back way."

"Thank you," he said, plucking the key from my hand. "I'll bring this back in a moment."

I waited to see if he'd volunteer any additional information, but he smiled and remained silent. "What exactly are you looking for?" I asked.

"I just like to check things out thoroughly in cases like this."

His enigmatic smile was raising my hackles. "Cases like what?" I persisted.

"Any unusual death where there are no witnesses. As I said, I'll return this in a moment."

I'd run into a wall. "Fine. Okay." I was tempted to follow him to the shed and keep an eye on him, but I couldn't imagine he'd take anything, and even so, what could he possibly want with a collection of gardening tools?

The doorbell rang again as the detective left by the kitchen door. This time it was the doctor to check on Evandra. I explained again that Dorothy was resting but asked that he talk to me before he left. He nodded and headed up the stairs.

I poured another cup of coffee and put two pieces of bread in the toaster. When they popped up, I slathered on some butter and jam and wolfed them down. The detective hadn't returned, but after a bit, I heard the doctor's steps from the second floor and waited in the hallway for him to descend.

He spoke while he shrugged into his coat. "She seems quite lucid now. I suggested that I arrange to have her admitted for a few days' observation, but she was having none of that."

"That sounds like Evandra. What do you think is causing her symptoms? She's confided some of her fears to me."

"Anxiety is still one of the most common afflictions of the elderly. And certainly, if there's failing health or loneliness, that's understandable. Symptoms can present as shortness of breath, trembling. And depression can be diagnosed as dementia."

"If she is suffering from depression, what would that look like?"

"The signs might be poor memory, a slow reaction time, difficulty communicating, maybe sleep and appetite irregularities. For now, I've prescribed an antipsychotic for her. It's mild, and we can see if that alleviates these symptoms. Her heart rate is rather fast and she does still seem disoriented, but otherwise she's fine. Oh, I might mention, she could also be a bit dehydrated. Make sure she drinks plenty of water."

"I'll tell Dorothy. Is that usual, prescribing an antipsychotic?"

"Very often. With older patients, it does help."

"She's seemed to have all her wits about her when I've spoken with her recently, so it's hard to understand that she could be talking to people who aren't there."

"To be perfectly honest, we often find it hard to distinguish conditions in older people, but I do know the medication I've prescribed will make her less anxious, and that should help."

I heard the door from the kitchen swing open and Detective Rinetti approached. "Thanks again," Rinetti said. He nodded to the doctor and handed me the key. "I'll give Mrs. Sanger a call later."

"I'll let her know you were here."

The doctor waited until the detective had shut the front door behind him and we were alone. "Have Dorothy give me a call if she has any questions. I'll call the pharmacy and have them deliver the prescription this afternoon." He picked up his bag. I followed him and locked the front door behind him.

I wasn't thrilled that the medical response to Evandra's condition consisted of adding more medication to the mix, especially since her problems could already be caused by too much medication. I returned to the kitchen and replaced the key to Luis's shed on the hook. My cell was ringing inside my purse. I dug it out before the call went to voicemail. It was Don.

"Hey. Got some info for you."

"Great. What?"

"Well, a birth date for starters. Your Reverend was born June 10th, 1969, in Baton Rouge."

"That's something. Anything else?"

"Seems a local paper published an article implying there were abuses at a shelter he'd opened. Another woman claimed she was beaten and sexually assaulted. She actually made a police report, so the paper was able to print the story. This happened after the first woman made her claim, the one who didn't press charges. A lot of local people were getting funny ideas about this guy around that time anyway."

"What happened? Was he arrested?"

"Apparently not. She ended up withdrawing her complaint too, and as far as anyone can figure, she left the area. Who knows, maybe she was threatened and got scared. So the whole thing had to be dropped."

"Very convenient."

"After that the Reverend decided Louisiana was not supportive of his preaching, so he headed for more fertile ground — California."

"Terrific. Now *we're* stuck with him."

"There's something else."

"What?"

"It's about your column."

"What about my column?" I didn't like the feeling I was getting in the pit of my stomach.

"I don't want you to get upset, because nothing's really been decided yet."

"Don. Spit it out. What are you trying to tell me?"

"Les has had the screws put to him to discontinue the *AskZodia.*"

My heart sank. "No!"

"Yes. He doesn't want to. He's fighting it. He's got a meeting set up for tomorrow. I'm sure the pressure's coming through local politicians, but we know who's behind it."

"I can't believe this."

"Believe it. Julia, be careful. The guy's dangerous."

I heard a loud knocking at the front door. "Don, listen, I'm not at home. I'm staying with a friend and there's someone at the door. This place is like Grand Central Station. I better get it. I'll talk to you later."

Before I could reach the door, the doorbell

rang in several short bursts. I finally opened it and came face to face with a young man in his mid-twenties with bleached blond hair. He was wearing jeans, a surfer T-shirt, and a windbreaker, with a knapsack on his back. He leapt across the threshold and enveloped me in a great hug.

"Auntie Dorothy! I'm so happy to find you."

"What?" I gasped.

"I'm Reggie." He spoke in a strong down-under accent. His smile was wide and generous. "Reggie Carrington. Your nephew from Australia." He spoke as if talking to a slow child. I was speechless. "And you must be my Auntie Dorothy."

"Uh . . . no. I'm not."

"Oh! I'm hoping to find the Gamble family or Dorothy Marshall. Did I come to the right house?"

"It's the right house all right, but I'm Julia, a friend of Dorothy's. Her name is Sanger now."

Reggie's eyes looked past me to the stairway. I turned as he and Dorothy locked eyes. Reggie smiled broadly. Dorothy, standing motionless halfway down the steps, looked thunderstruck.

"Who . . . ?" she demanded.

"I'm Reggie . . . Reggie Carrington. My

grandfather was Jonathan Gamble. I know he had two sisters, Eunice and Evandra. I'm hoping to locate them. If they're still alive, I mean."

"Oh, they're very much alive," Dorothy said. "But you're not going to see them unless I have some proof."

TWENTY-TWO

I couldn't decide if I should shut the door or wait to see if Dorothy booted the new arrival out to the street.

"Sure thing." Reggie smiled and pulled out his wallet. A car had pulled up in front of the house. I saw Richard climb out and breathed a sigh of relief. If nothing else, he'd calm the situation. I decided this was a good moment to beat a hasty retreat. I didn't want to wait around to follow the rest of the exchange. I needed to sort out my feelings about Don's news about the column, and, given the recent arrival, decide if it was still a good idea to stay on Telegraph Hill. I could fill Dorothy in later about Detective Rinetti's visit. What could he possibly have been looking for in the gardener's shed? I grabbed my coat and purse and headed out the door with a wave to Dorothy, who barely acknowledged my leaving.

The Zodia column was to have appeared

in the paper that morning, following its regular schedule. And Sam would have included my response to *Desperate in San Leandro,* the one that had started my troubles with the Prophet. If Les was under pressure to cancel my column, I had no doubt it was because of that.

I drove down the hill and through the tunnel heading for the Avenues. The thought of losing my column was more than depressing. I felt like a small boat with no anchor drifting through the city, unwilling to settle anywhere but afraid to go home. When I turned down 30th Avenue and reached my duplex, I parked across the street. I was leery of calling attention to my visit by pulling into the driveway, just in case someone was watching. As I crossed the street to climb the stairs, I spotted a piece of paper attached to the beveled glass of the doorway. I hesitated. Something told me this wasn't a party invitation. I trudged up the remaining stairs and ripped it off the glass, convinced the Army of the Prophet had left me another nasty message.

At the top of the page, in large capital letters, were the words *THREE DAY NOTICE TO PERFORM OR QUIT.* A different sort of fear shot through me. The letter went on for two pages, citing various county codes, but the gist of it was that if my presence caused any more disturbances in the neighborhood, the owner would regretfully file an unlawful detainer complaint against me and I would be evicted and lose my lease.

I felt as if I had been punched in the stomach. It was all I could do not to break down sobbing. I felt as if the earth had been yanked out from under my feet. I collapsed on the stairs and re-read the notice a second time to make sure I hadn't missed anything. The bottom line was that the owner had the right to evict me if she so chose because I'd broken the terms of my lease by creating a disturbance and by operating a business in a residential apartment. I had three days to cure these supposed defaults. Just great! Just what I needed.

I pulled myself together, grabbed a few pieces of mail out of my mailbox, unlocked the front door, and climbed the stairs. The apartment was undisturbed. Mercifully. The bubble wrap I'd taped to the broken pane of glass was intact, as was everything else. The light on the answering machine was blinking. I counted ten more hangups. I didn't have the heart to keep up with my log today. If it weren't for the threat of eviction — no, not a threat, a promise — I'd move back in today. The hell with Reverend

Roy and the Army of the Prophet. We'd see who's tougher. But the hard practical truth was that discretion was the better part of valor right now. If there was a slight chance of keeping my lease, it was smarter to stay away.

On the positive side, the apartment was warm and cozy and the pine wreath smelled wonderful. I stepped onto the brick hearth and stuck my face in the pine needles to breathe in the fragrance. For a second, it almost lifted my spirits. I plopped down in a chair with my coat still on and sat there a long time, staring at the wall. I mentally reviewed my letter to *Desperate in San Leandro.* I had given her good advice. The Prophet's Tabernacle was a con. What kind of church required its followers to sign over their worldly goods? Utter nonsense! But in the meantime, the Army of the Prophet was doing a pretty good job on me. I was about to lose my apartment and my newspaper column. And if these goons threatened my clients, I could lose them too. I shuddered, thinking of my night in the parking garage. And that could be just the beginning.

I finally stirred from my funk and sorted through the mail, tossing the junk in the trash and stuffing the phone bill and gas bill into my purse. Then I walked through the apartment, checking everything one last time, locked up, and drove away, heading for the Mystic Eye. I wanted to touch base with Gale and Cheryl and see how they were coping with the repairs at the shop. I also wanted some reassurance from my friends that we'd all weather this storm.

I pulled into a vacant parking space in the back alley and spotted Gale's Mercedes. I found her inside, in the tiny office behind the front counter going over inventory. Cheryl was at the front of the store unpacking more boxes. A side table in the office was spread with a napkin and four boxes of Chinese takeout. I sat in the chair across the desk from Gale. She was dipping into a paper container with a pair of chopsticks and expertly moving noodles and bok choy to her mouth without a drip. I was impressed.

"Help yourself," Gale said, waving to the side table with her chopsticks. "Cheryl told me about your phone calls and emails. I wish we'd had more time to chat after the meeting."

"It gets better." I handed her the three-day notice. She flashed me a quick look and picked it up, skimming through the legalese while scooping up a piece of broccoli with her chopsticks.

She passed the notice back to me. "Don't worry about a thing. I'll call my lawyer. Do you know when they posted this on your door?"

"No," I replied, close to tears.

"Well, if they couldn't serve you, they'd have to mail a copy as well, generally regular mail and certified."

"How do you know all this?"

"I worked in real estate, remember? So there's a good chance this was stuck on your door today, if there was no other mail. That means in three days the owner has the option of filing an unlawful detainer complaint in order to evict you. You'd still have another five days to respond. My guess is that she really doesn't care if you're seeing clients and probably doesn't want to evict you. Why should she? You're a good tenant, after all. I think she's done this just to cover her bases in case things get worse. In any case, you'll be able to fight this."

"I hope so," I replied without conviction. "On top of that, my editor's under pressure to shut down the Zodia column. But my problems don't hold a candle to yours. No one's firebombed my apartment as yet, but at the rate things are going, it wouldn't surprise me." I rubbed my temples. "Right now, I just feel so beaten down by all of this. It's awful not feeling safe in my own little nest."

"Don't worry, honey." Gale's eyes narrowed. "We'll find a way to put those creeps out of business."

I attempted a smile in response. "I stayed at Gloria's last night, but the furnace died so there's no heat or hot water. I'm planning to stay with Dorothy and her aunts up on Telegraph Hill until the furnace guy finishes."

"You should have called me. You can stay with me." Gale has a luxury penthouse at the top of Russian Hill with an extra guest room.

"You're allergic to cats. I had to take Wiz with me."

"Oh yeah, I forgot. Love him, but my sinuses can't take it." Gale scooped up the last of her takeout and tossed her chopsticks into the wastebasket. "Look what this is doing to our business. No one's come in all day. They're afraid of those nuts. They probably even burn books." Gale wiped her mouth and fingers with a tiny napkin and leaned forward on the desk. "Now tell me all about the threatening messages. Cheryl said it's because of the Zodia column?"

I groaned. "They quote the Bible. Stuff like, *'Thou shall not suffer a witch to live.'* "

Cheryl piped up from behind the counter. "Not very bright. Don't they know astrologers aren't necessarily Wiccan?"

"I don't know who I dislike more," Gale said. "People who use religion as a power base or their followers. There are so many wonderful churches and congregations in the city. Why not join one of them? A real church! Foolish I can forgive, but full of hate is another matter."

I grabbed a container with a small amount of rice at the bottom and added some beef and broccoli from another box. "I really stopped by to see if you can use any clean-up help in the storeroom."

"It's pretty much done. Edwin will be here later and I'm having the alarm people come today and give me an estimate."

"Have the police checked back?

"They've been stopping in, and that detective called too. They're treating it as arson, so at least they're taking it seriously. Maybe they'll even find enough evidence to make an arrest.

Cheryl joined us inside the office and piled a paper plate with fried rice and a vegetable mixture and squirted soy sauce over it all from a plastic packet. "Those people have figured out the identity of more of the readers who work our fairs. Maybe from the ads we post. And I got several calls this morning from people who couldn't make the meeting last night. They accused me of giving out home numbers. You know I would never do that!"

"I know," Gale replied. "Let's hope the Reverend's followers haven't taken over the phone company."

I returned to Castle Alley and packed up my clothes, laptop, and Wizard with his dishes and paraphernalia and lugged everything down to the car. I left a note for Kuan letting him know where I'd be and drove back up the hill. I was really getting this moving thing down.

I rang the bell and Alba opened the door. Before I could speak to her, loud voices carried from the living room. Dorothy was shouting. Alba's complexion was pale. She looked frightened and didn't speak a word, just helped me drag my belongings into the front hallway. Wizard started to howl, so I unzipped his carrier and he ran up the stairway to the second floor. As Alba shut the door behind me, the voices quieted.

I stepped into the front parlor. Richard was seated in an armchair and Dorothy was pacing back and forth. Neither one looked very happy. I was already regretting my decision to return.

Dorothy turned to me. "Julia, I'm so glad you're here."

"Are you sure this isn't a burden, my staying here?"

"Not at all! I'm so grateful for your company. If it weren't for you and Richard, I'd probably lose my mind."

I waited for a further explanation. Richard was staring at the carpet. I finally broke the awkward silence. "What's wrong?"

"What's wrong?" Dorothy's voice rose. "You saw him, didn't you? Can you believe this? Where the hell did he come from?"

Richard spoke up. "Now Dorothy, we don't know anything for sure as yet."

She ignored Richard's comment. "He's actually moved in. I made the mistake of letting him meet Evandra and Eunice. And now Evandra's insisting he stay here. Julia, he could be anybody. We don't know a thing about him."

"Dorothy, calm down," Richard said. "We can check out his story. That's perfectly reasonable under the circumstances. We can call the attorney and ask him to find an investigator. If he's not who he says he is, you can send him packing."

"You're right. I'm sorry. I've just been so upset."

"I'm sure Reggie won't cause any harm," Richard offered. "He seems like a nice young fellow. I'll stay here if you're nervous."

They'd obviously been batting around their concerns about the new arrival for some time. Dorothy could be quite intense once she put her mind to something. I decided it might be a good idea to change the subject. "Did the pharmacy deliver the new medication for Evandra yet? The doctor said to call him if you have any questions but he felt she needed an antipsychotic."

Dorothy ran her hands through her thick hair. "I hate to do that, I really do. She's so lucid most of the time. These episodes have come out of nowhere."

"I did try to question him about that. I asked if these were normal for the elderly."

"They're quite common. Many elderly people do suffer from dementia. It can be terrible. Family members are hoping to spend some time with a loved one before they pass, but that personality seems to disappear and something else takes over. I've certainly seen it. But my aunt . . . like I said, these episodes are unpredictable."

"I don't mean to harp on this, but with her transits and the fact that she's elderly and frail, she could be in danger from prescription medication."

"You mean, like the wrong medication was prescribed?"

"Not necessarily," I said. "Just that her system is extremely vulnerable right now and any medication could hit her hard. I'd keep an open mind about senile dementia. She's confused and paranoid, yes, but that could all disappear when the transit's over. Oh, before I forget, I've arranged for the séance tonight."

Dorothy groaned and rolled her eyes in response.

"Two people I know from the Mystic Eye will be here, Nikolai and Zora. Nikolai's very bright, very intuitive. He's a licensed clinical psychologist and he's also licensed to work with hypnosis. So even if you're not in agreement with his belief system, he's a responsible person."

"That's something."

"Zora's a bit more intimidating, but Nikolai says that we need her. And there's something else I should mention . . ." I hesitated.

Dorothy looked at me sharply. "What?"

"Nikolai has a local TV show where he performs exorcisms."

Dorothy blinked and plopped heavily into

one of the armchairs.

She stared at me.

"And he's a bit theatrical — he likes to dress up in robes."

"I'm sure he needs the drag," she replied flatly.

"He can be a bit much, but I'm told he's very talented."

"I can't wait." Dorothy heaved a great sigh, rose from her chair, and left the room.

TWENTY-THREE

Alba led me upstairs to the second floor, both of us loaded down with my things. I followed her down the hallway, in the opposite direction from Evandra's and Dorothy's bedrooms, into a room that was the size of my entire apartment. The ceiling had to be at least twelve feet high, if not higher, and the dark mahogany headboard of the canopy bed was nine feet tall. Tapestry drapes in a deep green material hung from the canopy, and matching drapes hung at the two long windows that overlooked the formal garden.

Wizard, hearing our progress, rushed into the room and hopped on the bed. Under instructions from Dorothy, Alba had already made up the room and spread two extra blankets across the foot of the bed.

"Thank you, Alba. This is fantastic."

Alba was a small woman, just barely over five feet, dressed in a plain black cotton dress with buttons running down the front, a white apron over all. Her skin was olive and unlined, making it impossible to narrow down her age. She could have been anywhere past her mid-thirties. It was only the weight gain around her middle that made me revise that figure upward. Her English was perfect, with only a slight touch of an accent. Today she seemed very subdued. I was certain she was upset about Luis's death.

"Did you know Luis very well, Alba?"

"Not well, but he was a very nice man." Alba quickly made the sign of the cross over her breast. "He's worked here for the sisters a long time. His family must be very sad."

I nodded. "Did you know he had a bad heart?"

"Is that what they say?" Alba replied dubiously. "No. He never said anything to me. Always very pleasant and kind. I always made sure he had some lunch when he worked. Very sad." She reached over to straighten out the extra coverlet at the foot of the bed and fussed until it lined up perfectly.

I watched her carefully, convinced there was something on her mind. "Alba?"

"Yes?"

"Is something wrong?"

She stiffened and turned to me. "Nothing is wrong."

I remained silent and watched her carefully. "Please tell me."

She looked down at the floor for several moments and finally seemed to make up her mind. "Luis . . . I saw him from the window that day."

"The day he died?"

"He was acting strange. I should have said something. I should have gone out there."

"Strange how?"

"He was walking in circles. At first I thought he was looking for something in the grass. But then he seemed to stumble. I watched him for a minute." She shook her head. "The mower was running but he wasn't paying any attention to it. Then someone called me. Gudrun, I think, and I had to go to Miss Evandra's room." She fell silent.

"Did you tell the police about this?"

Alba's eyes grew large and she shook her head negatively. "I don't like to talk to the police. I thought it was strange, but if they say he had a heart attack . . . I don't know what that looks like." She pointed to the intercom. "I sleep on the third floor, miss. If you need anything, just use this."

"Call me Julia, please. What's on the top

floor — the fourth floor?"

Alba stiffened. "Nothing. Just old things in the attic. Old furniture . . . trunks. I never go there." She turned away as if to hide her reaction to my question.

"Alba, what is it?"

Alba's shoulders sagged. She turned back to me. "Please don't tell Mrs. Dorothy I said anything."

"I won't. I promise."

"Sometimes I hear noises up there."

"What kind of noises?"

"Like . . . crying."

I studied Alba's face. The look of fear was unmistakable in her dark eyes. "Sometimes in an old house, noise can travel differently," I replied. "Maybe you heard Dorothy. She's had some hard times."

"I know, miss . . . Julia. I know. Mrs. Dorothy just laughed. Told me, no such thing as ghosts." Alba shrugged as if she didn't believe in such manifestations either and left the room, closing the door quickly behind her as if to avoid any more questions.

I sat on the edge of the bed and rubbed Wizard's ears. He started to purr. I've read theories about energies trapped on the physical plane, but frankly, I was more inclined to go along with Dorothy's belief system. I hoped tonight wouldn't prove me wrong.

I didn't know what to make of Alba's information about Luis. Her description of his behavior didn't sound like any heart attack I had ever heard of. Could he actually have been looking for something in the grass? Had he had warning of a heart attack and ignored it? The autopsy would take some time, but if there was anything suspicious about his death I hoped the coroner would find it. For now it might be better not to mention to Dorothy what Alba had seen.

I couldn't wait to get in the shower. I blasted the water until hot steam filled the room. I stripped off my clothes and climbed in. It was delicious. Afterward, foregoing my usual uniform of jeans, I dressed in a sweater and skirt. A little makeup and I finally felt a whole lot more presentable.

Wizard had made himself at home on top of the coverlet. I set up his bowls and litter box in the bathroom. I didn't mind if he had the run of the house, but if we were only staying for a few days, I planned to keep him in my room as much as possible. When my laptop and files were organized on the writing desk, I walked down the hall and knocked on Evandra's door, steeling myself to face the duplicitous Gudrun.

TWENTY-FOUR

When I entered, I spotted Reggie Carrington seated on the loveseat across from Evandra, sipping carefully from a delicate china teacup with a flowered saucer balanced on his knee. He was dressed in ratty jeans and a hooded T-shirt emblazed with the figure of a surfer riding through a pipeline wave. A tattoo of a blue shark stood out starkly on his tanned forearm. "I know this must be a great shock to you, Aunt Dorothy," he was saying. "But you see, I hired a private investigator to trace my family. Actually, I shouldn't call you that, because we're probably really cousins more than anything."

Evandra seemed excited and happy, although pale. Eunice and Gudrun were studying Reggie carefully. Eunice leaned forward and whispered to her sister, "He looks just like him, dear, doesn't he? Except for the blond hair. But the mannerisms . . . it's fascinating."

Evandra nodded, her face wreathed in smiles.

"Before my grandmother died, she told me all about my grandfather, Jonathan. Your brother, Aunt Evandra and Aunt Eunice." Reggie nodded in their direction. "It really wasn't hard once I knew his original name and where he came from. Before that, it was the great family secret."

"Our mother tried to locate Jonathan after my father died," Eunice volunteered. "She hired all sorts of people after he ran away, but no one was able to find him. She was broken-hearted over that."

"According to my dad, Australia was a pretty wild place in those days. In some parts, it still is. People went there to lose their past. No one cared who you used to be. My grandfather took the name 'West.' He became Jonathan West. He married and had one daughter, my mother, Lillian West. She married and her name became Carrington, hence me."

Evandra gasped when she heard the name Lillian, her face drained of color. "And my brother? When did he die? And how?"

"Heart attack. He was only thirty-four. I'm so sorry to bring you sad news."

"Oh no, you're a godsend. I can't believe you're here, sitting here with us. Jonathan's grandson! We had no hope of ever seeing him again, but to think he lived a lifetime that we never knew of."

Eunice had a faraway look in her eyes. "Did he have a happy life?"

"I think so. By all accounts. He made some money in ranching. My mother told me her parents always seemed to be very happy with each other."

"I have so many questions." Evandra's voice quavered. "But for now, dear, you're here with us. We want you to stay forever . . . or as long as you possibly can."

My eyes shifted to Dorothy. She was studying Reggie, a suspicious look on her face. Reggie turned and flashed a brilliant smile in her direction, apparently oblivious to her mood.

"And of course you'll join us this evening, won't you, dear?" Evandra added.

"Is there a party?"

"Not exactly. We're holding a séance. Hopefully to communicate with another long lost relative."

Reggie paused with a cookie halfway to his mouth, his eyes growing wide. "Oh . . . ah, good-oh. I'm up for it. Thank you for inviting me, Aunt Evandra."

TWENTY-FIVE

I made my excuses to Dorothy after the family reunion in Evandra's sitting room. Gudrun had been present as well, but sat quietly in a corner. I was still shaken about seeing her at the Prophet's Tabernacle meeting and determined to keep a close eye on her while I was at the house. I explained to Dorothy that I had a few holiday errands to run and a client to meet later at the Mystic Eye, and she followed me to the front door.

"I don't believe him for a second, Julia," Dorothy fumed. "Did you hear how he's sucking up to them? Aunt Evandra this and Aunt Eunice that! And now he's staying here!"

I let Dorothy vent.

"He could be anybody," she continued. "He could be a complete imposter. Our family history isn't a secret; anyone could have discovered that my uncle ran off to Australia and made up this damn story."

Dorothy's face betrayed her emotion. Bright red spots appeared on her cheeks and her voice rose as she reviewed the possibilities. She was gripping my arm so tightly, I winced.

"That's true." I agreed. "But you need to calm down. Getting so upset isn't going to do anyone any good."

It was as if she didn't hear me. "There's got to be some records somewhere, even if it was Australia seventy years ago . . . a passport photo, an ID, birth and death records . . . something. I don't know how to go about it, but I'm sure he's an imposter."

"Why don't we wait until he's shown us his research into the family tree and decide then? You can still hire someone to check it out."

"Julia, you don't understand. In the meantime, he's ingratiating himself with my aunts. It'll break their hearts if they find out later he's a fake. I'm worried what it'll do to them. There's too much at stake to take him at face value."

"I agree. You'll have to call your attorney and investigate his story."

Dorothy could have gone on for another hour with her diatribe. I could tell she was overreacting, in an obsessive manner that I'd witnessed before. I needed to escape. We reached the front door, and I pulled on my coat and grabbed my purse.

"Listen, I'll be back early," I said. "Please don't grind about this for now. We'll put our heads together and figure out what to do."

Dorothy took a deep breath. "You're right. Come back for dinner around five if you can make it. Richard will be here and he wants to cook. When are we starting the séance?"

"They'll be here at eight thirty."

"Fine." Dorothy's expression indicated she still wasn't happy about hosting, but she seemed to have become slightly more resigned to the household circus.

It was two p.m. by the time I reached Union Square to search for the sweater for Cheryl. The sky had darkened, promising yet another storm that afternoon or evening. Once again I parked in the underground lot, making sure to get a spot on the upper level where many people would be walking by. I certainly didn't want a repeat of the other night. I didn't spot any of the Prophet's followers as I emerged from the garage. In my current mood, I might be tempted to commit assault and battery.

The sidewalks were crowded all around

the square but I managed to maneuver my way across Geary. Inside the department store, the aisles were decorated with fake greenery and large shiny balls hanging from the ceiling, and piped-in music sang of snowmen and church bells. I found a friendly saleswoman on the second floor. How anyone could manage to smile this time of year was beyond me. When I explained my errand, she brightened and said, "You're not going to believe this! One was just returned. Let me dig it out from the back." She left the desk and returned a few minutes later with the lovely sweater scattered with pearls.

"Thank you! This was worth the trip down here."

The saleslady re-wrapped the gift in fresh tissue and placed a folded gift box inside my bag. I pictured Cheryl's face when she opened the present and smiled to myself. And I breathed a sigh of relief that I could cross one more thing off my list. After retrieving my car without incident, I paid the fee and headed along Market to Fisherman's Wharf. Only Gale was left on my list, and I had no ideas. The Wharf would be a zoo. It always was; just a bigger zoo this time of year. But there were several nice shops and street artists and perhaps something would call to me.

The light turned red at the corner of Columbus and Stockton. I hit the brakes. A group of young people with the bright blue armbands of the Army of the Prophet were shoving flyers into the hands of passersby. What was the appeal? Particularly for the very young? A need to belong? Some twisted tribal urge? How easy it is for the power-hungry to seduce those who want answers. But were they that different from myself? We all want answers, we all want the "truth" — confirmation that the universe is a good place and that we're protected from harm. We all want to believe there is an order. After all, isn't that what astrology is all about? Who are you, Julia, I thought, to judge and look down your nose? You're one of the lucky ones. You have no need for a Reverend Roy.

At Fisherman's Wharf I managed to find a parking space near the Maritime Museum; nothing short of a miracle. I walked toward the old Ghirardelli chocolate factory, now converted into artisan shops, and me-andered through a warren of small stores in a brick-lined alley. I was pretty sure I hadn't been followed the last day or so, but I glanced over my shoulder occasionally to reassure myself. In one window I spotted a small lamp fashioned from deeply tanned goat skins and shaped in an asymmetrical, three-sided pyramid. It cast a lovely muted light. I knew Gale would love one of these. It would appeal to her taste for the exotic and tribal. Discreetly, I checked the price tag and was overjoyed to find it reasonable. I paid and, clutching my find, hurried back to the car. At the corner, I saw yet another group wearing the armbands of the Army of the Prophet and passing out more flyers. I crossed the street and ignored them, as did many others. A stray flyer flew through the air and landed on the sidewalk in front of me, marked by the same bold Gothic lettering. The Prophet was everywhere.

I pulled out of my parking space and maneuvered to get free of the bumper to bumper traffic. As I reached Columbus, I hit a red light and heard sirens. Across the divided street, a police car had pulled up in front of a building that housed a women's clinic. Two patrol cars were already double parked there. Again I spotted the bright blue armbands in the crowd. The clinic, I happened to know, offered low-cost medical care, family planning, and abortions. A young woman sat on the curb, crying, blood running down her face. The police had lined four men up against the wall of the building. An officer had cuffed one of the men and was moving him into the back of a patrol car. A curious crowd had gathered to watch. No one seemed to notice the young woman at the curb. A horn blasted behind me. I looked up quickly. The light had turned to green and an angry driver was glaring at me. I hit the gas and didn't stop until I turned the corner on Broadway.

At the Mystic Eye, twenty or so people were kneeling outside on the sidewalk. The Army's dance card was really full today. I drove past slowly and rolled down my car window to get a better look. One man held a large sign that read *"BLASPHEMERS."* I saw two transvestites in full gear prancing around the prayer meeting, laughing and shouting epithets. An angry man came out of a Vietnamese restaurant two doors up, lugging a large bucket of bilge water which he aimed downhill toward the Mystic Eye. The small flood got everyone to their feet. The action had halted traffic. I sat in my car, transfixed by the scene, until a horn blared behind me again. I pulled around the corner on Stockton and drove down the alley to park in back of the shop.

This wasn't good. The client I was meeting would be completely freaked, and I wasn't even sure she'd manage to make her way through the crowd. This had to stop. It would deal a serious blow to the shop's budget, not to mention what it would do to my income. I turned off the engine, hopped out, and pushed on the Eye's back door. It was unlocked. I could hear Gale shouting as I came through from the back room.

"They've had it. Reverend Roy and his followers are *finished,*" she hissed. Cheryl was manning the counter of the empty shop.

Gale rushed to the front door and pulled it open. "Barbarians!" she screamed at them. "Freaks! Go back to whatever hole you crawled out of. I've called the police!" Her outburst seemed to have no effect. The crowd was singing a lugubrious hymn as they moved in a circle.

Gale returned to the threshold and slammed the door behind her. "Julia!"

"I'm supposed to be meeting a client here, but I doubt she'll show with this going on." As if on cue, my cell phone rang.

"Hi, Julia?"

"Yes."

"My God, what's happening? I just drove by the Mystic Eye and there are people out there singing and blocking the entrance."

"I know. I'm here now. If you pull into the alleyway, you can park in back. I'll meet you at the back door. The police are on their way, so no need to be afraid."

"This is too much, Julia. I really don't want to go anywhere near that crowd."

"I apologize. I'm very sorry this is happening. Would you like to reschedule for another time?"

"I really don't think so. You can't possibly expect me to go anywhere near that shop. I don't know what I was thinking. I'm not even sure I believe in astrology." The line went dead. She'd hung up.

I groaned.

Gale glanced over. "What's wrong?"

"Just lost a client."

"Well, it's her loss. Don't dwell on it. But do get away from that window. Who knows what they'll do next."

While I watched, a few passersby shouted obscenities at the picketers. A woman wearing a white apron came out of the Italian café across the street and shook her fist. Then she pulled two overripe tomatoes out of her apron pocket and, waiting for a break in traffic, walked to the middle of the street, then hauled off and pelted a couple of the marchers. It had no effect. They stared at her and called out "Join the Lord" as they continued marching.

I walked to the back of the shop and peered out. None of the Prophet's followers were in sight. They probably thought they'd get more attention in plain sight on Broadway. I heard sirens and returned to the front. The police were busy dispersing the crowd, most of whom had skittered away as soon as they saw the police.

Gale rushed outside and I followed her. She stood with her hands on her hips talking to one of the patrolmen. "Look, I want someone here at all times. Aren't there off-duty cops that want some extra work? I know they'll work on film shoots."

The two men listened patiently. One of them finally spoke. "You'll have to talk to the watch captain about that, but I'm sure you could arrange it. It'll cost some money though."

"I don't care. I just don't want those crazy people anywhere near my shop. I don't want them in the city at all."

"We can cite them for gathering without a permit, or interfering on city property, but other than that, they're entitled to their opinions."

"Like hell they are." Gale was spitting mad. The second cop slid his eyes to the other to gauge his reaction. The first officer seemed more sympathetic.

"I agree with you," he said. "I don't like them either. They've caused a lot of problems in other locations too. But unless they break the law, there's not much we can do. Do you know who any of these individuals are? Can you give us any information about them?"

Gale took a deep breath. I could see she was struggling to calm down. "They're connected to the Reverend Roy and the Prophet's Tabernacle, but other than that, I don't have any names. I want you to talk to the detective in charge at the SFPD. I'll get you his name. He's the one investigating the arson attempt."

The second patrolman, not so well informed, asked, "You mean the guy with the TV show? What do they call it . . . *Prophet TV*?"

"He's hassling everybody, especially in this part of town. He holds his meetings up on Mason. He says he's waging war on sin in San Francisco," Gale replied sarcastically.

"He's got his work cut out for him then," the older officer guffawed. "But seriously, we've had a lot of complaints all over town and everyone says the same thing. The Reverend's behind it. Hard to believe. He does a lot of good things in the city. He helps a lot of people."

Gale nodded. "Sure he does, as long as

you're in complete agreement with him. He's got a mandate from God."

TWENTY-SIX

By the time I returned to the Gamble house, the wind had picked up and the sky had darkened to a deep charcoal color. It suited my mood. Come to think of it, I hadn't seen the sun for several days. The possibility of a rare thunderstorm had even been predicted — rare for San Francisco, that is. Dorothy was again in the kitchen, but this time she wasn't working. She sat while Richard chopped herbs and sliced lemons.

"Julia, come on in." She smiled, but her eyes looked tired. "Dinner will be ready soon."

Richard wore a long white apron and waved a spatula at me. He'd made himself at home. I wondered what kind of pressure he might be putting on Dorothy to move her aunts out. I was curious, but Dorothy was overly sensitive on the subject. If I said anything at all to her, I'd have to tread carefully.

"I'd love some, Richard," I said instead. "What are you making?"

"Chicken with lemon and capers. We have some mashed potatoes and broccoli too. Simple stuff, nothing fancy."

Dorothy laid three large dinner plates on the table. "Gudrun brought up a tray earlier for herself and my aunts, so we can eat in peace."

"What time are your friends arriving?" Richard asked.

"Nikolai said eight thirty. Hope that's not too late."

"No, that's fine," Dorothy replied. "Gives us time to straighten up before he gets here. Richard, you'll stay, I hope."

Richard doled out the chicken breasts on each of our plates, adding a large scoop of mashed potatoes and small broccoli trees. "Wouldn't miss it for the world. I'm sure Evandra will be very happy if she's able to contact Lily across the void." He gave me a conspiratorial wink. "What does one do at this type of soirée?"

I shook my head. "Don't ask me. It's my first and only experience. I just hope it doesn't upset your aunts, Dorothy."

Dorothy cut the tender chicken with her fork. "Uh . . . something I should mention . . . Eunice and Gudrun will not take part."

"Really? Why?"

"The Prophet doesn't believe in séances, or so he's conveyed to both of them."

"Don't forget what I told you."

"What's that?" Richard turned from the stove.

"Oh, Julia saw Gudrun at one of those meetings," Dorothy replied.

"You did?" Richard looked at me quizzically. "You went to one? Are you converting?"

I snorted. "Hardly. I just wanted to warn Dorothy to keep an eye on Gudrun. I don't trust her at all."

"Why didn't you tell me about this?" Richard demanded.

Dorothy seemed flustered. "I don't know. It doesn't really worry me. So what if Gudrun is a believer?"

"I have to agree with Julia. I don't like it at all," he replied.

Dorothy made an effort to change the subject. "All that aside, if Gudrun and Eunice won't attend the séance, then there's just the three of us, plus Evandra, Reggie, and your friend — what's his name?"

"Nikolai. And he'll bring Zora with him. She's the medium."

Dorothy heaved a sigh. "Well, it'll be nothing if not entertaining."

"Speaking of Reggie, where is he?"

"Out. And he can stay gone for all I care. Evandra's been making a fuss over him all day and I can't stomach it. At the very least he's a freeloader, at the worst . . . well, we'll see, won't we? And before I forget . . ." She leaned over and spoke quietly, pulling a piece of paper out of her pocket. Richard had turned away and was running water in the sink to soak the pans. "I managed to get some information from Reggie's passport while he was in the shower." She passed the folded piece of paper to me under the table.

I wasn't so ready to let the subject of the Prophet go. "Dorothy, how long has Gudrun been with your aunts?"

"I guess about a year now. The last woman we hired moved out of the city, and I found Gudrun through an agency. She was highly recommended."

"She's very involved in that cult, Dorothy."

"She's never said much about it to me. And from what Eunice has said, it all sounds harmless enough."

"Let's talk later," I whispered.

Richard picked up our dinner plates. "Anybody for coffee and dessert?"

"I'll get some cookies." Dorothy started to rise from her chair.

"Relax. I'll get them." I went into the pantry and found a tin decorated with sprightly reindeer cavorting across a snowy landscape. Richard followed me in.

"Oh, no, not those." He plucked them quickly out of my hand. I stepped away from him. "Those are Evandra's special cookies I make for her," he explained. "Dorothy helps me, of course — she's the expert baker. But Evandra would never forgive you for eating them." He reached up to another shelf and passed me a square tin. "Go ahead and put these out. Chocolate."

I nodded and carried the tin to the table. This was the first I'd heard that Evandra had a special diet. I opened it and put several of the cookies on a plate and passed them to Dorothy.

"Julia, you look as tired as I feel. You need some sleep."

I'd caught a glimpse of myself in the mirror in the hallway and I had to agree. The strain of moving twice, threats to my life, staying in a strange house, broken sleep, and running around town had more than left me drained. "Maybe I will rest for a bit. Richard, thanks for dinner. It was delicious."

I left the kitchen and climbed the stairs. The door to my room was open, and Wizard was curled up in a ball on a knitted throw on top of a chair. When he saw me he leapt up on the bed, purring, and pushed his head into my hand.

I shut the door, kicked off my shoes, and pulled the comforter over me. Wizard burrowed under the covers with me, poking his nose out from the edge. Right now my cat was the only soul who gave me a sense of home. I rubbed his fur. "I don't blame you, Wiz. We have to get our home back soon."

The storm had arrived. I heard the rain, gentle at first and then increasing in fury, lashing against the windowpane as I slid into unconsciousness and a deep, dreamless sleep.

TWENTY-SEVEN

Tapping at the door woke me. I was disoriented for a few seconds. I wasn't sure where I was or what day it might be. I called out, "Come in."

The door opened and Dorothy stepped into the bedroom. She sat on the edge of the bed. "Feel better?"

"Oh, yes." I rubbed my eyes.

It's almost eight o'clock. Thought you'd like a wakeup call."

"I really did crash. Dorothy?"

"Yes?"

"Can I talk to you about something?" Her expression became serious. I pushed the comforter back and sat up on the bed. "This is really hard for me to ask you."

"What is it?"

"I looked over your family's charts recently. And I noticed that Richard's Neptune connected with two very sensitive points in Evandra's chart."

"What are trying to say?" Dorothy's eyes darkened.

"Is there anything she's taking in, whether food or meds, that Richard gives her? Something that no one else in the house eats? Perhaps she's allergic to something, like I've mentioned earlier."

Dorothy's jaw dropped. "Julia, I can't believe this is coming from you. Are you saying you think Richard is *poisoning* her?" Her face flushed red.

"I'm only exploring possibilities, Dorothy. Richard mentioned she has special cookies that no one else eats, and he might not be careful enough with her condition. It's just that Evandra was fine before . . . when exactly did Richard start coming here?"

Dorothy's face turned beet red. "The only thing he's made just for her are those cookies. The ones with the little caraway seeds. She loves them. And no, they're a lot of work, that's why we save them for her." Dorothy's voice had risen. "Julia, if there were anything wrong with those cookies, she'd have a reaction immediately, or certainly within twenty to thirty minutes. If you think they're poisoned, you're wrong. I'm a nurse. It's just not possible that her symptoms wouldn't appear quickly, rather than several hours later!"

"Please don't be upset that I asked," I said quickly. "I'll take your word for it. It's just that I didn't like the connections between their charts."

Dorothy stood. "You've never liked Richard. That's what it is. And to think I've listened to your advice all this time. I can't believe you could even think something like that."

My face stung as if she'd slapped me. "Dorothy, that's not fair. I've always given you thoughtful advice and been completely honest with you." I'd stuck my head into a hornet's nest. Dorothy was obviously hoping against hope that she and Richard could reconcile, and I was pulling a scab off an old wound by implying her husband might be capable of an unthinkable act.

"And if that's how you feel about Richard, maybe you should find another place to stay." Dorothy stood up and marched out, slamming the door behind her.

"I will. As soon as the séance is over, I'll leave," I answered to an empty room.

Twenty-Eight

I threw off the comforter and stomped around the room gathering my clothes. I was angry. Why couldn't I ask the questions I'd asked? I'd never really accused Richard of anything; I merely asked if Evandra could be allergic to something he wasn't aware of. Why did Dorothy react so vehemently? She was being obsessively protective of Richard and not listening to reason. Maybe she was under so much stress she'd overreacted to my questions. All I wanted to do that minute was pack my suitcase and head home to my apartment. The hell with the Army of the Prophet and my landlady. I certainly didn't need to stay here and be insulted.

Unfortunately, I couldn't exactly leave now. I felt responsible for the séance I'd arranged. But as soon as it was over, at the very least, I'd go back to my grandmother's. It was probably only one more night in a cold house. I'd survive. The new furnace would be installed in another day or so.

I washed my face and brushed my hair and pulled on a fresh sweater. Then I straightened up the bed, packed my laptop and folders away, and put all my clothes into my overnight bag. If I couldn't leave immediately, I'd at least be ready to go. As I descended the stairway, I heard Richard's voice calling up to me. He was standing on the lower step of the staircase.

"Julia, Nikolai's here . . . and Alba and Reggie have already set up everything in the library. We'll use the round table with chairs all around. Does that sound all right?"

"That'll work," I responded.

Richard moved closer and spoke quietly. "Julia, what's going on? Dorothy seems really upset and won't tell me what's wrong."

"We can talk later, Richard. This isn't the best time." I was sure Dorothy would tell him what it was about, but I'd leave it up to her.

He shrugged and turned away, and I headed into the library. Dorothy stood by the fireplace, her jaw set, refusing to meet my eyes. Zora was walking in circles around the table, murmuring to herself. Nikolai had donned purple robes and placed several large candles around the room. He cut a very impressive figure. He caught my eye and winked. I knew that Gudrun and Eunice were closeted upstairs in Eunice's room while everyone else waited in the parlor. I was fairly certain Nikolai would put on a good show. Depending on what happened, I just hoped it wouldn't be too upsetting or disappointing for Evandra.

Zora turned to me. "There are strong energies close by. I feel sure we'll have some communication tonight. Julia, will you ask everyone to come in, please?"

I nodded and left the room. I found Reggie chatting happily to Alba in the front parlor. She nodded occasionally but seemed distracted. She looked frightened, and I was sure she was only here under duress.

Richard led Evandra slowly down the stairs and into the library and helped her sit. Her face was flushed with excitement. Richard sat next to her and Dorothy took the seat on the other side of her aunt across from Reggie. Alba hesitated in the doorway but finally took a seat at the round table next to Reggie. I sat on Reggie's other side. When we were all seated, Nikolai and Zora sat down across the table from each other. Outside, the rain pelted furiously against the library windows. I caught a flash of lightning and the lights in the chandelier flickered for a moment. It happened so quickly I wasn't sure I hadn't imagined it.

Nikolai had turned off the lights in the front parlor and dining room. A small lamp was still lit in the front hallway. No light could reach us in the library. Candlelight cast eerie shadows against the bookshelves and ceiling. No one spoke a word. We waited for Nikolai's instructions. He stood and raised his arms. In a booming voice, he spoke. *"As I pass through the vays, I feel the presence of the gods. They are vith me and I vith them forever."* He glanced around the table at each of us, and finally, with a nod from Zora, said, *"May vee in this circle be protected from any and all harm."*

He sat down. "Please. Take hand of the person next to you." He reached over and took Richard's hand on one side and Alba's on the other. He nodded once to Zora. "Be patient, everyone, and vhatever you do, this is most important, do not break circle."

Zora closed her eyes, breathing slowly and deeply for several minutes. We watched her intently. No one spoke a word or appeared to breathe. Nikolai studied Zora's face. After several interminable minutes, Zora's head dropped to her chest. Her breathing was faster.

Nikolai spoke. "Is someone here? Do you haf message for us?"

We waited. Zora continued to breathe rapidly. Nikolai asked again, "Is anyone vith us tonight?"

Zora raised her head slowly, and her expression had shifted. She rose higher in her chair, her head slowly turning from side to side with a coquettish air. Her neck appeared to lengthen. *"I'm here. I've been trying . . ."*

I stared, not sure if what I was seeing was a trick of the light. Dorothy gasped. Nikolai shot her a warning look.

". . . to reach you."

"It's Lily!" Evandra cried.

I glanced at Reggie and Alba. Reggie's mouth hung open in disbelief. Alba looked frightened, as if she were about to flee the room.

Nikolai spoke. "You haf message for us?"

"Yes." The voice was not Zora's normally rough tone. It was several octaves higher. The skin on my arms prickled. What was happening? I struggled to stay in this reality. Could Zora really be channeling Lily's spirit?

"Danger." Zora's head dropped to her chest.

"What nonsense," Dorothy muttered

268

under her breath. Richard shushed her.

"Danger for whom, spirit?" Nikolai asked.

Zora raised her head, her eyes blazing. *For all.*"

"Lily!" Evandra cried.

Nikolai asked again, "Vhat danger?"

Still in that girlish voice, Zora said, *"Danger . . . death is planned."*

A tremendous thunderclap struck, shaking the entire house. A bolt of lightning lit up the sky beyond the library windows and threw the stone statuary in the garden into high relief. A cold draft swept through the room. The candles flickered in the sudden rush of air and were extinguished. Evandra cried out and collapsed in her chair.

TWENTY-NINE

Dorothy put her arms around Evandra. Nikolai shouted at her, "Do not break circle. Vee must close portal properly."

Dorothy glared at him but said nothing as she gently lifted Evandra's head. Nikolai stood and, holding out his hands, murmured unintelligible words.

Richard pulled a lighter out of his pocket and stood to re-light the candles. He hit the light switch but nothing happened. "Maybe a fuse blew. I'll check the box."

Zora sat quietly in her chair, her eyes closed, her chin resting on her ample bosom. Nikolai circled the table and knelt next to her. Taking her hands in his, he checked her pulse. She seemed to be sleeping. He cradled her face and called her name. Her eyes flickered open.

"What happened?" she asked. "Did anything happen?"

"Yes, dear. Are you all right?"

"I think so."

He turned to the rest of us. "This could haf been very dangerous, breaking the circle. I varned you." He glared at Dorothy, who ignored him. Evandra's eyes opened.

"It was Lily, wasn't it?" she asked plaintively. "What happened?"

"You fainted, dear, that's all," Dorothy responded. Richard returned and hit the electrical switch again. The room was flooded with light from the chandelier.

"It was Lily. I know it was." Evandra's voice rose in pitch, her breathing fast. She looked at me pleadingly. "Julia? It was Lily. Wasn't it! Please tell me!"

Dorothy shook her head to warn me not to say anything, then helped Evandra from her chair. "Help me get her up to bed, Julia. This has been too much for her."

I wondered if her request indicated a truce between us. Together, our arms around Evandra's slight frame, we walked her slowly up the stairs. Dorothy undressed her aunt and helped her into a nightgown while I pulled down the bedcovers.

"Stay here for a moment, Julia. I just want to look in on Eunice and make sure she and Gudrun are set for the night. It'll just take me a moment."

Evandra looked up at me beseechingly

271

from her bed. "I know it was her, Julia. I know we're in danger. Make sure Richard stays here, Julia. I'll be safe as long as he and Reggie are in the house. Now I know our family didn't die out. Reggie really is the image of my brother as a young man."

I heard Dorothy call my name from the hallway. There was an urgency to her tone. I hurried out to the hallway and saw her, pale-faced, standing outside the door to Eunice's room, holding a slip of paper in her hand.

"They're gone!"

"Gone?"

"Eunice and Gudrun. They've gone to the Prophet."

THIRTY

Dorothy wordlessly handed me the note, written in Eunice's spidery hand. "Should I call the police?"

"Yes." I quickly scanned the paper. I think you should."

My dear Dorothy,
I have decided to take up residence at the Prophet's Paradise. Thank you for all you have done for us and please forgive my leaving in this fashion.
Your loving aunt,
Eunice

Still, I wasn't sure what the police might be able to do about bringing Eunice back. Dorothy could accuse Gudrun of abduction, although the note would shed a completely different light on the situation.

"I'll do that right now." Dorothy hurried down the stairs to the telephone.

"What's happening? What's going on?" Evandra called out from her bedroom.

I returned to her room and sat down next to her on the bed. "Eunice and Gudrun have gone to the Prophet's Paradise. Eunice left a note."

"That silly woman. Never did have the sense God gave a billy goat. I suppose she thinks she'll be raising bees, no doubt."

"If that's the worst that happens, I'll be happy," I replied. "Stay here, Evandra. I'll come back and let you know what's going on."

I returned to my room, debating what I should do. I couldn't very well pack up and go, leaving Dorothy to deal with Eunice's decampment. Perhaps she had recovered from her earlier outburst, but I no longer wanted to stay where I might not be welcome. Her rebuke still stung deeply.

Wizard was sitting on the floor, at attention, staring at me, well aware that something was wrong. I picked him up and sat on the bed, holding him on my lap while I thought about the best course of action. I was torn between staying at the Gamble house tonight to see what came to pass and moving back to Castle Alley tomorrow morning, or sneaking away now like a gypsy in the night. I weighed both options and finally decided to stay long enough to make sure Dorothy didn't need any help, but remain ready to leave as soon as possible.

Several minutes later, I heard Dorothy's voice downstairs. She was talking to the police. I wondered what she'd said to cause them to arrive so quickly. I hesitated but finally decided to join them.

Downstairs, every light in the house was blazing. Nikolai and Zora stood in the archway of the parlor. Nikolai still wore his robes. Two police officers, an older man and a young woman, were questioning Dorothy.

"Do you know if your aunt left of her own free will?"

Dorothy hesitated. "Well, she left a note, but I still consider it an abduction. She's eighty-seven years old and she gets addled easily. Her companion is an employee, not a relative. She had no right to take her any-where, particularly at this time of night."

"Has anything happened that might have upset her?"

"No more than usual," Dorothy replied. The young female police officer had turned and was staring at Nikolai and Zora. Nikolai smiled his most charming smile as he scanned her trim figure.

"Ma'am, I don't know that there's much we can do. If your aunt left a note, she's a free agent. Unless you think she might have been coerced."

"Not coerced in the way you mean. Just led astray. There must be something you can do to find her."

"If you have any suggestions as to where she might have gone, we'd be happy to talk to her in the morning, just to make sure she's operating with all her faculties."

"That's just it. I don't. If I knew where she was, I'd go there myself," Dorothy shouted. "They go to that church up on Mason. Maybe she took her there."

"Well, we can check that location tonight and see if anyone's around, but it's more than likely closed. We'll have someone go there first thing tomorrow. Do you have a home address for this . . . companion?"

"She lives here. The agency I hired her from will have her other information."

"Give us the name of the agency, and we'll check with them as soon as they open in the morning. There's not much we can do tonight. We'll have someone contact you first thing. If you don't hear from her in twenty-four hours, we can report her as a missing person. That might help you locate her."

The officers took down the agency information and departed, and Dorothy's shoulders slumped. Holding on to the banister, she sank down on the stairs and started to sob. Nikolai shook his head sadly. Zora looked on silently, along with Richard and Reggie, who'd joined the group in the hallway while Dorothy pled with the police.

I approached her and put an arm around her shoulders. "Dorothy." She turned into my arms and I held her while she sobbed. "There's nothing you can do tonight. We'll figure it out in the morning." She nodded silently. Richard took her hand and led her up the stairs, his arm supporting her. I looked at Reggie. His face was white and drawn.

"Do you think I should go walk about, Julia?"

"No. I think you need to stay and see what you can do to help Dorothy out. I know she's been anything but gracious, but hang out for a little while till we see what's needed, okay?"

He nodded and climbed the stairs to his room.

Nikolai approached. "Julia, vee should leave."

I nodded. I helped him and Zora find their coats and watched them brave the rain as they ran to Nikolai's car. Then I walked through the first floor, turning off lights and checking that doors and windows were locked. I climbed the stairs to my room. As exhausted as I was, I wasn't able to sleep. I was haunted by my conversation with Dorothy, regretful that I had broached the subject of Richard, but there were questions that needed to be asked. Was it just a coincidence that Evandra's strange behavior coincided with Richard's presence? Was their connection truly an unhealthy one, with Richard's Neptune affecting Evandra's Ascendant and Moon? Was Dorothy right in her defense of Richard? After all, she was a nurse. She should know how long it would take a drug or poison to enter the system and symptoms to become obvious. She had said twenty to thirty minutes at most, not three hours or more. Nothing made any sense. How typical of a Neptune transit! I shed my clothes and climbed into bed, eventually falling into a fitful sleep.

THIRTY-ONE

I wasn't sure at first what woke me. My hand groped around the bedcovers, trying to feel Wizard's sleeping body. He had curled up in a ball next to me as I was falling asleep. I reached up and turned on the light next to the bed and called his name. He was across the room, standing at attention, staring at the door to the hallway. I called to him softly, but he ignored me. He stood, hair on end, and emitted an atavistic howl that made my blood run cold. Was someone outside my door?

I leaped out of bed and stroked his head. "Stay here, Wiz." I grabbed my robe and cracked the door open. Making sure to keep Wizard inside the room, I stepped out. The hallway was dimly lit by only one wall sconce. I listened carefully, but heard nothing. Moving cautiously toward the stairway, I peered up into the darkness at the top, but could see nothing. I shivered involuntarily.

When I turned to go back to my room, I caught a faint floral smell. I couldn't place it at first, and then it came to me — the smell of gardenias. Was I imagining that? What was it Evandra had said when she spoke of Lily? *When she's present, you can smell gardenias.* I shivered again and rushed back to my room, shutting the door firmly behind me.

I was wide awake now, adrenaline coursing through my system. There wasn't a chance in hell I'd be able to get back to sleep. I put a sweatshirt on under my robe and some socks and turned on my laptop. I clicked on Evandra's chart. We were now in the very four-day period that had so concerned me when I'd set up her lunar return chart. On top of that, she was in the thick of the Neptune transit that was draining her physically and causing mental confusion. I opened Richard's chart and superimposed it on Evandra's. His Neptune falling exactly on her Ascendant was one of those things that could go either way or both. Could his very presence in the house exacerbate her symptoms? Or was it simply elder psychosis as the doctor had suggested?

I found the piece of paper Dorothy had handed me earlier with Reggie's passport number and birth date. From one generation to the next, there are often similar themes, and even similar placements in family charts. Skipping a generation, an astrologer can sometimes find more similarities in charts between a grandparent and a grandchild than a parent and child. I set up a solar chart for Reggie and studied it for a few moments. Nothing struck me as significant; I could only compare it to Dorothy's and Evandra's charts, and they weren't in a direct line with his parents or grandparents. But I did notice that Mercury was very prominent in Reggie's chart. He was a Gemini, the sign ruled by Mercury. His Moon and Venus were in Virgo, also ruled by Mercury, but Neptune formed a hard aspect to his Mercury. Neptune is the planet of illusion and delusion. Reggie was clever and bright — that much was obvious. But was he lost in a Neptunian fantasy? I wondered how much of what he'd claimed about his family and his research was embroidery, and how much was a deliberate out-and-out lie.

I was well acquainted with Dorothy's Mercury-Pluto square. She had a tendency to bend reality and perceive it in a way that made no sense to others. She was stubborn and not one to listen to advice, and she bordered on obsessive when it came to the subject of her marriage to Richard. And speaking of Richard, no matter how courteous he might be on the surface, he was just as stubborn as she. Perhaps even more controlling. The combination of their charts created something I'd never liked. But had I been too judgmental of Richard? Dorothy undoubtedly played into his personality in a way that exacerbated it. Takes two to tango, as the old saying goes. Dorothy had explained that Richard's business involved the sale and rental of hospital equipment for home use. His employees handled most of the functions of the business, which allowed Richard a great deal of freedom. Yes, he was always there, always around, always trying to be so helpful but subtly controlling nonetheless. Were his intentions simply well meaning? Was I judging him too harshly?

I remembered what Don had told me about Reverend Roy's birth date and place. I had no birth time, but decided to set up a solar chart. Nothing would be exact, but I had my suspicions as to what his chart would look like. As the program generated a full-color chart, I realized I hadn't been that far off. He was a Gemini too; another Mercury-ruled individual. His physical appearance, I was sure, indicated a Leo rising.

He had the broad shoulders and distinctive mane of hair typical of that rising sign. I rectified the chart to place Leo on the Ascendant. His Mercury was in Gemini, its natural sign. A stellium of Pluto. Jupiter and Uranus in Virgo in his solar third house. Tremendous ability to sway people with his words and a conjunction of Mars and Neptune, the ability to manipulate. Enormous charisma. Not surprising that he used his gifts to gain power. Was he a con man, a sociopath, or insane?

More importantly, I realized it was Eunice's chart I should be looking at. A feeling of dread settled over me as her chart appeared on the screen. Pluto was exactly on her Capricorn ascendant. I mentally kicked myself. Why hadn't I looked at this earlier? Mars was only a few minutes away from an opposition. Even more dire, the Sun, useful as a timing device, would reach her ascendant in less than forty-eight hours, exactly coinciding with a solar eclipse at the new moon. Eunice was without a doubt in danger. Something had to be done to find her. I knew now what I had to do.

I kept my robe on and burrowed under the covers in an effort to finally get some sleep. Wizard stared at me quizzically. He was still sitting in the very same spot by the door. I patted the bedcovers and called to him. He meowed once and sprang onto the bed. I rubbed his ears, his favorite thing, as he climbed onto my stomach. I decided to leave the lamp on, half afraid to sleep in the dark. My neck and shoulders started to relax as sleepiness overcame me.

Just as my eyes closed, a shriek cut through the night air.

THIRTY-TWO

I bolted out of bed, my heart racing, and ran to the window. The sound had come from the garden below, the formal garden. The rain was over, but clouds now blotted out the stars and moon. As dark as it was, the pale statuary in the garden was still clearly visible. Something floated in the breeze near one of the sculptures at the far end.

I slipped on my shoes and left the bedroom, once again making sure to keep Wizard inside, and raced down the stairs, taking them two at a time. I hurried through the parlor and into the conservatory. I pushed aside the plastic sheets covering the outside door to the garden. I should have thought to look for a flashlight in the kitchen, but I was here now. I stepped carefully down the stone steps, which were slippery with dew, and moved toward the far end of the garden. The ground was wet with the recent rain and my feet sank into the earth with each step.

Evandra was balanced on a stone bench, walking back and forth on it and tilting her head as if speaking to someone behind her. She punctuated her nonsensical speech with shrieks and bursts of harsh laughter. Why hadn't anyone else in the house come running? Had I heard her only because my window overlooked the formal garden?

I spoke softly. "Evandra. It's me. Julia."

She spun around, almost losing her balance. There was a moment of connection between us, and then it was gone.

I reached up and offered my hand. "Come down, Evandra, slowly." She grasped my hand, but her head turned quickly in the opposite direction and she stared into space.

"Evandra. Come down."

She started to laugh. I watched her struggle to form words.

"What is it?" I asked.

"Flower."

"Yes?"

"Flower . . . house . . . comes . . . late . . ." She looked at me as if I could understand.

I reached up, put my arms around her waist, and lifted her toward the ground. Her skin was icy. She was dressed in a night shift and no robe, her feet bare.

"Let's go in." I led her slowly down the path toward the house. Her head jerked rhythmically.

"She . . ."

"Yes?"

". . . Lily . . ."

We reached the entrance to the conservatory. I let go of Evandra's hand to move the plastic sheeting to the side. When I turned, she was wandering back into the garden. I ran to catch up with her and turned her back again toward the house. I led her slowly inside, through the darkened conservatory and into the parlor by the stairway.

Something would have to be done. Evandra could not be left alone during the night. Or she would have to be locked in her room. It wasn't possible for Dorothy to stay awake day and night to keep an eye on her. I was annoyed that Dorothy hadn't yet done something about securing Evandra's room.

As we reached the stairway, the lights in the hallway chandelier blazed on. Dorothy came down the stairs, sleepy-eyed, tying her robe around her as she descended.

"Julia, what happened?"

"I found her in the garden. I can't figure out what's going on — she's not making any sense."

Dorothy peered into her aunt's eyes. "Her

pupils are dilated. Let's get her upstairs to the bedroom. I'll have a closer look at her."

"Have you started her on the antipsychotics yet?"

"Not yet. But her eyes and that involuntary twitching . . . I don't know what's wrong with her." Dorothy finally maneuvered her aunt into bed. I found a washcloth in the bathroom and ran the water until it was warm, then gently washed the grass and dirt from Evandra's feet. She lay against the pillows, exhausted but trying to communicate with us without the ability to form words.

"Could she have had a stroke?"

"Possible, but I don't think so. There are indications that aren't consistent with a stroke. If anything, she's hallucinating. I'm going to try to calm her down and get the doctor here first thing in the morning. But if she gets any worse, I'm calling an ambulance." Dorothy turned to me. "Julia, I'm sorry . . . about earlier. I didn't mean to bite your head off. I'm really sorry. It's just the tension of everything that's happening here."

"I do understand. I'll stay tonight and we can talk in the morning."

Dorothy nodded. "I'm staying right here for the rest of the night." She pushed an ottoman close to the armchair. I dug into a chest at the foot of the bed and found several blankets. I shook them open for her. Evandra was talking quietly to herself but no longer seemed to be aware that we were in the room.

"Go back to bed, Julia," Dorothy said. "Try to get some sleep. I'll prop a chair against the door as soon as you leave, just in case I fall asleep and she tries to get out. I'll call a locksmith in the morning too."

"No argument from me." I closed the door behind me and returned to my room. I climbed under the covers once again, certain I wouldn't be able to sleep at all. That's the last thing I remembered until the first gray light of morning filtered through the windows.

THIRTY-THREE

I stretched and winced. My muscles ached from tension and interrupted sleep. I climbed into the shower and let very hot water course over me. Then I dressed in jeans, boots, and a warm sweater and finished packing my bag. I had slept on the problem and knew there was no choice. I headed down to the kitchen and found Dorothy making toast. A carafe of coffee sat on the counter. She looked at me wordlessly and poured a cup, placing it on the table in front of me.

"The doctor's on his way. She finally fell asleep last night. Richard's taken over upstairs and I'm waiting for the police to come by. I insisted they come back." She seemed to notice me for the first time. "You're all dressed? Julia, truly, I'm so sorry about last night. I don't want you to leave. I didn't mean to lose my temper."

"It's forgotten."

"I don't know what I can do. I can't leave here with Evandra in bad shape. Richard has a business trip coming up tomorrow. Alba isn't up to dealing with Evandra and the police don't seem to offer any help with Eunice."

The kitchen door burst open and Reggie, looking tanned and fit and bursting with energy, bounded into the kitchen. "Ga'day, Aunt Dorothy. What's for breakfast?"

Dorothy's face flushed beet red and her lips turned into a thin line. "Nothing for you. That's for damn sure. Get the hell out of this kitchen."

"What did I do?" His eyes opened wide. I couldn't tell how much of his expression was the result of hurt feelings or how much was disingenuousness.

"You turned up on our doorstep." She moved menacingly toward him. Reggie took a step backward and beat a hasty retreat.

"No need to be nasty, Auntie Dorothy," he mumbled as he retreated from the kitchen.

"Sorry, Julia. Just can't stand that little bugger, and I'm not in the mood to put up with him right now. He can go somewhere else for his breakfast. Do you think they headed straight to that place last night? Prophet's Paradise or whatever it's called?"

"Yes, I'm sure they did. Dorothy, I've come to a decision. I'm going after them. I'm driving up there today."

"Oh, Julia, I can't ask you to do that."

"You're not asking. I checked Eunice's chart last night and I'm convinced she's in great danger. There's no time to waste. She needs to be brought home immediately."

Dorothy stared at me speechlessly.

"Besides, what else can I do? I've had it with Reverend Roy and his people. They've infected everything that's good about this city. I've been uprooted from my home, and I could possibly lose it. They've interfered with my business. Prophet's Paradise can't be that hard to locate. I'm going to find it. I'm sure that's where she's been taken, and whatever I need to do, I'm getting her out of there."

Tears came to Dorothy's eyes. "I'd go with you if I could."

"You're needed here. What you can do is pack me a lunch for the drive and ask the police to contact the sheriff's office in Mendocino County and let them know the situation. She may not want to come back, but then again, she may have had a change of heart. We really don't know until we locate her and talk to her."

"The police! Lot of good they are. When I

292

called them this morning, they told me to contact a lawyer. If I'm not her legal guardian, there's nothing they can do. Same nonsense as last night. According to them, she may be eighty-seven but she still has rights. Damn that Gudrun. If there's any way, I'll have her prosecuted . . . that's if I ever see her again. It's downright criminal what she's done. Leading an old lady astray with this nonsense. No sense of responsibility."

"I'm not sure it's an issue of responsibility," I replied.

Dorothy stared at me. "What does that mean?"

"I told you how I saw Gudrun at one of those meetings."

"Yes, I know."

"But I think she's more than a member. I think she works for them . . . targeting people . . . particularly the elderly and the wealthy. I think that's what this so-called nature community or retirement shelter is all about."

"Dear God." Dorothy slumped into a kitchen chair and rubbed her hands over her face. "What can I do? I should have listened to you."

"You mentioned real estate holdings once. Is there anything in Eunice's name?"

Dorothy's eyes grew wide. "Why, yes, actually. I believe there's a commercial block downtown somewhere. I'm not sure exactly. Somewhere just south of Market."

I remembered Don mentioning the Reverend's company, Revelations LLC. It all made sense now.

"Does Eunice have access to bank accounts?"

"Yes, but she's never bothered with any of that. All the bills for their needs and the house go straight to the accountant. She's so frail, Julia. She could never survive if she were put in an abusive situation."

THIRTY-FOUR

"You are so naïve." I had called Don on my cell just to hear a friendly voice, hoping he'd have more detailed information about the specific location of the so-called Prophet's Paradise.

"Thanks a lot."

"No, I mean it. You really are. But I guess Sagittarians are so busy leaping to the next thing, they don't see what's right in front of them."

Holding my phone in one hand, I was packing up Wizard's things and the last of my belongings with my free hand, getting ready for the ride up north.

"You just don't get it, do you? This guy donates a ton of money to politicians. They wouldn't care if he practiced human sacrifice as long as they get their votes. As far as the media goes, he's a golden boy. Her aunt needs to hire a lawyer. You shouldn't be the one going after her. Haven't they caused you enough grief?"

"Don, please," I begged. "I just need to know where this place is. Don't lecture me."

Don sighed loudly at the other end of the line. "It's in a town just across the Mendocino line . . . Ardillas, I think. Squirrelville."

I smiled in spite of myself. Leave it to Don to translate the Spanish word.

"As a friend, I'm telling you to leave it alone."

I didn't respond.

"You know, I don't even have to be in the same room. I can see that stubborn look you get on your face."

"What look is that?"

"The one where your teeth clench and your jaw shuts and your eyes glaze over."

"You know me too well."

"Yeah . . . well . . . frankly, this is a matter for the police or the lawyers. If your friend were appointed her aunt's guardian, she'd have the right to go in there and haul the silly old lady's butt home. But without that, good luck. Even little old ladies have rights." He was silent for a moment. "I hope you don't think you're gonna charge in there and demand to take her home."

"Why not? Dorothy's hands are tied. She's stuck here with her other aunt and can't do it herself. The police won't do anything.

Eunice took off of her own free will, or so they say."

"They're right."

"But Don, she *was* abducted. I saw that woman Gudrun at the Mason Street theater. I'm sure she's involved up to her eyeballs. She timed it perfectly. She knew we'd all be busy downstairs with the séance."

"The séance? Okay, I want to hear about that."

"I'm not sure what to make of it myself, but Evandra is sure the ghost of her aunt Lily is warning of danger."

"She's probably right. And you could be putting yourself in danger. The rumors I've been hearing are scary. Supposedly the Reverend's followers are required to sign over everything they own."

I flashed back to the letter from *Desperate in San Leandro,* the woman who was alarmed about her mother's involvement in the cult. Little did I think it would be a forerunner of Dorothy's situation, or mine for that matter.

"By the way, I found a few more articles with some nasty details. One, about the woman who claimed she was held against her will, said she was forced into hard labor and beaten."

"And no charges ever brought?"

"Nope. Nothing came of it. And she disappeared. In fact, both of them haven't been seen since. Maybe they were threatened or worse, and maybe the local cops or politicians were paid off. Who knows? That was a few months before the Reverend headed for California. You be careful. He may be a crackpot, but he's a very dangerous one."

"Later, Don. I'll keep you posted."

THIRTY-FIVE

It took two trips to the car to load Wizard's litter, food, and bowls. I planned to bring him down the hill to Kuan's apartment. Dorothy had said she didn't mind Wiz roaming the house, but I felt better with him in more stable territory.

On my last trip to the car, I glanced into the library. In the confusion of the previous evening, no one had cleaned up or cleared the candles away. What *had* happened last night, anyway? I had nothing to compare it to. I've certainly never been a devotee of séances, so I'd approached it with no preconceived notions. Was Zora truly a medium? Were there really such individuals, able to call forth the dead? In my heart of hearts, I didn't believe that was possible. I'd like to think we're no longer bound to the earth when our physical body expires, but mentally, I shrugged. Who knows? It's all just a best guess. Had Zora actually channeled a spirit? The changes in her voice and demeanor were chilling. And if so, was that spirit Lily, as Evandra believed? I ran my fingertip over the tabletop, half expecting ghostly writing to appear.

I shook off my mood. There were practical things I could do. I said goodbye to Dorothy before lugging my overnight bag to the car. I stowed it in the back and headed out.

When I reached my grandmother's house, no sign hung on Kuan's door. I knocked, and a moment later he stood in the doorway smiling. Wizard meowed piteously from his carrier. "I decided to take you up on your offer."

Kuan glanced at the cat carrier and then at me. "Come in, Julia. You look frazzled. Have some tea."

I followed him wordlessly into his immaculate and spartan kitchen. Bundles of herbs lay on the counter; he was preparing to hang them on a rod in the window to dry. I sat at the small kitchen table overlooking the back garden he'd created. Tall hedges of pale green outlined the perimeter. A gravel path wound through plantings of indigenous bushes and flowers, leading to a stone bench and small koi pond in the center. Herbs and vegetables were planted among the flowers, in scattered spots, and

Kuan harvested these for his teas.

He took another cup from the shelf and poured a steeping brew from a stoneware pot, then placed it in front of me.

"Do you believe in ghosts?" I asked.

"I do." Kuan lifted his teacup to his mouth and took a small sip. His hands were strong, with long delicate fingers. "Although I've never seen one personally. Have you?"

"No." I shuddered. "Although I may have heard one speak last night."

"I keep an open mind," he said. "The material universe we inhabit is only one very small portion of existence." He smiled. "Frankly, I don't rule anything out. Some people believe ghosts are trapped energies of the no longer living. I prefer to believe they are simply not focused in our linear time or physical reality. Perhaps they never lived, as we think of living."

"Supposedly this woman did."

"Don't worry your head about it, Julia. Astrology is enough of a discipline in itself."

"You're right. Thanks for taking Wizard in. I'll be back in a day or so to pick him up."

"He'll be fine with me. We get along. Your man Jerry called. He's installing the new furnace tomorrow. I'll be here to oversee. It's a quiet week for me."

I breathed a sigh of relief. "Thank you. Thank you. I've got enough on my plate without waiting for a furnace to show up."

"Where are you going? Back to your apartment?"

"No. Mendocino County."

Kuan raised an eyebrow. "To visit a ghost?"

"I hope not."

THIRTY-SIX

The ribbon of the 101 northbound stretched out before me. A ray of sunshine shot across the road, breaking through the storm clouds that had been plaguing the northern part of the state for days. The more I drove, the lighter I felt. The exits for Novato and Petaluma sped by, the surrounding terrain climbing imperceptibly higher as I drove. By the time I passed Santa Rosa, the air had warmed, a false hint of spring. Rolling green and brown hills stretched into the distance.

I hit the button on the car radio and heard only static. My stations were all tuned to the city and my CD player was out of commission. I made a mental note to get it fixed when I returned. As I drove, the tension in my neck lessened and my shoulders relaxed. I kept hitting buttons and finally found a country western station that came in loud and clear with twanging guitars and lyrics of love lost. I'd driven this road before a few times, and each time had the sense that I'd been transported to an alien universe. If someone were to tell me I'd been dropped in Utah or South Dakota or New Mexico, I'd probably believe them. Had my world narrowed? Had I been in San Francisco so long that any other vista seemed strange?

We're isolated on a narrow peninsula surrounded by water. It's easy to forget what the rest of the state looks like. Easy to forget that agriculture is California's largest and most important industry. Our politicians and real estate developers have a tendency to forget as well. Over the years, developers have industriously poured concrete over the most valuable topsoil on the planet to create expensive housing developments and gated communities with pretentious names in Spanglish, like Park Granada and Ensenada Acres.

I glanced down at the map with one eye on the road. I'd covered a lot of ground. The turnoff to Ardillas was ten miles away. My cell phone rang and I glanced at the number. It was Don. I hit the button to answer.

"Julia. Where are you?"

"On the 101 about ten miles from Ardillas."

"Listen. I've dug up some newspaper articles from the New Orleans area about a couple who got involved with the Prophet. Then I discovered they'd written a book — an exposé, really — about six years ago."

"That's great. I'd love to get my hands on that."

"Julia . . ."

"Maybe I could locate them and talk to them."

"That might be difficult."

"Why?"

I was greeted by silence. "Don? You there?"

"I'm here, Julia." Don was silent but I could tell the line was still open. "They were murdered about a year after the book came out."

A cold knot formed in my stomach. "Murdered? How?"

"Home invasion. At least that was the official verdict. No one was ever charged. A lot of people still harbor the suspicion it was an execution for betraying the Reverend Roy." Don was quiet for so long, I wondered if I had lost reception. "I think you should turn back."

I wasn't used to being worried about, much less someone asking me not to do something. Don had a point, but I know what a stubborn cuss I can be. Just his asking nicely felt like an order, and it put my back up. It's not a trait I'm proud of, but I have an irresistible tendency to do the exact opposite of what I'm told to do. Sheer contrariness, I guess. Don's pleas were falling on deaf ears.

"I can't. I can't see the point of turning around now that I'm almost there. Don't worry. I plan to talk to the sheriff and scope things out. Maybe I can get help from that quarter. Mostly I just want to locate Eunice. And if I can get in and talk to her, then I can at least tell Dorothy where things are at."

I heard his exasperated sigh. "Stay in touch, okay?"

"I will." I clicked off just as the sign indicating the town's one exit sped closer. I flicked on my turn signal even though no other cars were near — force of habit — and moved over to the far right lane. The exit appeared and I turned off, heading east onto a two-lane road. On the left, an old farmhouse appeared, protected from the road by a stand of ancient oaks. A dilapidated truck full of chicken cages, its front bumper tied up with a rope, passed in the opposite direction. Somewhere in the last few miles I'd crossed the county line from

Sonoma to Mendocino. If there'd been a sign, I'd missed it.

The road toward Ardillas was lined with scrub oaks and chaparral. I passed small industrial shops — an auto repair operating out of a garage, a rambling barn with dusty windows, and an "Antiques" sign hanging lopsided by the door. Eventually I passed a gas station and, another half mile on, arrived on Powell Street.

The main drag boasted a Frosty Freeze, another gas station, a one-story concrete block building that housed municipal offices, a diner, a motel called the Bide-a-Wee, and a bar aptly named Cowboy's End. I cruised slowly down the street and spotted the local firehouse, a two-story building with a large automatic door at street level. When I got to the end of the municipal attractions and saw more scrub oaks lining the two-lane road, I knew I'd gone too far.

I made a U-turn, drove down the main street again, and parked in front of the concrete block building. I had no idea where the Prophet's Paradise was located and this place seemed the most promising for my inquiry. I turned off the motor, stretched, cracked my neck, and climbed out of the car. A sign inside the glass double doorway announced the hours of the office of Mendocino County Sheriff/Coroner Leo X. McEnerny. I was willing to bet the X stood for Xavier. I've always wondered why Xavier crops up as a middle name for so many of Irish extraction. Was he a Catholic saint? I'd have to look that up. For me, the name conjures up visions of Cuban conga players in poofy-sleeved outfits.

Inside, a long counter separated the large room from civilians. A middle-aged woman in a gray sweater, with matching hair cut in a short bob, looked up.

"Can I help you?" Her edgy tone seemed to imply she had no intention of doing so.

"Yes. I'd like to talk to the sheriff."

"And the nature of your business?"

"It's private." *It's certainly none of your business.* For all I knew, she worshipped at the Reverend's altar herself.

"I'm sorry, but you'll have to explain your request."

Why was I surprised that bureaucracy didn't end at the city limits? I debated how much to tell this woman whose creed was obstruct and obfuscate.

"I need some information about a local group."

"And what group might that be?"

I could feel the beginnings of a raging headache. "Look, just tell me if the sheriff is available or not."

She passed a message pad across the counter. "Please leave your name and number and when he's available, he'll call you."

A door opened at the side of the large room and a tall man, well over six feet, with huge arms and a beefy but pleasant face, stood in the doorway.

"It's all right, Millie. Send her on back."

Millie gave me a fixed smile and hit an invisible release under the desk. A gate opened in the counter, allowing me entry. Sheriff McEnerny didn't look like a man who stood on ceremony. He smiled as I approached and held out a hand the size of a large ham. We shook hands and he stood aside politely as I entered his office.

"Don't mind Millie. She does her best to protect me." He shut the door behind him as I took a seat. "Sometimes she takes her job too seriously. What can I do for you, miss?"

"I'm looking for a place called the Prophet's Paradise."

"Hmm." The sheriff scratched his chin. "Hmmm."

"Something wrong?"

"Can I ask what this is about?"

I gave him the short version of my connection to Dorothy's family and the disappearance of Eunice. He paid close attention. From the concerned frown on his face, I could tell it was news to him. It was obvious he hadn't been contacted by the San Francisco police.

"Well . . ." Sheriff Leo scratched his chin once more. "I'm not sure what I can do for you, other than to tell you how to get there. If the San Francisco Police can't bring her home, I'm not sure I can either. Their community is on private property. I don't have any right to enter unless they agree, or unless I have a warrant. And they're a very private group."

"Any trouble with them up here?"

"Trouble? Oh, no. Couldn't be better citizens. Wish everyone obeyed the law the way they do. I'm real sorry about your friend, but unless her aunt was taken there against her will . . . not much I can do."

The exhaustion of the last few days and the drive swept over me. It must have shown on my face. Sheriff Leo looked sympathetic.

"Look, here's what. Today isn't possible, but maybe tomorrow I can take a ride out there and ask about this little lady. Can't force my way onto the property, but I can ask if she's there, and maybe I could speak with her."

"Tomorrow?" I squeaked. I couldn't imagine spending the next ten minutes in Ardillas, much less another day. And I really didn't want to wait until the sheriff managed to amble over. I wanted to know if Eunice was there now, and if so, I hoped to talk her into coming home.

"You need to understand a few things. That church group donates money and the food they grow to the community. There's a lot of poor folks up here. No employment to speak of. The only industry in this damn area is marijuana."

I was taken aback. "You're kidding, right?"

"No, not at all. Sixty percent of the population is in the growin' business. Legally, I mean. Unfortunately, a lot of 'em grow more than they're allowed and that's where I come in. And even worse, they don't stop with weed. There's a war going on up here, if you don't already know."

"I didn't. I had no idea."

"You oughta get out of the city more, if you take my meaning. You folks from San Francisco . . ."

"What makes you think I'm from San Francisco?"

Sheriff Leo let a huge belly laugh burst forth. "Well, I'm not such a yokel I don't know designer sunglasses when I see 'em."

"Point taken."

"As long as they stay to themselves and just grow vegetables and fruit, I've gotta leave 'em alone. You know, that Reverend's got some politician friends and I don't want to mess with any politicians, or lawyers either for that matter. Government's in our shorts enough as it is. Besides, some of the local people have jobs at that place. Much-needed jobs, as you can imagine."

"Maybe I could talk to someone who works out there."

"Maybe." The sheriff scratched his chin a few more times. "People here . . . they're very religious. They might not be followers of the Reverend, but they like what he's doin.' They're mighty protective of him and they really don't take to outsiders butting in."

I was getting the picture. "How about if you tell me how to find the place?"

"Sure. I can do that." He reached across his desk. It was littered with files, piles of paper, and empty coffee cups. He rummaged through one pile and pulled out a lined yellow pad. He sketched out a rough outline of the road that led out of town and marked a turn-off a few miles north. "Follow this road. It dead-ends into another two-lane road. Turn right and go about half a mile and you'll see a dirt driveway on your left. At the end of the drive there's a chain-link gate and usually there's someone posted there. You can talk to them and see if they'll let you in to talk to the lady you're lookin' for."

"They have a guard?"

"Just someone keepin' an eye out."

"Paranoid, are they?"

Sheriff Leo didn't respond. He scratched his chin yet again. "Nice meetin' you, Miss . . . ?"

"Bonatti. Julia Bonatti."

"Well, Miss Bonatti. I wish you luck finding your friend's aunt. Come on back if there's anything I can help you with." He hesitated. "Ya know, there's a family near here who took in a woman and her daughter from that place. They told the family some crazy story. I tried talkin' to the mother, but she clammed right up."

"Really?"

"Maybe you should go talk to that family. They've got a small ranch on the other side of town." The sheriff picked up the ballpoint pen and drew another quick map. "Name's Walker. Nice people. That woman and her daughter wouldn't still be with 'em, but maybe the Walkers can tell you more."

THIRTY-SEVEN

I was suffering from afternoon narcolepsy and needed a triple cappuccino thrown in my face. There was slim hope of finding such a delight here, but I hoped to grab some form of caffeine-to-go at the local eatery. I left my car parked in front of the sheriff's station and walked the two blocks to the diner. On the way, I noticed a drugstore and a hardware store I hadn't spotted on my first round.

The diner was a melody in turquoise, from the vinyl-padded booths to the stools and countertops. The windows were covered with painted leaping reindeer, candy canes, Christmas trees, snowy hillsides, snowflakes, and Santa on his sleigh piled high with toys. I just love this stuff. There were few patrons. A young woman with two squalling children under the age of five occupied a booth in the middle near the large front windows. The older of the two was doing his best to lick the painted snow off the window with his tongue, his mother oblivious to the possibility of toxins. An elderly man alone at the counter stirred a steaming bowl of soup. The lone waitress approached as I slid onto a stool. Her uniform echoed the aqua décor of the diner, while her hair, as if rebelling against company policy, was an odd shade of raspberry.

Through a hatch behind the counter, I saw a man in a white cap moving from one area to another as he worked. I ordered a large coffee to go and when it was delivered, I was told to pay at the front cash register. The waitress, doubling as the cashier, followed me and took my money. Trudging back to my car, I gently wiggled the hot paper cup into the cup holder, revved the engine, pulled a U-turn, and headed out of town in search of paradise.

I placed the sheriff's hand-drawn map on the passenger seat. His directions were simple and accurate. I reached the point where the road ended, leading into another two-lane country highway, and turned right. I continued to drive, watching the odometer. I have to confess I wouldn't know how much a half mile is if my life depended on it. I have no perspective when it comes to distance. The black and white numbers clicked over and I slowed to ten miles an hour until I saw a clearing at the side of the road and a wide drive leading up a short rise into the trees.

I pulled to the side of the road directly opposite the drive. From this perspective I could see only the top of a chain-link fence. I turned off the engine and silenced the car radio. The only sound now was the wind rustling in the trees and the scampering of little creatures in the woods nearby, perhaps the squirrels the town was named for. Then I heard dogs, more than one or two, barking in the distance.

Now that I was actually here, my nerves jangled and I felt a level of dread. This did not feel like a very welcoming place. I climbed out of the car and walked slowly up the drive. At the top of the rise, the land leveled off. The rest of the way was blocked by a high chain-link gate and fence that continued in either direction into the dense trees. The chain-link was topped by barbed wire. Not a great advertisement for a welcoming religious community. In spite of what the sheriff had indicated, the gate itself was unmanned and secured by a chain and padlock.

Inside the perimeter of the fence, the road curved down toward the right. Clinging to the fence and standing on tiptoe, I could just make out the tops of a couple of primitive cabins. Hopefully, there were more promising buildings out of my line of sight. I called out but no one answered or appeared. I waited a few more minutes and hollered out again. No response.

Frustrated, I returned to the car. The sun had disappeared behind bleak clouds as the day shortened. I huddled into my jacket, turned on the engine to start the heater, and waited, very glad I had thought to put on socks and thick-soled tennis shoes. I wasn't sure what to do next. It was late afternoon and just possible the Prophet's followers were doing something productive like praying. As tasteless as the coffee was, it had helped to keep me warm, but I knew it would soon do its other magic and force me to search for a restroom. There was no way I was going to trudge into the woods to find a private spot. I just might get buckshot or worse in my rear end.

As the minutes passed, the overhead pines and bare branches cast a deeper gloom over the road. I hunkered down into my jacket a bit more and waited. Three-quarters of an hour passed and just as I was about to throw in the towel, I heard a car. From my vantage point, I saw the top of the chain-link gate open. I put the Geo in reverse and backed up a discreet distance, to a spot partially hidden by bushes on the shoulder of the road.

A late-model sedan that needed a paint job and sported splashes of mud on its sides moved slowly down the drive, cautiously inched onto the road, and turned in the opposite direction from me. A lone woman was at the wheel. As she turned, she pulled a white cap from her head and threw it on the seat next to her. I started the engine and put the car in gear. Waiting for a few moments, I followed from what I thought was a safe distance. As I passed by the dirt drive, I caught a glimpse of a man in jeans and western hat winding a chain around the opening of the gate.

The sedan was ahead of me, disappearing occasionally as the road curved. I stayed a good distance behind. Only one other car passed in the opposite direction as I kept the sedan in my line of sight. The last light of the sun was disappearing quickly as we headed east. The sedan took a fork to the south and I followed. I realized we were heading back to town from the opposite direction.

This road led to a street that paralleled Powell. The car turned right on a side street and then pulled into a parking lot behind the same diner where I'd bought coffee earlier. I slowed and then pulled in at the far end of the lot. I shut off the engine and pretended to rummage in my glove compartment while the other driver got out of her car, slammed the door, and walked purposefully toward the back entrance to the diner. She was wearing white nurse's shoes and a white uniform under a dark gray jacket.

I counted to twenty and then entered the diner through the same rear door. Christmas carols were playing on a boom box at the end of the counter. I made a beeline down the main aisle to the restrooms, grateful the nurse had chosen a spot with facilities. I washed my hands and splashed some water on my face. The towel dispenser was empty, but at least the restroom was clean. I dried my hands on some toilet paper.

The woman with the two young children and the elderly man were gone. Two men in overalls now sat in a corner booth. Other than the men, the waitress, the woman I'd followed, and myself, the diner was empty. The nurse sat alone in one of the turquoise vinyl booths halfway down the aisle. I took a seat at the counter a few stools away, where it was easy to keep an eye on her.

The same waitress was still on duty. She dropped a menu in front of me, giving no indication she'd seen me an hour or so before. She reached under the counter and placed a heavy white cup and saucer in front of me. Then she poured coffee from a full pot without asking. Something greasy and wonderful was frying on a grill in the rear and I realized I was starving.

"What'll it be?"

I ordered the special — meat loaf and mashed potatoes with gravy. Comfort food. It came with a side dish of peas and tiny carrots. I skipped the vegetables and dove into the mashed potatoes and gravy. They were real potatoes and real gravy, and the whole dinner was delicious. I must have inhaled my food, because when I glanced up, the waitress had just served a plate to the nurse in the nearby booth. I left some bills next to my plate, enough to cover the meal and a tip, and walked over to the booth carrying my coffee cup in hand.

"Excuse me. Could I talk to you for a moment?"

The woman looked up, surprised. She had a long angular face and dark eyes. Dark straight bangs covered her forehead, and the rest of her hair was pulled back in a low ponytail.

"Have a seat." She seemed curious but reserved. Tiny lines around her eyes tightened when she looked at me.

"My name is Julia. I've driven up from San Francisco and I'm hoping to locate someone who might be at the Prophet's Paradise."

She was buttering a roll. I noticed her hesitation as I mentioned the compound. She shot a look at me and returned to buttering her roll. "Why don't you talk to them?"

"I would if I could. I went out there, but I couldn't find anyone and the gate was locked." She'd ordered the same special I had. She picked up her fork and, unlike me, ate her vegetables first. I waited, but she offered no further information.

"You work there."

She stared at me. "So? A lot of people do. How do you know that anyway?"

I hesitated to tell her I'd followed her. Either she already knew that, or she assumed there were no secrets in a town like this.

Ignoring her question, I ploughed ahead. "I'm looking for an elderly woman. Her name is Eunice. She disappeared from her home yesterday."

"A relative of yours?"

"My friend's aunt."

"Maybe you should call the cops."

"We have. They can't do anything. She left a note."

The woman shrugged. "There are lots of elderly people out there."

"Have you noticed anyone who might have arrived recently? Today maybe? Or last night? She's a tiny woman, white hair. Her name is Eunice." I was repeating myself.

"I can't help you." The nurse wiped her mouth daintily with the rough brown napkin and started rummaging in her purse.

I had run into another wall. What was it with this town? "Look, I wouldn't be bothering you if I had another option. I get the distinct feeling they wouldn't let me in there anyway. I don't know who else I can ask."

"I told you. Call the cops." Her voice had risen slightly. The waitress stopped in her tracks and stared across the counter at us. The nurse threw some bills on the table, placed the salt shaker on top, and scooted out of the booth, heading for the back door. I thought about going after her and giving it one more try. The compound couldn't possibly be that large. If they used the services of a nurse, surely that nurse would know of any new arrivals. On the other hand, she seemed fairly determined to get away from me. I took a last sip of my coffee and slid out of the booth. The waitress was standing with her arms folded, staring suspiciously at me as I left through the back door.

Outside, the sun had sunk below the horizon. The wind had come up and the temperature was dropping to a frosty level. I got back in my car, turned the key in the ignition, and cranked up the heater. I pulled out to the main street. The few retail shops had all closed. I passed by the Sheriff's Station, dark now except for an overhead light above the front door. Further down the street, flashing multi-colored Christmas lights outlined the blacked-out windows of the local bar. I heard a blast of country music emanating from within as I cruised by.

The biggest light source in town was the Frosty Freeze, empty except for one teenage clerk wiping off the counter. He looked out the window as my car drove by, as if yearning for something to happen. What did kids do at night in a town like this? For that matter, what did the big people do? I drove out the main road and again headed back toward the Prophet's Paradise, a misnomer if ever there was one.

The road was pitch dark. I parked my car

on the shoulder and walked back to the locked gates. I peered through the chain-link fence, hoping to see or hear something. I wasn't certain, but I thought I saw light coming from one of the rustic cabins. The gate was unmanned as before. I debated climbing over the eight-foot fence to gain entry. I could probably do it, but the thought of getting cut up on the barbed wire gave me second thoughts. I couldn't imagine Eunice surviving in a place like this unless the interior of the compound was a lot more comfortable. Most of all, I couldn't ignore the pattern forming in her chart. I had to find her.

An owl screeched in the tree above. I shivered. I was sure Eunice was here, but I had no way to get to her. As I stood there in the dark, frustrated, going over my non-existent options, I heard the dogs barking. They sounded like big, nasty dogs that I didn't want to mess with. Once again, I beat a hasty retreat to the warmth of my car.

What could I do? I could admit defeat and drive back to the city. It would only take a couple of hours. Maybe I could even sleep in my own bed. What a thought! Or I could check into the Bide-a-Wee Motel and try again in the morning. Talking to the Walkers tomorrow sounded like a plan, and maybe I could light a fire under Sheriff Leo and ride along with him. In any case, I wasn't at all willing to give up. The Bide-a-Wee it was.

I followed the road along the route the nurse had taken. In the dark, I hoped I could find the turnoff to town. I missed it on the first pass and didn't realize until I passed an abandoned farmhouse that I hadn't seen earlier. I pulled a U-turn and retraced my route, driving slowly until I spotted the turn. When I arrived on Powell Street, I pulled into the courtyard of the Bide-a-Wee. A green neon vacancy sign hung in the window of the office. I pushed through the glass door and, over the sound of a television blasting from somewhere inside, I heard a buzzer.

I dumped my purse on the counter and waited. A small fake evergreen decorated with tiny lights and mini cookies stood on a table in the corner. I moved in to get a closer look, wondering how long the cookies had hung there. I was tempted to pick one off the tree but worried what the etiquette might be. Did one wait for Christmas to eat the goodies? Or were they packed away to be rehung the following year? I hoped not. While I wrestled with this dilemma, the volume of the television ceased. The door opened. A diminutive woman with glasses on the end of her nose approached the counter. Her head was a mass of tight curls in a color somewhere between her original blond and silver. She smiled when she saw me and raised her glasses to get a better look. She wore a fuzzy yellow cardigan covered with embroidered bees. My heart lurched, remembering Eunice's collection of jeweled bee pins.

"Hello, dear. I'm glad I wasn't hearing things when the buzzer went. My hearing isn't what it used to be."

I smiled and didn't comment. Given the volume of the television, it was no wonder. "I'd like a room for the night, please."

"Just one night?" The overhead neon lights cast a purplish tinge over her hair.

"Yes. I think so." *I hope so.*

"Well . . ." She pulled a large register out from under the counter. "I can give you room 202. It has a full-sized bed. Would that be all right?"

"Yes, that's fine. Thanks."

"Just sign the register and fill out this form." She slid a piece of paper toward me. "That'll be $39.50. Oh, and the pool isn't open this time of year. It's not heated, so we have to drain it in the winter."

I hid my disappointment that I wouldn't be frolicking in an unheated pool in December. I filled out the form and pushed my credit card across the counter, opening my wallet so she could check my ID. She readjusted her glasses and peered at my driver's license.

"You're from the city?"

"Yes."

"What brings you up this way, dear?"

"Just looking for someone."

"Hmm." She regarded me more thoughtfully. "Someone in town? Maybe I could help you. I've lived here my whole life and know everyone."

"Well . . ." I debated how open I could be with her. "I'm looking for an elderly lady who might have gone to the Prophet's Paradise. She disappeared from her home last night."

"Are you a detective?" she whispered.

"Oh, no. Just a friend of the family, but no one could leave to come up here right away."

"That's terrible. That family must be so worried."

"They are, believe me." I thought about Dorothy and felt a pang of guilt that I hadn't called her all day.

"I go to a regular church. And I'm not much of a joiner, so I don't really understand what all the hoopla is with these people. But they seem all right when they come into town. Don't bother anyone, at least."

"I understand from the sheriff that some people from the town work out there."

"Yes, a few. You've met our sheriff?"

"Yes, ma'am." A few more days and I'd be talking like a local.

"Come on down to the office tomorrow morning around ten. You can meet Duane. He's my handyman. Does odd fix-it jobs here at the motel. He works out there occasionally. Maybe he could give you some information. I'm Gladys, by the way."

"Nice to meet you, Gladys." I reached across the counter and we shook hands. "I'd appreciate any help I can get."

She indicated the doorway behind her. "I just want to catch my show, dear, but you come on down tomorrow morning. And there's coffee and donuts here till nine thirty, if you'd like some."

"Thanks. That would be nice."

"Good night." She smiled and scurried away to the room in the rear. I picked up my key and heard the volume of the television return to stun level as I pushed through the glass doors. A chill blast of wind whipped through the entryway as I hurried back to my car. I pulled the car inside the goldfish bowl courtyard and parked on the opposite side from Room 202, better to keep an eye on it if I heard any strange noises in the night. I turned off the engine and dialed Dorothy's number. She answered on the second ring.

"I was hoping that was you! Have you found anything out yet?"

"Not much. I've located the compound and made friends with the sheriff, but I haven't been able to get onto the grounds. I'm staying at the Bide-a-Wee Motel tonight. So don't worry that I'm not back in the city yet."

"Julia, I don't know how I can ever repay you. And again, I'm sorry I snapped at you last night. My nerves are just frazzled."

"No worries. And you don't owe me! I'll call you at some point tomorrow when I know more." I clicked off.

Next I dialed Don and got his voicemail. I left a message that I was well and the name of the motel where I was spending the night. I tried Gale's number. She didn't answer. I left another message that I was out of town and not to worry. I'd call her in a day or so to explain.

I shoved the room key into the pocket of my jeans, popped open the trunk, and pulled out a down jacket and a scarf I keep in there for emergencies. Swapping it out with my lightweight jacket, I closed the trunk and walked out of the courtyard down Powell Street, heading for Cowboy's End.

THIRTY-EIGHT

As dark as the street was, it still took a minute for my eyes to adjust to the interior of the bar. Rows of bottles that needed dusting were lined up in front of a long mirror. A brightly lit moving diorama advertising beer hung on the opposite wall from the bar. And at the end of the room, a jukebox had pride of place. Two men in jeans and denim jackets lounged at a table in the corner, several empty beer bottles in front of them. One sat with his booted foot resting on a nearby rickety chair. A couple danced listlessly in the center of the floor, clutching each other to the strains of a twanging rendition of unrequited love. Peanut shells and sawdust littered the floor along the length of the bar. I groped for a stool as my eyes adjusted. One woman sat alone at the bar with an untouched beer in front of her, cracking peanut shells in her teeth. It was my nurse. I decided to take another chance.

I sat on the stool next to her. "Hi."

She turned slightly unfocused eyes in my direction. "Oh. It's you."

I raised a finger to the bartender who ambled over. "What kind of wine do you have?"

He snorted. "Merlot and Chardonnay."

The nurse giggled.

"Merlot, please."

The nurse turned to me. "What's your name?" The phrase seemed flat, more like a statement than a question.

"Julia. What's yours?"

"Edie."

"Look, I didn't mean to bother you earlier. I just didn't know who to talk to."

The bartender returned with a glass that looked like an empty peanut butter jar filled with a dark red substance. I took a sip. It wasn't bad, or maybe I was just desperate.

"Better if you don't talk to anybody here." Edie cracked a peanut shell in her fingers and popped the fruit into her mouth, washing it down with a swig of beer. "In fact, you're only the third person who's talked to me in the seven months I've been in this stinking town."

"Where are you from?"

"L.A."

"What brought you up here?"

"Oh . . . I don't know . . . I went through a break-up and I guess I had some crazy idea I needed to be close to nature. Some place simpler. So . . ." Another peanut shell cracked. "I answered an ad for a local doctor who needed someone who could double as a nurse and office manager."

"How did you end up out at the compound?"

"I visit there two afternoons a week for an hour or so, whatever they need, or if they call for me. You know, if someone gets sick. Check some of the people, blood pressure, vitals, that kind of thing. I still work for the doc." She spoke carefully, slurring a word here and there. She'd managed to down a few beers since I had seen her at the diner.

I glanced around the bar. "So is this what they call nightlife here?"

Edie grimaced. "Yeah. Can you believe it? They're all chicken farmers or some such thing. To bed at sundown and up at dawn. I guess I thought I'd find some real men up here. But they're either drunk or taken." She shook her head. "What was I thinking?"

"Far cry from L.A."

"You can't even imagine. Look, I'm sorry if I was rude to you. It's just . . . I didn't want to talk about that place." She leaned closer. I could smell the beer on her breath. "They scare me."

"Have they threatened you?"

"No. Not directly. It's just . . . I've mentioned it to the doctor I work for. He's a decent guy, but . . . he doesn't want to do anything."

"What do you mean?" A small knot gathered in my stomach. Was she about to confirm my worst fears for Eunice?

"It's like this." She swiveled on her stool and looked straight at me, lowering her voice. "I'm only allowed to see the people they choose. I can't just check anyone I want. They put me in a little room and bring people in. They're mostly elderly, but not all of them. A lot of them seem to be in decent shape when they first come, but after a while . . ."

"What?"

She hesitated and looked over her shoulder, then turned back to me. "I think they're being drugged. And some . . . are maybe overworked. They have a farm out there. But I can't prove anything. I'm not allowed to draw blood or do anything like that. Today . . . well, I made a stink. There's a man out there. He needs further care — he needs hospitalization. I told them that, but they didn't want to hear it."

"Could you go to the sheriff?"

"Oh, him!" She waved her hand dismissively. "He's not gonna stir up any shit. They all just wanna get along, that's all. But today . . ."

"So what happened?"

Her lips set in a thin line. "They scare me. That's all. And I'm not going back. I'm supposed to be there tomorrow, but I'm not going. I'm gettin' the hell out of here."

"Back to L.A?"

"Nope. San Francisco. I have a friend there, and I can stay with her while I look for a job. I'm an R.N. I can work anywhere. I must have been out of my mind to come up here."

A plan was starting to form in my mind. "What time are you supposed to be there tomorrow?"

She looked at me carefully. "Four o'clock. Why are you asking?"

"I'm thinking that maybe you could loan me one of your uniforms and I'll be the next visiting nurse."

"Are you crazy?" She leaned closer. "These are not nice people."

"They may not be, but I've got no other option. I promised to do my best to find my friend's aunt. She's very frail. If she's being drugged or overworked, I've got to get her

335

out of there. My friend can't do it. She's a nurse too, but her other aunt has been ill and she can't leave her."

"It's your funeral, then."

THIRTY-NINE

I raced back to the Bide-a-Wee, got my car, and drove the one block back to the bar, where Edie waited for me. I was half-afraid she might change her mind. Once again, I followed her, but this time on the road leading out of town. When we reached the fork, she turned left, away from the route that led to the compound. We drove a short distance. Edie's car slowed and a blinking light indicated she was turning left again. She pulled into a narrow drive leading to a settlement of rustic cabins.

I parked next to her, climbed out, and followed her to a door painted bright blue and lit by a hanging lantern. She turned her key in the lock and pushed the door open. "This used to be a motel. Now they rent them out."

"Quaint," I replied, following her in.

She glanced at me quickly. "No, really. They are. Very cute. Little hobbit houses."

"The best thing is, they all have fire-places," she said.

Inside, the tiny cottage consisted of a small living area furnished with a worn sofa, a chair, and a lamp; a kitchen the size of a roomy closet; and one small bedroom.

"It's been fine for me, staying here. Can't complain, but it's time to move on." We entered the bedroom. A built-in wardrobe took up half of one wall. Curtains in a flowery print covered the one window. Edie opened the wardrobe door and pulled out two uniforms. "These are old. I was getting ready to dump them. This one has pants and a top. The other is a dress style."

She was about my size, but taller. I was afraid the pants would be too long. I reached for the dress. "I'll take this one. I'm sure it'll fit me."

"Take one of these too." She threw a small white cap that turned up at the edges onto the bed. Then she leaned down and rummaged on the floor of the wardrobe, emerging with a pair of scuffed, white lace-up shoes.

"Won't you need your cap?" I asked.

"Nah. I just have these 'cause the doctor's old school. He thinks it looks more professional. Nurses wear all kinds of gear now, sometimes just hospital scrubs."

"I really appreciate this." I dug into my purse and pulled out a business card. "I wish you the best in San Francisco. Here's my number if I can ever return the favor."

Edie stared at my card. "You're an astrologer?"

I nodded.

"Thanks. I'll give you a call soon. I can use all the help I can get. I just hope you know what you're doing."

I shrugged. "I don't. I just don't know what else to do."

She stood in the doorway of the cottage and watched as I dumped the uniform, shoes, and cap into the back of the car and belted myself in. I started the engine and turned the car around to head out to the road. Edie approached as I started to inch down the drive. I stopped and rolled down the window.

"You better be careful. What do you think they keep those dogs for?"

"To keep people out?"

Edie shook her head. "To keep them in."

FORTY

I headed back to the Bide-a-Wee, wondering why it didn't have a cute Scottish theme instead of the mid-1950s motif of white stucco with orange trim. There were only two other cars in the courtyard. No wonder the vacancy sign was lit. I parked in the same spot opposite my room, grabbed my nurse's uniform, and trudged up the pressed concrete steps. I unlocked the door of room 202 and flicked on the light.

I gasped. My room was a riot of red plaid — walls, bedcover, and drapes. Gladys should have warned me. I'd need sunglasses to sleep. The bathroom, on the other hand, matched the white and orange décor of the building. To think I'd hoped for a cute Scottish theme. This was Glasgow on acid. I shed my clothes, brushed my teeth, and slid under the covers. In seconds I slid into unconsciousness, hoping tomorrow would be my last day in Ardillas.

■ ■ ■ ■

I woke the next morning to a red plaid haze as early light filtered through the drapes. I fumbled for my phone to check the time. I had slept until nine o'clock! Duane the handyman was due to arrive by ten, as I recalled, and I desperately needed coffee. Time was running out and I was suffering from a rising level of anxiety. I had one day to find Eunice. Less than twenty-four hours before that solar eclipse and new moon was exact. I couldn't ignore it. I was sure that if I was unsuccessful in bringing Eunice home, she would come to permanent harm.

I climbed out of bed, jumped in the shower, and dressed in record time. I brushed my teeth, pulled my hair back into a ponytail, and pulled on my socks and sneakers. I was craving cappuccino. I loped down the stairs to the office and pushed through the door. The aroma of coffee filled the room. A small pot still stood on the counter with paper cups, plastic stirrers, and real cream. Next to the coffee pot was a plate with a generous stack of donuts. I poured a cup of coffee, grabbed a jelly donut, and wolfed down a mouthful of jelly and sugar.

Gladys entered from the back room, followed by a man in his thirties who towered over her. He wore work clothes and a leather tool belt. He creaked when he walked.

"Hello, dear. Glad you finally woke up. This is Duane." I quickly swiped my hands on the back of my jeans before the giant shook my hand.

"Pleased to meet you, ma'am."

Ma'am? "Please, call me Julia." I was sure I wasn't much older than he.

Gladys busied herself wiping off the counter and rearranging the donuts. Duane nodded in her direction. "Gladys tells me you're askin' after that crowd out at the compound."

"I'm looking for my friend's aunt. I think she might be there. In fact, I'm sure she's there, but I can't seem to get in."

"No, it's not easy. I work there sometimes. When they call me."

"What do you do for them?"

"Odd jobs. One time I fixed a pipe that broke. Another time I fixed a busted door on a cabin. I guess they asked around town and got my name."

"You ever get to see inside any of those cabins?"

"Not really. Someone'll meet me at the gate, let me in, and take me to where they need the work done. Never seen anybody who lives there. It's like they want to keep me away from all the people. Somebody, usually one of the men, stays with me while I work and then they escort me out. There was one time, though . . ." Duane glanced at Gladys as if conveying new information to her. "Everybody was busy and they asked me to stand at the gate. They were expectin' someone and needed somebody there to watch the gate and open it."

"Did anyone come?"

"A big black Caddy pulled up that day. Saw a driver and a red-haired man in the passenger seat. I did like I was told. I opened the gate and then relocked it with the chain and the lock and just went home."

"So if someone's expected to arrive, there's somebody waiting to let them in?"

"Seems so."

Gladys turned back to us. "Thank you, Duane. I'll call you if I have any more problems with that faucet."

"I'll take off then." We both watched him through the glass door as he climbed into his truck and drove away.

"That man's a Godsend, I tell you," Gladys said. "I couldn't keep this old place running if it weren't for him. Did he help you any?"

"Just confirmed the impression I already had."

"Well, dear, be careful where you nose around. People here are a little suspicious of outsiders. We just don't want any trouble."

"Let's hope Prophet's Paradise doesn't bring some serious trouble to your doorstep."

Gladys nodded and returned to her living room.

FORTY-ONE

I shrugged into my jacket and headed down the street toward the diner. For a weekday morning, it was crowded. Another waitress, in addition to the one I'd seen yesterday, was on duty. I sat at the counter, squeezed in between two large men who overflowed their stools. Belatedly I realized the man on my left was Sheriff Leo.

"Hello," I said.

"Good morning. How you makin' out?"

"Haven't learned much."

"Didn't think you'd have any luck." He chuckled. "You interested in taking a ride out that way this morning?"

I thought about the nurse's uniform in my room and decided that riding along with the sheriff might not be the best idea. If I planned to get into the compound masquerading as a local nurse, I didn't want to be spotted in the sheriff's car, and I certainly didn't want to fill him in on my plan.

"Thanks, I appreciate that, but I don't think so."

He looked at me questioningly. Just then the waitress arrived and I was saved from having to offer an explanation. I ordered a hearty country breakfast of bacon, two eggs, hash browns and toast. If I kept up all the good work, I'd easily grow another couple of dress sizes.

"Suit yourself." He took a sip of his coffee. "What do you plan to do today?"

I decided to be honest — for a change. "I think I might take your advice and drive out to see the Walker family — the family you told me about."

"Hmm." Sheriff Leo scratched his chin, as I expected. "Okay. That's good. I'm sure they'll talk to you, tell you whatever they know."

"You really had no luck at all with it?"

"Well, the Walkers couldn't do much. The woman and her daughter didn't want any fuss made. They just wanted to call some relatives and get out of town."

"Do you think they might have told the family more?"

"Maybe. But unless they made a complaint, my hands were tied." He took a last swig of his coffee cup and rose from the stool. "Check back with me later. Let me know how you made out."

"I'll do that."

Back in the car, I dug the sheriff's handwritten directions out of my purse. The farm was a few miles north of town, probably a half mile in a straight line due west from the compound. If someone needed to escape, it would be logical they'd end up at the Walker house if they headed in that direction.

I slowed as I neared the area the sheriff had described. I spotted a sprawling ranch style house with yellow clapboard siding. An old well stood in the front yard, a bucket hanging from its tiny roof. I couldn't tell if it was decorative or once was the real thing. Small bushes outlined the front, covered in nets of tiny multi-colored lights. A Christmas tree filled the large picture window, and a St. Nicholas doll the size of a small child rested in a hobbit-sized chair by the front door. I made a U-turn and pulled up in front of the house, as far off the road as possible. I climbed out of the car and walked to the front door, where an evergreen wreath hung, topped with a large bow. I rang the bell and soon I heard footsteps approaching. A trim woman in her forties opened the door.

"Yes?"

"Mrs. Walker? I hope I'm not coming at a bad time. Sheriff McEnerny gave me your name."

"Leo?" She looked puzzled for a moment. "Okay. Why don't you come on in. We can sit in the kitchen. I just made some fresh coffee."

I followed her through the front hallway. A teenage girl peeked out from another room, and, realizing it wasn't someone her own age, disappeared.

"Coffee?"

"Yes. Thanks. Love some."

"And please call me Janet." She wiped her hands on a dishtowel and placed a full mug in front of me, moving the creamer and sugar bowl closer. "What can I do for you?"

I explained the situation and told her the sheriff had told me about the people they had sheltered. She nodded and regarded me carefully, slowly stirring cream into her own cup.

"I don't know what to think about those people out there. That was about a year or so ago. We called Leo because we really didn't know what to do with them. The woman claimed she escaped because they'd beaten her daughter."

"Escaped . . . not left?"

"That's the word she used," she replied

348

drily. "I found them hiding behind our barn. They were so frightened. It was all I could do to get them in the house and get them to eat a little food. The sheriff wanted to talk to them, maybe get them to press charges, but they were having none of that. They were really terrified."

"What happened to them?"

"We took care of them for almost a week. They wouldn't leave the house — afraid to be spotted, I guess. They wouldn't talk much at all. They didn't have anything but the clothes on their backs. The little girl was only about ten years old. Frankly, I wondered what other kind of abuse might be going on out there, but there wasn't anything anyone could do." She took a sip of her coffee. "The day after we took them in, two people, a man and a woman, nicely dressed, perfectly normal looking, showed up. They claimed the woman and the girl had gone for a walk and hadn't come back. They said they were worried they might have gotten lost."

"What did you tell them?"

"Not a thing. I didn't invite them in. After I saw the condition that poor woman and child were in, and the fact that they ate like they hadn't had a decent meal in a while, I didn't buy that story for a minute. Just told 'em I hadn't seen a thing and made sure the door was locked afterwards. I did suggest they talk to the sheriff, though."

"Did they?"

"They did not. I called the sheriff the next day and asked if anyone had contacted him. And I checked again a week later. He never received any reports of anyone missing." She paused. "That woman and the girl, they were poor. She was a single mother, and I guess she hooked up with that group because they promised shelter and some sort of religious community. Whatever it is, those people must have a good rap, but the reality seems quite different. Anyway, long story short, the mother finally managed to locate some relatives down in Daly City who offered them a place to stay. My husband drove them down on one of his trips to San Francisco."

"Was that the last you heard of them?"

"Yes, it was. Except about a week later, the same two people came around again. Tell you the truth, they gave me the creeps. Real friendly and laid back, just to tell me not to worry, their visitors were fine. I said, 'That's good, because I was worried and I let the sheriff know some people might be missing.'" She chuckled. "You should have seen the look on their faces. Not so friendly then, and they took off in a hurry." Janet brushed a crumb off the tabletop. "I wish you luck finding your friend's aunt. I know there's a lot of elderly out there too. I can't imagine putting old people in those drafty old cabins. It was a kind of campground years ago, but after the owner died, the buildings were never fixed up. They might have running water and maybe electricity, but it's not a good place for old people. Not a good place for anybody, if you ask me."

"You talking about that compound?" A tall, lean man in overalls entered the kitchen and, taking a mug from the counter, poured himself a cup of coffee.

"Jim, this is Julia. The sheriff sent her out. She's looking for her friend's aunt."

He leaned over to shake my hand, then took a seat at the end of the wooden table and looked at me seriously. "You think she's there?"

"We're pretty sure. She left a note."

"Damn. Good luck with that." He shook his head.

"Your wife just filled me in about the woman and her daughter you took in."

"We tried to find out as much as we could. Maybe get 'em to press charges if there was anything strange goin' on."

"Did you believe them?"

"I sure did. That little girl never spoke one word the whole time she was here. The mother . . . well, she explained enough. I could tell she was real scared they might find her and grab her back. She didn't want to talk to the sheriff at all." He stared into his coffee cup and looked up. "She did tell me some strange stuff though."

"Like what?"

"Guess you'd call it brainwashing. This preacher . . . he had 'em all convinced they owed their lives to him. That he could do anything he wanted to them and he had complete control over everything. If they ever tried to leave or talk to any outsiders, they'd be betraying him and the Lord would strike them dead. He did a real job on those people."

"It's so sad," Mrs. Walker added. "They were simple people, religious — that's how they were able to hook them. It is brainwashing. I hate to think what else is going on. I just don't understand why people put their trust in any stranger who talks about God and give up control over their own lives. I just don't understand it."

"Maybe 'cause they have nothing else." Her husband replied, reaching over to squeeze her hand.

■ ■ ■ ■

I said goodbye to the Walkers and headed back to town the way I'd come. These country roads wound around so much I was afraid I'd lose my sense of direction if I didn't retrace my steps, like Hansel and Gretel dropping bread crumbs. Because the road curved in a semi-circle, the Walker ranch was at least two miles from the compound by the road, even though closer in a straight line than any other inhabited property.

Instead of turning toward town, I stayed on the road, following it as it circled around. I passed the entrance to Prophet's Paradise and continued on. I took the first right turn I could find. This road again followed the property line. Between breaks in the trees, I spotted more chain-link fencing. The entire compound was fenced off from anyone who might accidentally wander in — or deliberately attempt to get out.

After completing the circuit, I headed back to town. I pulled up at the one hardware store the town boasted and wandered up and down the aisles looking for wire cutters. I wasn't sure what size I needed for the job I had in mind and was finally forced to approach the counter. A rotund man of about fifty, wearing an extra-large T-shirt that hung over his belly and a baseball cap, spoke up. "Whatcha' lookin' for, lady?"

"I need a wire cutter that'll work on a chain-link fence."

"Hmmm . . . that'd be about a number nine wire, I guess. What do you need that for?"

"We're taking down a section of fence to put in a gate." I'm so honest. I hoped I looked like a do-it-yourselfer.

"You doing that by yourself?"

"Mostly."

"Well . . . show you what I have. Lotta ranchers use these, works on barbed wire too." He disappeared through a door behind the counter and returned with a two-foot-long, double-handled implement. "This might be kinda heavy for you. Give it a try."

I picked it up. It weighed about twelve pounds. "Not bad, but do you have anything lighter or smaller maybe?"

"Not here, miss. You'd probably like a Felco, maybe a twelve or sixteen inch. They only weigh a couple of pounds, but they have carbide blades that can cut through links pretty easy."

I sighed. "Do you happen to know where I could get one of those?"

"Well . . ." He rubbed the back of his neck while he thought. "There's a place over in Cloverville that sells sporting and climbing gear. Those guys use 'em. Not cheap though. Other than that, maybe you'd have to drive down to Santa Rosa."

"Oh." My disappointment must have shown.

"Tell you what. I'll give 'em a call. I know the guys over there. If they have 'em in stock, you want them to hold one for you?"

"Yes. Please."

"Wait here." He disappeared again through the rear door.

If I had to, I'd buy the twelve pound wire cutters, but the lighter tool could make any task easier. I might be jumping the gun and the tool might not be necessary at all. At least I was hoping it wouldn't come to that, but if I had one shot to get into the compound, I wanted to be prepared for the worst.

The clerk returned a moment later. "They'll hold one for you. Ask for Al when you get there. I forgot to ask the price, but it'll probably run about sixty bucks or so."

"Thanks!"

"Just head back to the freeway, go under the overpass, and it's about ten miles to Cloverville. Can't miss the place. Big yellow sign two blocks down."

I waved and ran back to the car. I followed the clerk's directions and in thirty minutes I was driving down Sebastopol Street. I spotted the yellow sign two blocks in and parked in front. Only one man was at the counter.

"You must be Al."

"Sure am." He smiled. He reached under the counter and pulled out a shiny, twelve-inch-long tool. "You won't have any trouble with this. Great tool. These carbide blades will cut through anything pretty quick." I pulled out a credit card, waited for Al to run it, and then signed.

"No need to wrap it up. I'll just carry it. Thanks." I jammed it into my purse and jogged back to my car. Forty minutes later, I pulled into the courtyard of the Bide-A-Wee. I'd have just enough time. I parked in one of the many empty slots and loped up the stairs to my room. I had nothing to pack, and if I stuffed everything I didn't need into my overnight bag, I could check out of the Bide-a-Wee before going out to the compound.

Once inside my room, I dialed Dorothy's number on my cell. It rang several times until the answering machine picked up. I left a message that I'd have more news for her later in the day. She might be busy with

Evandra or maybe out doing errands. I didn't want to tell her what I planned. I didn't want her worrying about me as well as Eunice.

I shed my clothes, pulled the white uniform over my head, pinned my hair in a bun, and pulled on the rubber-soled orthopedic shoes. I tied the laces and winced. They were half a size too small and started to pinch after a couple of steps. I was wishing I'd brought some tights or pantyhose to keep my legs warm, but I didn't want to take the time to try to locate a store. If Edie arrived at four o'clock on the nose, I would too. I used two more pins to secure the little white hat. I checked myself in the mirror. I thought I looked quite professional — Julia Bonatti, R.N. — nurse without a license. Hopefully no one would ask me to do anything more complicated than check a pulse.

I emptied the contents of my purse into the overnight bag. Then I grabbed my sneakers, a pair of socks, jeans, a knitted cap, a T-shirt, and a thick sweater and stuffed them in my large purse, along with the wire cutters and the scarf I'd discovered in the pocket of my down jacket. Thank heavens for big purses. I stuck my cell phone into a side pocket. All the rest I stuffed in the overnight bag. I walked quietly down the stairs to my car, hoping Gladys wouldn't spot me in my get-up and ask any questions. I threw the overnight bag in the trunk and dropped the key to my room in the night box. The office was vacant, but the noise level through the glass told me Gladys was pinned to her television. Prime time for soaps.

I followed the original route mapped out by the sheriff. As I neared the turnoff to the drive, my palms became sweaty. If I stopped to think about what I was doing, I'd lose courage. I wasn't sure what my plan was, but I had to get inside. I was sure Eunice was there, and I was also sure she'd be ready to come home without a fuss. The difficulty would be getting her out unseen. I reviewed the possibilities in my mind. Worst case scenario, I could be attacked and hurt. If not by humans, then by dogs. Another possibility was that Eunice wasn't there, but her note and my instincts told me she was.

If I were caught, what would they do? Call the sheriff? Charge me with trespassing? It wasn't against the law to impersonate a nurse. Not like impersonating a police officer. As long as I didn't try to practice medicine, I couldn't see that I was doing anything terrible. I took a deep breath, pulled the car onto the shoulder of the road where it was hidden by a curve and some overgrown bushes, and turned off the engine. I rummaged in the glove compartment and found a short cord. I laced my car key onto it and tied the cord around my neck, tucking it under my uniform top. I found a small, flat mini flashlight and shoved that into my purse with the rest of the paraphernalia.

I climbed out and walked down the road to the driveway, and then walked casually up the rise to the chain-link fence. An older man with gray hair, wearing jeans and a heavy, checked shirt, was standing by the gate. I raised a hand in greeting. He looked at me cautiously before he undid the lock and chain. I wondered if he was part of the group or another local, like Duane.

"Where's the other nurse?"

"She was called out on an emergency. I'm filling in."

He hesitated a moment, looking my uniform over, then swung the gate open. "Let them know when you want to leave."

"I will." I smiled. Hitching my purse further up on my shoulder, I walked down the dirt drive toward the cabins. I could feel the guard's eyes on my back as I walked. I continued on and resisted the urge to turn around. Near the bottom, the dirt road leveled out and curved slightly to the left. After I had walked several more yards, I glanced cautiously over my shoulder to make sure I was out of the guard's line of sight.

Ahead of me, the road was lined on both sides with tiny cabins, reminiscent of the dollhouse cabin that Edie had rented. There must have been a time when Ardillas had been a tourist stop. But unlike Edie's rental, these cabins were dilapidated, raw. Weather-beaten wood was evident where the paint had peeled. Many of the wooden steps had rotted from exposure. Some of the small windows were cracked, pieces of tape holding them together. I doubted these cabins had any heat source, perhaps not even electricity. I shuddered to think what this environment could do to old bones.

On an impulse, I ducked behind the first cabin on the right. The weeds and brambles came up to my knees. The Army of the Prophet was in serious need of landscape help. I pressed my way through, thorns scraping my bare legs, and ducked into the trees behind the cabin. I kicked off my uniform shoes, which had already caused some blisters, and pulled on my socks, jeans, and sneakers. I took off the cap and dress and pulled on my T-shirt. I wrapped the long silk scarf in an X around my chest and, using it as a holster, stuck the wire cutters in a loop of the scarf under my arm. I wiggled around to make sure they were secure. Then I pulled my heavy black sweater over my head with the black knit cap. I shoved my cell phone in a front pocket of my jeans and the flashlight in the other. Then I balled up the uniform, cap, and shoes, stuffed them into my purse, and hid it under a bush. I made sure my car key was secure on the cord around my neck and tucked it into my bra under the T-shirt and sweater.

I tiptoed carefully toward the back of the cabin. Each one had the same small window in the rear wall. When I reached the cabin directly in front of me, I stood on tiptoe to peek inside. The walls of the room were unfinished. A naked light bulb hung from the ceiling. I noticed a hook on the back of the door, a cot, and a thin blanket. I walked carefully to the back of the next cabin, doing the best I could to tread softly, careful not to step on any twigs that might give my presence away. This cabin was empty as well, and displayed the same lack of personal belongings. These seemed to be nothing more than sleeping quarters. The real action must take place somewhere else.

I clambered up the rise and back into the stand of trees. It was growing dark by now and I could hear voices at a distance. From the trees and the higher vantage point, I saw a group of twenty or so people, all sizes and ages, walking toward a large building at the far end of the road. Several of them carried gardening tools. Behind them was a field of dark, loamy, freshly turned soil.

Once I was sure I was out of the line of sight of anyone returning from the field, I hurried out of the trees and down the slope to the last cabin, the third one in the row. Before I reached the back window, I heard a door hinge squeak. I ducked and held my breath. Then I peeked carefully around the corner of the building. On the other side of the dirt road stood an identical cabin. A woman stepped out and stood on the rickety wooden stairs. I recognized her instantly. It was Gudrun.

She peered up and down the road, more than likely searching for the vanished nurse. I waited, terrified of making any sound. After a few moments, she stepped back inside the primitive cabin and pulled the squeaking door shut.

I decided to huddle down and wait for the sun to set. In the dark, I might be able to check the rest of the cabins without difficulty, particularly if anyone turned on an interior light.

I managed to squat in a comfortable position behind the cabin. The minutes crawled by, and finally I heard the same door open across the way. I peeked cautiously from my hiding spot in time to see Gudrun striding down the road toward the larger building. Perhaps sunset signaled a time for an evening meal or prayer meeting. If Eunice was in that larger building, this could be a very long evening.

As soon as Gudrun was out of sight, I crept cautiously toward the dirt road and then darted across. No lights burned inside any of the cabins. I moved to the door of the first cabin in the row. It was bolted with a primitive wooden latch. I opened it and peeked inside, turning on my small flashlight. It was a repeat of what I'd seen across the road. There were two cots in this room, with thin blankets. No heater, one window in the rear, and a light bulb hanging from a long wire in the center. The second cabin was exactly the same and unoccupied.

The third cabin was the one I'd seen Gudrun leave. I opened the door, expecting to find it empty like the other two. But when I waved the flashlight over the cot, I saw a small form under the thin blanket.

I crept toward the bed and carefully lifted the threadbare blanket. My flashlight illuminated a cloud of soft white hair. It was Eunice, her hair in disarray. She was dressed only in a cotton shift. She made a small mewling sound and tried to focus her eyes. She was barely conscious. I shone the flashlight up to my face.

"Eunice, it's me. Julia. I'm getting you out of here."

Her eyes widened at the sound of my voice. "Julia?"

"Dorothy sent me. We're going home." I hoped I sounded more confident than I was. I pushed back the blanket and helped her to a sitting position. She was conscious, but her eyes were unfocused. She had been drugged. I was sure of it.

"Do you think you can walk?"

Eunice nodded and moaned. She clung to my sweater with both hands while I moved her legs carefully, placing her feet on the floor. Her bare legs and feet felt ice cold. I shone my small light around the floor and under the bed, but could find no shoes or slippers. I kicked myself for leaving the nurse's shoes behind. "I'll help you."

I wrapped the blanket around her shoulders and lifted her to her feet. I could tell she was willing, but she seemed to lack the necessary motor skills. I wasn't sure I was strong enough to carry her, but I could hold her up and if her feet would move, we could make it out.

We moved toward the door of the cabin at an agonizingly slow pace. With one arm holding Eunice upright, I opened the door and peeked out. No one was nearby. With both arms, I hugged her to myself and lifted her down the stairs and around the corner to the back of the shack. She couldn't weigh more than ninety pounds, but ninety awkward pounds would be more than I could carry for any distance. Half lifting, half carrying, and stumbling with my burden, I reached the wooded area behind the shack. Eunice was now able to put one foot in front of the other, and we moved slowly into the trees.

My plan had been to head toward the main gate and find a secluded spot where the chain-link fence could be cut. Now I was afraid that this plan would take far too long. Gudrun already knew the nurse was missing and soon would realize her elderly convert was gone. The main gate would be the first place they'd look.

So I headed in the opposite direction. If I could reach the edge of the property at the rear, where the road ran past, perhaps I could leave Eunice safely for a few minutes and circle the fencing to retrieve my car. I realized with dismay that I should have parked on the road behind the compound and walked the distance to the main gate. With luck, maybe I could flag down a passing motorist. As I debated, I heard a shout and my blood ran cold.

FORTY-TWO

Footsteps pounded along the dirt road and another voice answered. Two men. We'd managed to put only thirty feet between ourselves and the shack. They would know Eunice was missing. They wouldn't know I was with her.

Eunice was doing her very best to stay conscious and walk. "Eunice," I whispered. "Climb on my back when I bend down." I stopped, and, squatting, I hoisted her up piggyback style. She wrapped her arms around my neck. I was treading carefully in an effort to not give our position away.

I weigh about a hundred and twenty pounds, but I'm strong and can carry a lot of weight. Even so, in less than a minute, my knees and back were aching. I was moving as fast as I could, but I knew it wouldn't be fast enough. Sooner or later the men searching for Eunice would figure we'd gone in the opposite direction from the gate and catch up with us. I stumbled through the trees, bent almost double. My lungs and thighs burned from the exertion. I stepped forward and felt the ground give way beneath my feet. I struggled to keep my balance. I had reached the edge of the ploughed field, my feet sinking slightly into the loamy dirt. Our journey had just become more difficult.

I recalled the figures I'd seen working in the field. From my vantage point in the trees, I'd seen tools and a wheelbarrow. If I could find that wheelbarrow now, we could move a lot faster. I strained to make out shapes in the darkness. It was the dark of the moon, the last few hours before the new moon. The eclipse would be exact. I had to somehow find the strength to get Eunice to safety. Her very life was at stake. There was no time to waste. I sank to my knees, helping her lean against a nearby tree trunk while I reached for my flashlight. It was small but gave off a concentrated light. Shielding it with my hand, I raked it slowly over the edge of the cultivated stretch of ground. The wheelbarrow was there, only ten feet away.

I ran to it and grasped the handles, dragging it back to the tree where Eunice stood. The wheel on it had been well cared for and well oiled. It was nearly silent. I took the blanket from Eunice's shoulders and stretched it over the bed of the wheelbarrow. I tipped it forward and led her closer, gently easing her into its cradle. She was shivering. I covered as much of her as I could with the edges of the blanket, maneuvered the wheelbarrow around, and headed straight across the field. The soft ground protected us from noise. The path between the cultivated mounds offered slightly firmer footing. Eunice sat quietly, doing her best to curl up and present no impediment to our travel.

A dog howled in the distance, greeted by other dogs barking in response. I registered the sound but forced the full meaning of it out of my mind. We had to get across the field and through the trees to the road. I was sweating profusely in spite of the cold and afraid to move faster for fear of tipping over the awkward carriage. I was mumbling prayers under my breath.

The barrow hit a hard bump. We'd reached the opposite side of the cultivated field. The road could not be far away. The barking of the dogs carried through the cold night air. Was it my imagination or were they closer? Somewhere in the trees behind us? Were they leashed? Could the dogs follow our scent? If so, and if they were trailing Eunice, would that scent have disappeared when she climbed inside the wheelbarrow? I hoped that was the case.

I pushed my burden into the thicket. Branches tore at my face and arms as I continued on, hitting a rock here and there, but I managing to keep the cart upright. I stopped. I listened and tried to quiet my breathing. Voices carried across the field, but they weren't heading in this direction. The edge of the property had to be very close. I needed to reach the fence.

I leaned close to Eunice's ear. "Don't move," I whispered. "Stay very still until I come back for you." I pulled off my heavy sweater and wool cap, and, reaching down, helped Eunice into a semi-sitting position.

"You need this to keep warm."

"Thank you, dear," she replied in a breathy whisper. I quickly pulled the sweater over her head, helping her slide her arms into the thick sleeves. Then I pulled the wool cap over her head.

"Give me a few minutes. I have to find a way to get us out to the road."

I moved as quietly as possible through the dense bushes until I reached the metal links of the fence. I pulled the wire cutters out of my makeshift holster and tore the scarf from my neck. Methodically, I clipped through

370

each of the links from the ground to my shoulder height, and then cut several of them across at a right angle. The tool quickly snapped each link. I dropped the wire cutters and grasped the flexible chain-link, pulling it toward me to create an opening.

I wasn't sure what to do next. The wheel-barrow might not fit through the opening and I didn't want to take the time to cut more links. I was afraid to leave Eunice bundled up in the wheelbarrow inside the fence for fear she'd be discovered. And I couldn't leave her unprotected on the road while I ran around the property to reach my car. That's when I heard a motor and saw a flash of headlights coming toward me on the road.

I stood on the shoulder of the road and waved frantically as a pickup truck neared. It didn't slow but continued past. My heart sank. Except for my T-shirt, I was dressed in black. The driver must not have seen me. I turned and saw a flash of red taillights. He had seen me! The truck moved into reverse gear and backed up very slowly. I ran to meet it. The driver hit a button and the passenger window opened. In the interior light, I saw a man dressed in work clothing: well-worn overalls with a work shirt and a heavy denim jacket. He was in his mid-fifties. His hair was gray, and his calloused hands rested on the steering wheel. The smell of the exhaust hit my nostrils.

"Do you need some help, ma'am?"

"Yes. Please. I do. Can you give us a ride?"

"Us?" His glance became more cautious.

"Yes. I have an elderly woman with me. Please, wait for me. I have to help her."

"Sure thing. I'll give you a hand." He reached down and turned on blinking hazard lights. He left the engine idling and climbed down from the driver's side.

I rushed back to the opening in the fence and pushed through. A few strands of Eunice's white hair were visible in the dark. I ran to her. "It's all right now. I have help."

She didn't reply but let me lift her slowly out of the wheelbarrow to a standing position. With my arm around her waist and guiding her, I pushed branches away and led her to the opening in the fence. My good Samaritan was waiting at the side of the road. He still had not asked any questions. I led Eunice through the fence, and when the driver saw she could barely walk, he lifted her with ease, carrying her like a child. He nodded to me, indicating that I should open the passenger door. He slid Eunice across the seat.

"Hop in, ma'am."

I didn't need a second invitation. I clambered into the truck, putting an arm around Eunice to hold her upright. Her thin hand gripped my T-shirt as if she were clinging to life. The driver resumed his seat, hit the door locks, and put the truck into gear, picking up speed as he moved forward on the road.

"Can you take us to the Sheriff's Station?"

He glanced at me, nodded, and turned his eyes back to the road. At the next bend, he turned right. We were still circling the Prophet's property. At the end of this road he slowed the truck, and instead of turning left to head into town, he took a right.

My stomach knotted in fear. "Where are you going?"

The man glanced at me quickly but didn't respond. We passed my car, barely visible on the dark road.

"Stop!" I shouted. "Stop right now." I clutched Eunice protectively. Before I could say another word, he hit the brakes, slowed, and turned into the same dirt driveway I'd entered just a few short hours ago.

The sickening knowledge hit me. We'd walked into a trap. I hadn't managed to rescue Eunice, and we were now, both of us, prisoners of the Prophet's Paradise.

FORTY-THREE

The driver pulled to a stop, his headlights illuminating the locked metal gate. He gave the horn three short bursts.

I turned to him. His features were lit only by the dash lights. Those same features that had seemed benign a few moments before now took on an evil cast. I was sure the driver's door lock controlled the passenger door, and even if I were able to jump out and run, I couldn't leave Eunice alone. I had no options. I was trapped.

Anger welled up inside my chest. "How could you do this?" Anger was better than tears.

He shot a glance toward me. "I get paid, lady. The rest is none of my business."

I was tempted to spit at him. "I will get out of here," I hissed, "and when I do, I swear I'll find you." I was very close to tears.

There was movement on the other side of the chain-link fence. Two men were running from the camp toward us. Gudrun was right behind them. One man reached the gate and pulled a set of keys from his pocket. He unlocked the hasp and swung the gate open. The driver hit a button and unlocked the doors of the pickup. The second man passed a shotgun to Gudrun and yanked open the passenger door. He grabbed my arm and pulled me out of the truck. Eunice had been leaning into me and almost tipped over on the seat. The man who'd opened the gate reached in and slid her toward the door, lifting her in his arms. I heard her cry out.

I yanked my arm from the first man's grasp. "Let go of me!" I was furious now. I was probably going to get hurt, but I didn't care. I wanted to inflict some damage. I took a quick step closer and attempted to kick him in the groin. He jumped back. I'd missed the mark.

I turned to Gudrun. "What do you think you're doing? I've already called the sheriff. He's on his way."

She was momentarily confused and looked questioningly at the driver. The driver had not moved from his position. He shook his head in response. "I doubt she had time."

What an idiot! If I hadn't been so panicked, I would have called the sheriff. It would have been worth the loss of time to try to reach him. Even if no one answered, I could have left a message and then someone would at least know where we were and bring help.

The man with the keys grabbed my arm and reached into the pocket of my jeans. He extricated my cell phone and hit buttons to check the call log. He laughed. "She's bluffing." He dropped the cell on the ground and crushed it with the heel of his boot.

Gudrun leveled the shotgun at me and nodded to the two men, indicating they should bring us inside. I struggled to break free but his grip was too strong. Half pulling and half dragging me, he forced me down the dirt road while the other man carried Eunice in his arms. She was crying quietly and called my name.

We reached a cabin just beyond the one in which I'd found Eunice. Gudrun removed a heavy padlock from the door handle, opened the door wide, and stood back. Eunice was carried in and placed on a cot. I was forced up the two short steps and shoved hard. I flew across the tiny room and fell against the opposite wall. The door slammed shut behind us. We were in total darkness.

As the lock clicked into place, I heard

voices outside the door, then Gudrun's response. "The Prophet . . . coming tonight . . . decide what to do."

I took a deep breath and took stock. My elbow was badly scraped. My cell phone was gone. The one tool I had was the wire cutters, and those were on the other side of the compound by the chain-link fence. I felt in my other pocket and almost cried in gratitude — they hadn't discovered my tiny flashlight. I reached in and dug it out, shining the narrow beam around our prison. This cabin was exactly like the others, except it had no window. I put my ear to the door and listened carefully. It was possible they'd posted a guard outside, but also possible they hadn't. I hoped they were convinced we were safely imprisoned for the night.

Eunice had stopped crying. I felt my way to the cot and, kneeling down, stroked her head. "I know you're afraid." I felt her nod. "Try to stay calm. I swear, Eunice, I'll figure something out." She shook her head in a hopeless gesture. She seemed less confused than she had been an hour ago. I counted that as a good sign. Whatever drugs she'd been given were wearing off.

I pointed the light at the door and checked the frame. This door was heavy and fit solidly into the jamb. It wasn't something that would give way to a few well-placed kicks. The ceiling was built out of heavy boards that seemed newer, as if they'd recently been replaced. I turned off my flashlight, anxious I might wear down the tiny battery. On hands and knees, I crawled back to Eunice's cot. I wanted to keep her quiet and make as little noise as possible in case Gudrun or the men returned.

One of the boards under my knees creaked. I pressed on it several times, and it seemed to give slightly. I turned on my flashlight again to get a better look. The floorboards were very old and pitted, but some had been secured with newer nails, the shiny newer steel reflected the light.

Starting at the side of the cot, I crawled slowly around the perimeter of the room, inspecting each floorboard carefully. They were uniformly old and mostly eaten by dry rot and mold. If I could locate one that hadn't been recently nailed down, then perhaps I could dislodge it. There was a crawl space under each cabin, maybe only two feet high but big enough for me.

Eunice was moaning. She called my name. I crawled back to the cot on my knees. "Shhh. Stay calm. I think I have an idea."

"Julia?"

"Yes, I'm here," I whispered.

"So foolish. To come here . . . it was for the bees, dear."

"I know."

"They promised me."

"What did they promise?"

"To let me care for the bees." Eunice's one passion had been used to seduce her. There has to be a special hell, I thought.

"Listen to me. I don't know how yet, but I promise you, we'll get away and I'll make sure Dorothy lets you keep bees."

"You will?" she replied breathily.

"I promise."

"I want them to feed on lavender. They'll make such nice honey then."

"Lavender it is." I almost laughed. The thought of a fragrant lavender bush on a warm sunny day seemed light years away from our current predicament. "Just keep imagining lavender. I'm going to be crawling around on the floor looking for a way out, so be patient, okay?"

I turned and started my maneuver once again. There were a few creaks and groans but nothing that looked promising under the light. I'd reached the opposite wall. I planned to move in tighter concentric circles until something looked viable. I reached the far back corner and almost missed it — one spot where the wide boards had not been reinforced.

My flashlight was dimming. The battery was losing power. I took one last look under the light, wedged my fingernail into the edge of a corner board, and flicked off the light. I could feel the board wiggle back and forth. Perhaps the nails had fallen out. I felt for the short edge of the floorboard, wedged two fingernails into the end, and pulled it toward me. I heard the rough creaking of rotten wood and the squeak of a rusty nail. I managed to lift one end half an inch when a fingernail broke and the board fell back into place. I didn't care if my fingers turned into bloody stumps — I intended to find a way out.

I remembered I had one other tool. No one had spotted the cord around my neck. I reached inside my T-shirt and took the long car key out. Once again, I wedged an unbroken fingernail into the end of the board and managed to get the tip of the key into the crack. I had to be careful not to damage the key, though, in case I was able to reach my car. Using the key as a lever, I lifted the board enough to insert a finger into the gap. With my other hand, I tucked the cord back under my T-shirt. Maneuvering on my knees and gripping the edge of the board with both hands, I pulled it up another inch. Once again, a stubborn rusty nail squeaked. I was making progress but hoped no one was outside the door listening to my efforts. I took a deep breath, then grasped the end of the board and pulled with all my strength. The board came completely loose. It was only one wide plank, but it was a start. A trickle of something warm ran down my palm. I was bleeding.

Still kneeling, I changed positions and, using both hands, grasped the long edge of the next board. I pulled with all my strength and felt the resistance of the ancient nails. After three tries, the board came away, cracking in two. Half was in my hand, the other half a jagged tear.

A rush of air, damp earth, and dead leaves hit my nose. I put my foot through the opening and touched the earth below. Using my knee, I kicked upward until the next board loosened, easier now that I had leverage. I felt the edges of the opening. It was time to give it a try. I could squeeze through the hole. I was only afraid someone might have heard my struggle.

I crawled back to the cot. "Eunice. I'm not going to leave you here alone. I'm going to crawl under the cabin to get out. I'll get you free somehow. I won't leave you here. Just trust me, okay?"

She gripped my hand in the dark. "I'll try to be brave, dear."

I turned back to my newly created escape hatch and pushed the thought of black widow spiders out of my head. California was rife with them and piles of construction material and logs were one of their favorite nesting places. Once bitten, emergency care would be necessary within minutes, or vomiting, blindness, even death could result, depending on body mass. I put both feet through the hole. If I could squeeze my hips through, I could make it the rest of the way. The jagged edge of the broken board pressed against my thigh. I turned and kicked it up, dislodging it. I now had just enough room.

Kneeling on the cold ground beneath the shack, I squeezed the rest of the way through, holding my breath. Now only the upper part of my body was above the floor. I had to make it the rest of the way. Painfully, I twisted my body until I could stretch my legs out on the ground. Lifting my arms above my head, I squiggled my bottom along the dirt until I was completely under the cabin, lying on my back. I prayed I had not disturbed a nest of any kind of creepy crawly things. If I had, I'd require hospital-ization long before I could escape, with or without Eunice. Given the ethics of the Prophet's Army, I was certain they'd do nothing to help me.

I turned slowly onto my stomach and, brushing cobwebs from my face, crawled the few feet to the rear of the cabin and the night air. I emerged and frantically brushed leaves, dirt, and cobwebs from my face and hands, hoping nothing had nestled in my hair.

I sat on the freezing ground for a moment, hugging my knees and catching my breath until panic subsided. I looked up and down at the backs of the cabins. There were lights on in two of them. As I watched, they were extinguished. I heard a door slam in the distance and voices carried on the cold night air. Adrenaline had made me unaware of the cold, but now I was shivering in my light T-shirt. I had to keep moving or the cold would slow me down.

I stood and tiptoed along the side of the cabin, aware of Eunice lying silently inside just on the other side of the wall. My eyes were adjusting slowly to the darkness. Farther up the road I saw the wavering beam of a flashlight. I waited and listened. Then I distinctly heard Gudrun's voice. She was walking toward our cabin with another person. I heard a man's deep voice in response to hers, although I wasn't able to make out the words. She was coming closer. I didn't know if she'd return to her former cabin, or if she'd unlock the prison door to check on us.

As she came near, I crawled behind the cabin. My knee hit a sharp rock. The pain shot up my leg. I almost cried out from the shock. I turned back and picked up the rock, gripping it in my right hand. It was small enough that I could grab it in one hand, but heavy enough it might serve as a weapon. I peered into the darkness around the side of the cabin, Gudrun's footsteps were coming closer. She passed our cabin and climbed the steps of the cabin next to us, then there was the telltale squeak of the door opening. I crept along the side toward the front of the cabin and peeked out. Her door was open. The light made an elongated yellow rectangle on the dusty road.

I hunkered down once again, trying to formulate a plan. I might be able to escape on foot by myself and get help, but I'd promised Eunice I wouldn't abandon her. I had no idea how long it would take to reach the town and enlist aid, but the thought of leaving Eunice here frightened me. If I could find a way to get the cabin door open, perhaps I could get her to safety.

As if in answer to my prayers, Gudrun stepped out of her cabin. I ducked back. She hesitated a moment, and then, clomping down the three steps, strode toward our makeshift prison. She fished a large keyring out of her pocket and inserted it into the lock, swung the door open, and stepped inside. I caught a flash of light from her flashlight. It was now or never.

I crept quietly up the stairs behind her. She was standing inside the doorway, her flashlight aimed at the hole in the floor. She uttered an oath under her breath in German. I gripped the rock and bashed her squarely on the back of her head.

She wavered for a moment. Terrified I hadn't knocked her out, I slammed the rock into her head once more for good measure. She pitched forward, hitting the floor face down. Her flashlight dropped from her hand and rolled into a corner.

Eunice pushed herself up to a sitting position. "Bravo, my dear!" she whispered. I automatically put my finger to my lips, not sure if she could see me in the dark. I kicked the door shut behind me, grabbed the flashlight, and rolled Gudrun over. A trickle of blood was oozing from a cut on her head but she was still breathing. I wouldn't have been the least bit upset to learn she was dead, although I didn't particularly want to be the one responsible. I wondered if a self defense plea under these circumstances would be credible.

I rummaged in her pocket and found the set of keys. One of these had to open the front gate. I stuffed the key ring into my jeans. Under her skirt was a serviceable slip over a pair of thermal bloomers that would have done justice to a nunnery. Under those were pantyhose. I pulled off her bloomers and, grasping the edge of her pantyhose, struggled against the weight of her body. I finally managed to pull them off, shoes and all. I rolled her over onto her stomach and using the stockings, bound her wrists tightly behind her back and then tied them to her ankles. As a last touch, I stuffed the thermal bloomers in her mouth. I had to silence her. She could wake up in a moment or, I was afraid to dwell on this, not wake up at all. I couldn't afford to take any chances.

"Can you stay here just a few more minutes, Eunice? I'm coming back with my car. When I pull up, do your best to get down the stairs. If you have trouble, I'll help you. Keep the door shut till then."

"Yes," she whispered. I peeked out the

door, checking the dirt road in both directions. No one was stirring. I closed the door quietly behind me, making sure it wouldn't lock. I hurried down the dirt road, staying close to the cabins where I could duck between them in case anyone happened to come by. With no moonlight and no artificial light, it was difficult to follow the road.

By the time I reached the gate I was out of breath with anxiety. I pulled the flashlight from my pocket and, tucking it under my arm, aimed it at the lock that held the chain securing the gate. There were several very old fashioned keys, perhaps to these very outbuildings, and three newer ones that seemed to be made for a padlock. Whether from fear or cold or both, my hands were shaking and I was shivering. If I'd heard correctly, it seemed that Reverend Roy was due to arrive tonight and Gudrun had planned to wait for his decision. We had to escape. There wasn't a second to waste. If the rumors were true — if he was responsible for the murder of his disenchanted followers — he was capable of anything.

The first key wouldn't fit the lock. The second one fit, but wouldn't turn. When I tried to pull it out, it stuck and I was forced to waste precious seconds wiggling it back and forth until it released. The third key was the lucky one. It turned easily and the lock clicked open. I pulled the hasp off the chain and threw it into the bushes by the side of the gate, tossing the ring of keys after it. I looked over my shoulder but saw no movement in the dark. Carefully and slowly, I pulled one side of the wide gate open to its farthest extent. It was well oiled and barely creaked on its hinges. I raced down the drive and headed up the road to my car. I breathed a sigh of relief that I hadn't been searched and the car hadn't been discovered. I pulled the cord over my head and fit the key into the lock. Miraculously, it turned easily — the key hadn't been twisted in my struggle with the floorboards. I started the engine and headed up the drive toward the chain-link gate.

I drove as fast as possible down the dirt road with my lights off. I did a tight U-turn outside the cabin and opened the passenger door. Eunice stood in the doorway of the shack clinging to the door jamb. I ran around the car and and lifted her down the stairs and into the passenger seat. I didn't bother with a seat belt, just shut her door, ran around to the driver's seat, and hit the door locks. Turning on the headlights, I floored it. The Geo jumped forward and then its wheels started to spin on the dirt. I took my foot off the accelerator, turned the wheel, and accelerated a little slower. The tires bit into the dirt. We had traction and we were on our way.

As we neared the top of the rise, I heard men shouting. I looked in the rear view mirror and saw two figures running at full speed down the road carrying flashlights — probably the same two men who'd delivered us to the locked cabin. I heard dogs barking and could see their shapes on the road, low to the ground and highlighted against the wavering flashlights. They'd been let out of their pens again.

I was almost to the gate when the first shotgun blast went off. I hit the gas and pulled Eunice toward me, forcing her to lie down as much as possible in the tiny car. Her head was almost on my lap. I prayed they hadn't hit my gas tank or the tires.

"Stay down. Don't sit up," I shouted.

I heard a second shotgun blast as we flew through the open gate. The rear window shattered into a thousand tiny pieces. A thud hit the trunk. Eunice screamed. I looked in the rear view mirror and saw a dark lunging shape. I heard an unearthly growl as the Doberman pushed its head through the shattered rear window. Its snarling jaws dripped saliva, only a foot from my head. I gunned the car and sped down the drive, turning sharply onto the road, hoping to avoid skidding into the trees. The tires screeched as I hit the brakes just before the turn. The dog flew off the trunk, yelping as it landed in the thicket. I flicked on my high beams and drove recklessly, praying I wouldn't miss the turn that would lead me to town. I had one chance to get away. They'd pursue, I was sure, but if I could find help, we'd be safe.

I saw the road that would lead us to town and slammed on the brakes, made the turn, and accelerated again. I didn't slow down until I reached the main street. The Sheriff's Station was completely dark. The tavern was lit but I wasn't sure what help, if any, I could find there. I pulled up to the two-story fire house and stopped, facing the metal garage door. I leaned on the horn. I had no idea who manned the fire house at night, but I hoped the second floor was someone's sleeping quarters. I continued to lean on my horn in bursts.

An engine revved in the distance. A shot of fear ran up my spine. They were chasing us. I craned my neck to look at the second story and saw a curtain move, illuminated by a dim light from the interior of the room. A bulky figure came to the window, then reached down and pushed up the lower sash. A frizzled gray head poked out of the window. What was taking this guy so long?

"Please, help us!" I shouted.

"Is there a fire, ma'am?"

"No, it's an emergency, please let us in!" I was hoping he'd push a button and the heavy metal door would swing up. I glanced at the end of the street, the concrete ribbon disappearing into the black hole of the woods at the edge of town. Then I saw headlights flashing through the trees. They were coming after us. Was there anyone here who would help us?

"Just a minute. Let me get my pants on." He pushed the window down and moved away. Good thing there wasn't a fire — the whole damn countryside could burn down by the time this guy got a move on. My palms were sweating. I had to get both Eunice and myself to a safe place. I just didn't know where that was.

I heard tires squeal at the end of the road. They were here. There was no time. I gunned the engine, threw the car into reverse, and leaped forward, heading for the Bide-a-Wee two blocks away. As we approached, I saw truck lights in the rear view mirror. It looked like the same truck that had picked us up on the road. Tires squealing, I pulled into the motel courtyard, hoping there were witnesses about. I leaned on the horn, not letting up. The truck chugged in slowly behind us, leisurely, as if knowing we were alone and there was no way to escape.

"Eunice. I'm getting out and locking you in. Don't open the doors for anyone but me. And keep leaning on the horn."

Eunice nodded. Her face was flushed. At least she looked more alive than when I'd found her. I popped the trunk and hit the door locks as I climbed out. Reaching into the trunk, I grabbed the steering wheel lock and pulled it apart. If our pursuers came closer, I had a bludgeoning weapon and a nasty stabbing device. I only hoped I was strong enough and quick enough to buy us some time. I slammed the trunk and took a position behind the car. Eunice began to hit the car horn in erratic bursts. The truck lights blinded me. A man climbed out of the passenger side, the same man who'd carried Eunice into the compound. He walked slowly toward me.

"Now lady, don't give us any more trouble. We just want Miz Gamble to come back with us. She's joined them now, you know."

"Like hell she has," I shouted over the noise of the horn. "She's not going anywhere with you."

He glanced back at the driver of the truck and chuckled. His breath misted in the cold night air. "Who's gonna stop me? The old lady here is deaf as a post. We know she don't have no guests at all."

I stood my ground, the heavy steel weapon at my side. I hoped I could swing fast enough if he came any closer.

"Turn around and get the hell out of here. The sheriff is on his way."

That seemed to anger him. All humor left his face. He moved quickly toward me, his arm outstretched as if to grab me by the throat. I swung the heavy club down, striking his arm with a solid thunk. He cried out and fell back, clutching his forearm. He lunged at me again. I jumped back and heard the unmistakable ratchet of a shotgun.

A fiery blast roared from the direction of the motel office. The rear windshield of the truck exploded.

"Hey," the man yelled, turning with a surprised look on his face.

"Deaf as a post, am I? I'll show you." Gladys stepped around the truck. A flowered nightie hung under her pink velour bathrobe. Her head was covered in pink squeegee curlers. She ratcheted the shotgun once more and blasted the front windshield of the truck.

"That was birdshot, you losers. The next one is a live round. Now get the hell off my property."

The man ran back to the truck and jumped in the passenger side as the driver revved the engine. The truck reversed, tires screeching as it backed out of the motel courtyard.

"Are you all right?" Gladys called out.

"Yes." Hysterical laughter bubbled up in my chest. "Never better. Thank you."

"Those two," she sneered. "Old man Braddon and his mean-ass son. Figures they'd be doin' dirty work for those so-called Christians. I've known both of them their whole life, and I always knew they'd never amount to anything."

"Gladys!" I heard a voice call from the street, and the frizzled gray-haired man from the firehouse rushed into the court-yard. "What happened?"

"Oh, come on inside and I'll tell you all about it." Gladys waved her shotgun like a welcoming banner. "You missed all the ac-tion, you old fool."

FORTY-FOUR

Inside Gladys's parlor behind the motel office, we sank into a pink sofa covered with overstuffed embroidered pillows. Framed autographed photos of soap opera stars stood on a side table. Gladys had draped a crocheted throw around Eunice's shoulders and slipped her feet into fuzzy slippers. She cranked up the volume on the space heater in the corner of the tiny room. The interior temperature had to be eighty-five degrees, but at least Eunice had stopped shivering. I held a cup of warm tea to Eunice's lips, the warm fluid bringing her to life.

"I feel so foolish causing all this trouble. I was just so angry at my sister and I thought, I'll show her. I can do something on my own. Now I see Gudrun planned all this." Eunice shook her head. "I was so very gullible."

"Do you remember being drugged?"

"I must have been. They gave me something to drink and then I fell asleep. They kept me in that horrid room, and then Gudrun came in with someone else, some man — they wanted me to sign lots of papers. They said it was for their liability and I had to sign everything if I wanted to stay."

"Did you?"

"No, I didn't. Lord knows what they would have done to me if you hadn't found me, Julia. I didn't know anything was wrong right away. They told me the beehives were at the rear of their property. But when I asked if they had a smoker or queen excluders — I've been keeping up on this, you see — I could tell they had no idea what I was talking about. That's when I became frightened."

Gladys cocked her head at a sound I couldn't hear. I noticed the small plastic hearing aid in her right ear. She rose and opened the door to the outer office. Sheriff Leo filled the doorway like a large and friendly bear. I'd never been so happy to see law enforcement in my life. He listened grimly to our tale, then stepped out of the room to make a phone call. When he returned a few minutes later, he said, "I put calls in to the Santa Rosa sheriff and the FBI. The CHP is on the way now. I'm heading over to the compound to meet them. If half of what you've told me is true, we'll be making arrests tonight."

I stood. "I'm going with you."

"I don't think that's such a good idea. It might get dangerous. I'll come back as soon as I can. We need to take the little lady there over to the hospital and have her checked out."

I ignored his warning. "You forget, I know the layout of the place. I need to be there. Besides, I can identify the men who locked us up."

"Ha!" Gladys said. "I can tell you that. If they're not there, I'll give you their damn address."

The sheriff sighed. "All right. If you're coming, let's make it fast."

"Oh, Julia," Eunice said. "Don't go back there."

"I'll be careful." I squeezed her hand. "Don't worry. You just rest and we'll be back as soon as we can."

"I'll take good care of her," Gladys said to the sheriff. "You two get a move on. Don't let those people get away." She turned to Eunice as we headed out the door. "Do you like old movies, dear?"

I didn't hear Eunice's response as Sheriff Leo shut the motel door behind us and hurried to his car. I ran to catch up and climbed into the passenger seat. I belted up as he sped down the road, back toward Prophet's Paradise.

Before we reached the entrance to the compound, he pulled over. Three state cruisers were already parked at the end of the drive, blocking it. Sheriff Leo climbed out as an officer exited from the first car, and they conferred for a moment. I saw the sheriff nodding his head. He hurried back.

"We're going in. Ambulances are on the way in case we need them. You stay right here," he admonished. "You'll be safe. I'll come back for you if I need you."

I nodded and unstrapped my seat belt. The first cruiser drove up the dirt drive, its lights flashing and siren screaming, cutting through the still night. I heard an announcement and a warning through a bull horn. The other two cruisers followed, with only lights flashing. Then the sound decreased slightly.

I couldn't hear very much over the siren. I fidgeted. Impatient, I finally climbed out and followed the path up the drive. As I started to walk down the road past the gate, I could see that the cop cars had taken up positions along the main road. A few residents huddled in the doorways of the small cabins, thin blankets around their shoulders. They looked confused and frightened. Then I heard shouts and dogs barking. I wondered if Reverend Roy had arrived and if, right now, Gudrun was trying to explain what went wrong with our escape. I certainly hoped he was there — I wouldn't be happy until I could see him taken away in handcuffs. Not to mention Gudrun.

Then I heard a shotgun blast. Some of the cops took cover behind their vehicles. I couldn't tell where the sound had come from — farther away, maybe the large meeting hall. It struck me that they must have already discovered the hole in the chain-link fence I'd cut earlier. They would have wondered how Eunice and I had initially reached the road. Anyone curious enough would have seen the wheelbarrow on the far side of the field, leading straight to our path of escape. Surely the man in the truck would have told them where he had found us.

I raced back to the sheriff's cruiser and climbed in the driver's side. He'd been in a hurry — had he left the keys? He had. I'd just borrow it for a bit. I was sure he would understand. Just as I started the engine, I saw Sheriff Leo running back down the drive.

"Hey!" he shouted.

I shouted back, "Get in!"

He looked confused for a moment, but pulled the door open and jumped into the passenger seat. "What the hell do you think you're doing?"

"The hole in the fence. They must know about it by now." I revved the engine. It was so powerful, the car leaped ahead. I had to hit the brakes not to fly off the road. "We have to stop them." I turned right, driving as fast as I dared until we reached the rear of the property. I slowed and stopped the car just before we arrived at where I thought the break in the chain-link fence was. I held my breath and listened. "Hear that?" I turned to the sheriff.

He nodded. There was more crashing and movement behind the fence. A pale face showed itself in the dark.

"They're trying to escape. Hold on." I hit the gas and drove off the shoulder of the road, ramming the side of the vehicle into the fence, trapping whoever was trying to exit.

The sheriff pulled his weapon and hit a button on the dash. He aimed a spotlight at the movement in the bushes. Gudrun and the Reverend stood stock still, staring at us through the fence, like deer caught in the headlights.

"Police. Hands up. Now!" Sheriff Leo shouted. The searchlight was trained on Gudrun's face and I caught the hateful look she shot in my direction.

Then I heard the Prophet speak in his mellifluous tones. "Sir, I'm sure there's some misunderstanding. I can explain everything."

"You'll have lots of time to explain everything very soon," the sheriff replied. We heard more movement in the bushes behind the duo and two other officers arrived. They cuffed Gudrun and the Reverend and led them back into the compound.

Sheriff Leo breathed a sigh of relief. He holstered his gun and climbed back into the cruiser. He glared at me.

"I had a feeling they'd try to run," I offered by way of an apology.

"Just drive back around, will you? Jeez," he muttered, shaking his head. "Don't ever do that again. You coulda been shot for Chrissakes."

I did as ordered and drove back to our original spot to let the sheriff out. I watched as Gudrun, the Reverend, and four men and one woman were locked into the back of the Highway Patrol cruisers. Three ambulances and two vans arrived, and the residents of the Prophet's Paradise were led to the vehicles. The whole operation took no more than an hour and a half.

Finally the sheriff returned. "Let's get your friend over to Cloverville and have her checked out." He opened the driver's door. "And I'm driving."

I breathed a sigh of relief that it was finally over.

When we arrived back at the Bide-A-Wee motel, Gladys and Eunice were ensconced on the pink sofa watching a Thin Man movie. Eunice was smiling. She looked up at us. "Back so soon? My, that was quick."

"Thanks to Julia, the Reverend and his accomplice didn't manage to escape." He patted me on the back. "Good work. But don't ever steal my car again." He sat on the sofa next to Eunice. "Now I'm taking you to the ER at Cloverville. It's not far from here. You need to have someone take a look at you."

"I'm fine," Eunice replied. "Really. I just want to go home."

I'd noticed some dark bruises on her arms. I didn't know if they'd been caused by our escape attempts or administered by the caring staff of the Prophet's Paradise. "I think the sheriff's right, Eunice. Let's get you checked out."

"You're coming with me, dear, aren't you?"

I nodded. "I'll follow in my car. I'll be right behind you."

Eunice squeezed my hand and whispered, "Thank you."

Gladys turned to Sheriff Leo. "I gave her some warm slippers. Make sure you keep that afghan wrapped around her. She isn't wearing anything but a thin cotton thing and a sweater. You can return that stuff to me later." The motel owner followed us out to the patrol car, making sure Eunice was bundled up and strapped in with the seat belt, and then she walked me to my car.

"You sure you can drive that thing all right?"

"I think so. It's only the back window. It's got to get me back to San Francisco." I glanced over at the patrol car. The interior light was on, and the sheriff was leaning close to Eunice as if to hear what she had to say. I saw him smile and nod in agreement. The interior light went off and the flashing lights on the roof of the patrol car lit up.

I thanked Gladys profusely and hugged her. She had saved us.

"That's quite all right, dear. I'm happy to know I'm a better shot than I realized.

You're welcome back any time. We haven't had this much excitement here since one of the junior high kids stole a tractor and drove it into an open septic tank."

"Ah," was my response. My mind boggled at the vision. I hopped in the Geo, revved the engine, and turned the dashboard air on full blast. The exhaust would be sucked back into the car through the hole from the shotgun blast and I didn't want to collapse from carbon monoxide poisoning. I said a prayer for the state of my tires and, waving one last time to Gladys, followed the sheriff's car out of the courtyard of the Bide-a-Wee and onto the highway.

We exited at Cloverville, lights flashing all the way. I glanced at my car clock, shocked to realize it was only midnight. It felt more like the wee hours. I had been running on adrenaline and exhaustion was taking over.

The sheriff pulled straight into the emergency parking area and ran inside, returning with a wheel chair. He lifted Eunice from the car and wheeled her through the automatic doors. Inside, he showed his badge and explained our situation to the admitting clerk. While the clerk was doing her best to take information from Eunice, who didn't know if she had an insurance policy or not, I stepped outside to call Dorothy on the sheriff's cell phone. Mine, of course, was in little pieces in the dirt at the compound. I felt bereft without it. I wanted to let Dorothy know Eunice was safe; perhaps I should have tried to call from the Bide-a-Wee, but so much had happened so fast. I could fill her in on the gory details later.

The phone rang twenty times — I counted. There was no answer, and the machine didn't pick up. Surely Dorothy would hear the phone even if she'd gone to bed; that is, unless a storm in the city had knocked out power or the telephone lines.

I was shivering and hungry. I walked back to my car and put on my down jacket. I found the lunch Dorothy had packed still sitting in its thermal pack. Was that only yesterday? The food was over a day old but had been naturally refrigerated. I unwrapped the turkey sandwich and took a huge bite, not caring if I splattered mayo over my clothes. I was filthy and covered with dirt anyway. The sandwich wasn't spoiled, but it was definitely soggy. I tossed it back in the container and found the plastic bag of cookies. I wolfed them down. They were sugary, crunchy, and delicious.

Inside the ER, a nurse was wheeling Eunice into an examining area. I followed and helped her move onto the gurney. While the nurse took her pulse and blood pressure, I heard the sheriff speaking quietly to someone outside. A moment later the doctor, who looked as if he'd just woken from a sound sleep, stepped into the room and introduced himself to Eunice. I was sure the sheriff had filled him in on her recent escape, so I told her I'd be right outside and joined Sheriff Leo, sitting next to him on a hard plastic chair connected to a row of other hard plastic chairs.

"Did you reach your friend?"

I shook my head. "No. There was no answer. I'm a little worried." I passed the phone back to the sheriff. "Thanks for letting me use this."

"I've got an extra in the patrol car. I'll give you one."

"Thanks. I'll get it back to you." I shook my head. "I just don't get it. What drives people to abdicate authority over their life? What drives a man to create such misery in the world?"

The sheriff sighed. "Given my line of work, I've thought about that a lot myself. Power, I guess. Control. Sometimes it's a combination of energies. A few kids get together and do something horrible. You see it on the news all the time. Left to themselves maybe they'd never dream of doing anything but together they feed each other, feed off each other. Maybe it's as simple as that. If they had never met, never come together, would those crimes have happened? I don't think so somehow. I think something far more terrible comes to life when some people get together. Is that fate? Is there such a thing? I don't know."

I listened to him carefully. "Astrologers grapple with those larger issues too. How much is carved in stone? What does the birth chart describe and how much can the individual evolve? What energies are created when two or more people come together?"

Sheriff Leo looked at my quizzically. "You believe in all that stuff?"

I nodded and smiled ruefully. "We don't have any easy answers either."

We both looked up as the doctor approached from the examining room. He took a seat next to the sheriff but addressed both of us. "She seems fine, but I'd like to admit her for observation, just for a day or two. There's some bad bruising and she's extremely dehydrated. I want to make sure there's no organ damage. I don't think there is, but I'd like to be positive before I release her. Could either of you be responsible for her when she's released, and take care of getting her home?"

The thought of hanging around yet another small town for a few days didn't appeal to me in the least. It must have shown on my face. The sheriff spoke first. "I'll take care of it. I'll drive over tomorrow and check on her. Just give me a call when she's ready to go home. I'll take her there myself. Oh, and most of all, she's not to be released to anyone but me."

"Got it," the doctor replied. "I'll leave instructions."

We re-entered the examining room just as a nurse was attaching a plastic bracelet to Eunice's very thin wrist.

"Julia, I don't want to stay here. I want to go home."

"I know. But believe me, I'd feel better if you did stay, just to make sure you're stronger."

I didn't want to tell Eunice what my fears were. The sheriff had given me a clue, and suddenly everything was falling into place like the pieces of a puzzle. I had a sinking feeling in the pit of my stomach and I hoped I was wrong. I had to get back to the city. I still didn't know how, but I thought I knew why.

"Sheriff Leo will come over tomorrow to check on you. You're in very good hands, and he's going to take you home as soon as they let you go. Right now, I've got to get back to the city. I've been trying to reach Dorothy, but there's no answer at the house."

"Oh," Eunice groaned. "I'm so embarrassed. They'll think I'm such a fool."

"No, they won't. They'll be relieved you're safe. I'm driving back now and I promise you'll be planting lavender for your bees very soon."

Eunice squeezed my hand in response as the nurse wheeled the gurney out of the examining room.

The sheriff was waiting for me in the parking lot. "Maybe you should stick around. They'll want to question you, and you'll have to give evidence at some point. Believe me, Julia, I'm very relieved you both made it out of there. But if that's what's going on in my town, I'll be happy to see the whole lot of them locked up."

"I'm worried about what's happening in the city. I'd feel better if I went back right now, but I'll give you my address and home phone."

Sheriff Leo reached into the front seat of his patrol car. "Just write it all down. I'm heading back to the station now but I'll keep in touch." He opened his trunk. "Hang on, take this phone. I don't need it back."

"Thanks." I slipped it into my pocket. "I'll pick up a new phone tomorrow and let you know that number and I can drive back up if they need to talk to me." I followed the sheriff back to the 101 and flicked my lights as I turned down the ramp to head south. He flashed his lights in response. I did my best to quell the uneasy feeling in my stomach. Once on the freeway, I was able to keep up a good pace. The surrounding countryside was pitch black, but at least it wasn't raining. I would have loved some coffee to stay awake, but I didn't want to take the time to pull off the freeway at this time of night. There might not be anything to find out there at this hour anyway.

I reached Santa Rosa after an hour and the traffic became heavier. It would be another twenty minutes to Petaluma, Chicken Capital of the World. I put pedal to the metal and kept going, fighting off exhaustion and achiness. When the Novato exits flashed by, I had only another thirty miles to reach the city. As I came over the long hill and started down toward the Golden Gate Bridge, my eyes started playing tricks on me. I struggled to focus, but the spires of the bridge shattered and moved, then returned to their original place. Was I so tired my eyesight was affected? I shook my head and rolled down the window, letting the fog and the wind roll through the car. I hoped I wasn't breathing exhaust fumes from the hole in the rear windshield.

I struggled to maintain focus and stay within the narrow lanes crossing the Bridge. Back on land, I followed the road to the Marina and took Lombard to Van Ness. A second wave hit me as I entered the Broadway tunnel. The walls of the tunnel were melting. I felt panic rise up in my chest. Had an earthquake hit? Were the walls undulating from earth movement? I've never touched LSD, but I'd heard accounts from many people. Was I hallucinating? Something was happening to me. My head wouldn't stay still. My neck was spasming and my head was jerking involuntarily. I gripped the steering wheel tighter, trying to slow my breath and not panic.

Crossing Columbus, the noise and street lights jarred me. Everything was out of phase, but there was no sign of an earthquake. I drove slowly up Filbert, my vision disjointed. Everything that should have been solid was shattering like glass in front of me. The concrete of the road was undulating. I reached the spot where I hoped the

Gamble house stood and pulled over, turning off the engine, and saying a prayer of thanks I had managed this far. I was hearing voices, people chattering to me, but I knew no one was near.

I tried to climb out of the car. My legs were not cooperating. I managed to stand and did my best to cross the street. I reached the door that I knew was Dorothy's, but somehow it looked different — larger and more forbidding. The door was ajar, not shut and not locked. I pushed it open. The front hallway was dark. I stumbled. I couldn't get my legs to move properly.

I took a deep breath and pushed through the door into the kitchen. The lights were on but the room was empty. I retraced my steps and, clinging to the banister, forced myself up the stairs. I couldn't seem to call out Dorothy's name. Nothing was working right.

It felt like hours before I reached the top of the stairs and stumbled down the hallway to Evandra's room. I pushed open the door and found her tied to the bed. She was talking to herself, not making any sense. I clung to the bedpost and managed to survey the room. There was no one else there. I spoke to her but she didn't respond.

I sobbed. Something was terribly wrong. I

had to get help. I had to find Dorothy. Trying not to lose my balance, I clung to the banister and very slowly descended the stairway. I reached the kitchen and opened the door to the back garden. I couldn't see very well. Inanimate objects weren't holding still. I couldn't tell where I was. Was I close to the cliff? My legs seemed to give out. I stumbled and fell forward on the grass. The earth was spinning. I reached out my hand and felt the stones in the wall at the edge of the cliff. I managed to get up on all fours and headed in a direction that I hoped was away from the cliff. I crawled across the lawn toward the conservatory entrance at the side of the house. Grasping the edge of the doorjamb, I struggled to a standing position and pushed through the plastic covering over the doorway.

The light was dim, but I could clearly see Reggie. He was splayed out on his stomach, inching slowly across the floor. I watched as he clawed at the edges of the tiles as if trying to move through the floor. A dark shape loomed up and came toward me.

I stared, transfixed, willing my brain to work. It was Dorothy. Yes, Dorothy. My heart sank. Fear coursed through my veins. I turned away and forced my legs to move. I was tangled in the heavy plastic sheets and something was holding my head in place. Dorothy held my hair, pulling me back, dragging me into the conservatory.

"I'm sorry about this, Julia. You shouldn't have come back." She turned me around by the shoulders. I tried to focus on her face but it wasn't staying still. She shoved me to the ground, my fall stopped by a potting table. The room was splintering and moving. My heart was racing and now I was sure my legs were paralyzed. I watched helplessly as Dorothy calmly poured gasoline on a bundle of rags in the corner. Her movements were as efficient as if she were whipping up a casserole in the kitchen. Gasoline fumes filled the room.

I tried to form words. "Wh . . . ?"

"Such careless workers, leaving oily rags around."

My heart was racing faster. "Where's . . . ?"

She looked up from her task. "Richard? Not here tonight." She stopped her activity for a moment. "He was going to leave me again, Julia. I didn't want to hurt anyone, especially you, but I need the inheritance. I can't let Reggie take it all away. It's the only way I can keep Richard. You're young. You could never understand."

I shook my head negatively. "Not . . . marriage . . ."

"Of course it's a marriage. We are married, and he'll never leave me again."

I heard scratching and turned my head. Reggie had reached the wall and was now standing. His arms were moving as if he were attempting to swim through the molecules of the hard surface.

Dorothy turned and watched him carefully. Finally deciding that Reggie was no threat, she replaced the cap on the gasoline container and carelessly threw a few rags onto the floor near a stack of lumber and some paint cans.

My mouth was dry, I could barely get my tongue to move. "They'll . . . know."

"Know what? Nothing. That's what they'll know. When they examine what's left of you, there'll be no trace of the belladonna seeds."

Reggie pulled at the skin of his face. He howled madly and rushed toward Dorothy. She was smiling as she watched him in the dim light. By the time she saw the pitchfork in his hands, it was too late. The only sound she made was a gurgle as blood spurted from her neck. Reggie continued screaming, wheeling madly with the pitchfork. Window glass shattered as he struck at the windows.

I rolled over and pushed myself forward

onto my hands and knees. I crawled to the doorway and through the plastic sheeting. I kept moving until I felt the grass beneath my hands. Light from the kitchen windows fell in trapezoidal shapes across the damp lawn. I remembered I had a phone. Somewhere. Yes, pocket. My peripheral vision was fading . . . I was losing consciousness. I lay on my side on the grass and felt the smooth plastic. I couldn't be sure I'd hit the right numbers. I felt the numbers by touch, dialing 911. When a voice responded, I croaked, "Gamble . . . Filbert . . ."

The phone dropped from my hand. I could still hear a voice but wondered if I was imagining it. I rolled over onto my back. The sky was clear. The wind had swept away the fog and the stars overhead were wheeling through the heavens. It was the most beautiful sight I'd ever seen. I was sure I could see all the way to the Milky Way. Warmth flooded my body and I was overcome with a sense of well-being. I felt a soft brush against my cheek and could have sworn I smelled gardenias.

FORTY-FIVE

I woke in a hospital bed, a small box clipped to my cotton gown and a white plastic bracelet was on my wrist. I stared at the bracelet. My name was on it. How strange. It should be Eunice's name and not mine. Christmas carols were playing somewhere. I wondered what day it was.

The door opened and a nurse stepped in. "Welcome back, Ms. Bonatti."

"Where am I?"

"St. Francis. You were admitted last night."

"Last night?"

"The doctor says you'll be fine. There's still some medication on board, but I think we'll be able to take you off the heart monitor today. The doctor might let you go home tomorrow. Your friends are here too, right down the hall."

"Friends?" I sounded like an echo chamber.

"A young man and an elderly lady . . . uh . . ." She searched her memory. "Carrington and Gamble, that's it. They'll be fine in a day or so too. I'll come back to help you if you'd like to visit them. By the way, next time you decide to get high, stay away from the alkaloid poisons, okay? Good way to get dead."

The nurse left, her shoes squishing on the shiny tile. I heard carts being wheeled in the corridor outside my room and the clatter of trays and pottery. I was starving. A good sign, I guessed. I tried to remember the last time I'd eaten and couldn't. I did remember the crunchy cookies that Dorothy had packed for me. The special ones she'd helped Richard prepare . . . poor unsuspecting Richard.

I looked hopefully at the doorway, expecting a hospital worker to arrive with a tray, but instead I saw a tall, powerfully built woman. She wore a sensible navy wool skirt and jacket and her fair hair was cropped short. She approached the bed.

"Ms. Bonatti. I'm Detective Ursula Williams with the San Francisco Police Department." She opened a small leather wallet to show me her badge. "I wanted to catch up with you before you were released. We found your belongings in your car, but I'll need to talk with you later as the case develops."

"Call me Julia, please." I gave her my home number. "I don't have a cell anymore. I was using one the sheriff in Mendocino County gave me."

"Yes, we know. We found the phone and contacted him. He's told us about the events in Ardillas. I understand you had quite a time up there."

I felt a sudden frisson of fear. "Is Eunice all right?" Like a dream poorly remembered, everything was flooding back to me.

"That's the other Miss Gamble? Yes, she's just fine. Sheriff McEnerny has been to see her today and has agreed to break the news to her about the death of her niece."

I groaned in response, thinking of the effect this would have on both the sisters. Perhaps Evandra might feel vindicated in her suspicions of Dorothy, but Eunice was a far more delicate soul.

"I had a long talk with the sheriff, and I believe he'll be very gentle with her. He and his family have taken Eunice under their wing. The hospital is releasing her, so she's spending the holiday with them and after that he'll drive her back to the city."

I tried to imagine the Gamble house without Dorothy, and the sisters without their companion. As if she'd read my mind,

Detective Williams replied, "The husband — Richard Sanger, I believe — is pretty torn up, as you can imagine. But he's agreed to stay at the house for the time being and look after the two ladies, at least until suitable arrangements can be made."

"Thank you for letting me know. What about . . . ?"

"The Prophet's Paradise?"

"Yes."

She smiled widely. "You'll be happy to hear several arrests have been made and more to come. This has blown the whole organization wide open. Local emergency services have transported the . . . uh . . . residents to area hospitals, as needed."

"What about the Reverend Roy?"

"He's in custody."

"Good."

"Your doctor warned me to keep my visit short, but I'll be calling you in a few days to fill in some blanks." Detective Williams smiled and placed a card on my nightstand. "Give me a call if you have any concerns."

She turned toward the door and then hesitated, turning back to me. "One more thing."

"Yes?"

"What do you know about the young man who was admitted with you?"

"Reggie Carrington? He told us he's Australian and related to the Gamble sisters."

The detective nodded. "Well, it seems he was carrying a 'borrowed' passport. We think he's a Canadian citizen and we've been in touch with Homeland Security about him."

I nodded and collapsed back on my pillow. Why wasn't I surprised?

FORTY-SIX

Gale and Cheryl showed up at my hospital room that afternoon bearing food, wine, and flowers. Gale leaned over and kissed my cheek. "Honey, I was worried sick."

"How did you find me?"

"Don called the Mystic Eye. He'd been trying to reach you and panicked when your cell phone went dead. I went to your grandmother's house and talked to Kuan and then I drove up the hill to the Gamble house. When I got there, the police were cleaning up. They told me where you'd been taken. And I wormed most of the story out of them."

Cheryl grasped my hand, "I'm so sorry about Dorothy."

"It was . . . horrible." I fought back the tears. "I was so blind. I didn't realize until . . . it was something the sheriff said that made everything clear. We were speaking of fate, of crimes committed when two disturbed individuals hook up. Crimes that either person alone would more than likely never commit. I was so suspicious of Richard's being in the household, I simply couldn't see it was the effect of that relationship on Dorothy. But by the time I realized this, I'd already eaten the cookies she'd given me."

"If it's any consolation, I don't think she wanted to hurt you. She just wanted you out of the way."

"No. She never intended for me to come back in one piece." I leaned back against the pillows. My chest ached more from emotional injury than physical. Dorothy's desperation and obsessiveness, Richard's focus on money. Had she married anyone else, would she have taken the actions she did? Richard, for all his faults, would never have condoned murder. But the combination of their energies had convinced Dorothy there was only one path to take — she could not wait for her aunts' natural deaths.

So she had turned a blind eye to Gudrun's proselytizing of Eunice. If Eunice was foolish enough to be lured to Prophet's Paradise, Dorothy knew her aunt would never survive for very long. Perhaps she'd planned to have Evandra committed, based on the psychotic behavior caused by the belladonna seeds she'd substituted for caraway seeds in Evandra's cookies. All it took was a few thrown into the batter. The final catalyst was Reggie. His arrival meant that because of the stipulation of Elisha Gamble's trust, Dorothy would lose her inheritance to a male heir.

I was certain her shock over Luis's death had been genuine. The belladonna seeds — the coatings of which delayed symptoms for several hours — were meant only for Evandra. It was strictly an accident that Alba had unwittingly delivered the wrong snack to Luis.

Dorothy had succumbed to the madness of Mercury: a skewed, single-minded obsession that brooked no delay or impediment, an ability to warp reality to fit a desired outcome. She refused to see that all the money in the world would not make a flawed relationship work. I cast my mind back to all our meetings. Had I missed clues that would have warned me she was crossing the line into unthinkable acts? Were my perceptions so blinded by my affection for her?

"Why don't you get some rest now?" Gale said. "We'll be back tomorrow to pick you up and, no arguments, you're staying with me for a day or two.

"Oh, no. Wizard. I've been so worried about him. I don't know if I can —"

"Not a problem. I stopped by to see Kuan. Wizard's fine, and Kuan says to tell you not to worry. You can pick him up when you're feeling better. Oh, before I forget, I had your car towed to my mechanic's. They're fixing everything. My present to you for the holidays."

Cheryl spoke up. "We'll get you some fresh clothes tomorrow, and I'm cooking a big dinner."

I smiled in response. "I have presents for both of you too. Can we stop by Castle Alley tomorrow and pick them up?"

Reggie arrived at my bedside later that afternoon. My involuntary muscle spasms had lessened. I'd eaten almost three small meals and was feeling closer to normal. Best of all, the room wasn't spinning around and I no longer heard strange voices.

"I hope you don't hate me, Julia."

"Why did you lie?"

"I . . . I never meant for anything like this . . . If Dorothy hadn't been so threatened . . . none of this would have happened." I noticed the down-under twang of his speech had vanished.

"There's a good chance that's true," I

said. "I think it'll take me a long time to sort this out. What did you hope to accomplish?"

Reggie shrugged. "I figured the little old ladies had bags of money. Why shouldn't I get some of it? After all, I could have been Jonathan's grandson. They wanted to believe I was."

I was speechless for a moment. "What are you going to do now?"

"Head home. They told me there'll be an inquest, but they said under the circumstances they wouldn't be pressing charges. After that I should be able to go."

"And where's home?"

He smiled mischievously. "Toronto."

"Tell me something. How did you know the family history?"

"Well, here's the true part. My great-grandfather was one of the people the Gamble family hired to locate Jonathan in Australia. When my grandfather died, we had to clean out his house. In the attic, I found all the notes *his* father had kept from his investigation. He did find Jonathan, by the way."

"He did?" I was hardly ready to believe him.

Reggie nodded. "He did, he really did. Jonathan never had any children. He died

426

in a . . . let's say a house of ill repute. Heart attack. He was broke and was buried in a pauper's field. My great-grandfather interviewed witnesses who knew him. But here's the thing. He sent his report to the Gamble family, but I don't think they ever accepted it as true. Either their mother refused to believe it, or if she did, she never told the sisters."

"Pretty risky, what you did."

Reggie shrugged and smiled sheepishly. "Worth a try. Why shouldn't all that money come to me?" He brushed a blond lock from his forehead. "Besides, what I did? It wasn't illegal. Not really."

Handsome, young, and completely amoral.

I didn't feel any anger, though. Only a wave of indescribable sadness. If Reggie had never discovered the information about Jonathan Gamble . . . if he had stayed in Canada . . . if he had not decided to con the family . . . if Dorothy had never married Richard. All those if's, and now two people were dead, one of whom I'd cared for and trusted. It was only by the grace of the universe the rest of us were still alive.

Don showed up that evening carrying a steaming box of pizza and settled in a chair next to my bed.

"Julia, I was worried sick about you. I kept calling your cell but never got an answer. I got in touch with Gale, and, well . . . you know the rest."

"I'm sorry. I never meant to cause everyone all this worry."

"Well, damn it, you did. Now shut up and have some pizza." He tucked a large napkin under my chin and opened the box. The smell was indescribable. "I'm sure you're getting crap food in this place. By the way, the paper's running a story on this tomorrow. Wait till you see the headlines!" Then he saw the expression on my face and hesitated. "I heard about your friend. I'm really sorry, Julia. This must be hitting you hard."

"A story about Dorothy and her aunts?"

"No, not at all. Although I'm sure that will eventually come to light. No, it's much better. You'll be happy about this. The Prophet is now persona non grata." Don chuckled. "The politicians, the mayor, the chief of police are tripping over themselves trying to put some distance between themselves and the Reverend Roy. Never seen anything quite like it. They're all going on record to say they never *really* supported him. It's enough to make you sick. Bunch of disgusting hypocrites, worried about their own skins."

The events at Ardillas, as chilling as they were, weren't uppermost in my mind. I was gratified that the Prophet's days were numbered, but I couldn't share Don's excitement. The sight of Dorothy staggering, gasping in her own blood, would haunt me for a long time to come.

"Julia, this is big, real big," Don went on. "Major scandal, major investigation — there'll be finger pointing all over the place. The Reverend's finished in San Francisco, and anywhere else in the U.S. He has a lot to answer for."

I leaned back against my pillows and breathed a sigh of relief. "That is good news. Thanks, Don."

"Hey, you look tired. I'll leave the pizza and let you get some rest. Oh, by the way, we found the culprit." I must have looked blank. "At the newspaper. We found the guy who leaked your info. He worked, past tense, in the Accounting Department. You don't have to worry anymore. He's toast. I'll give you a call . . . do you have your cell?"

"No. It's gone. The sheriff in Ardillas loaned me one, but the police have it now."

"Well, call me as soon as you get a new

one. Come over and have dinner with us, okay? And get hold of me if you need anything at all." Don leaned over and gave me a kiss on the cheek. "I've got to do some shopping for the little guy. I promised Kathy I'd pick up a couple of things he wanted for Christmas."

I waved goodbye to Don as he left. I pulled the rolling tray closer and opened the pizza box. One slice remained. How did he do it? How did he manage to talk the whole time and still devour almost the whole box?

FORTY-SEVEN

The next morning, I walked — very carefully, I might add — down the hall to Evandra's room. She was sitting up in bed with the TV remote in her hand, channel surfing through morning talk shows, her complexion quite pink and healthy. I hoped I'd look as good in a few days. I'd had a glimpse of myself in the bathroom mirror and was horrified. My face was gray and gaunt and my eyes were bloodshot. When she spotted me standing in the doorway, she waved me over.

"Julia. How can I ever thank you? You saved us all."

"I'm so sorry, Evandra, that I didn't believe you about Dorothy." I felt close to tears.

"There, there, dear." She patted my hand. "I know you loved her. I did too, but as I told you, it happens more often than you'd think. I'm just so grateful her mother wasn't alive to see this. So grateful." She heaved a sigh. "As soon as we're all out of this place, come and visit, anytime you like. You know Richard will be staying with us, hopefully for a good long time."

"Yes, the police told me. I think they're letting me go today, but I'll stay in touch. There's one thing, though."

"What's that, dear?"

"I promised Eunice that I would talk to you about letting her keep bees. And growing some lavender bushes for them to feed on."

Evandra snorted and rolled her eyes heavenward. "If that will keep her happy, then fine. I'll arrange it for her."

"Thank you." I smiled, relieved I had kept my promise.

The doctor was waiting for me when I shuffled back to my room. He checked my vital signs and agreed to release me as long as I made sure someone was around to keep an eye on me. To tell the truth, if he hadn't let me go, I would have climbed out a window to be free. Gale and Cheryl arrived an hour later. Gale was lugging a Macy's bag with a pair of very fashionable skinny jeans, a sweater bedazzled with little gems, and a pair of boots.

"You shopped for me?"

"Sure. I didn't want to bring you home for Christmas dinner in a cotton hospital gown with a plastic bracelet on your wrist. Besides, the clothes you were wearing when they brought you in need to be burned. There's some underwear in there too."

"I'm paying you back for all this stuff."

"Like hell you are. I refuse to be repaid." Gale smiled. "Besides, I didn't have a key to your apartment."

I groaned. "My apartment. I hope I still have one."

Cheryl leaned over to give me a hug. "You won't have anything to worry about now."

Gale smiled. "She's right. Your landlady won't be bothering you anymore. Have you seen the paper?" She held up the front section of the *Chronicle*. The headlines blared across the front page: *REVEREND CHARGED WITH ABUSE. PROPHET'S PARADISE SHUT DOWN.* Underneath, the banner was a still shot of the Reverend Roy from his TV show and a photo of the barbed wire gates of the Ardillas compound.

"Don warned me this was coming."

Gale rattled the newspaper open. "And you're famous, my dear. Listen to this: 'San Francisco astrologer Julia Bonatti was instrumental in rescuing an elderly victim. Ms. Bonatti was imprisoned at the compound and shot at before she managed to escape. Once free, she enlisted the aid of Sheriff Leo McEnerny, who, with the intervention of the California Highway Patrol, shut down the Reverend's slave labor compound.' It goes on," Gale trilled.

"I don't want to be famous . . . not at all. Not like this."

"Ah, well, we can't always pick and choose." Gale's smile was brilliant. She leaned over and hugged me. I heard a catch in her voice. "I'm glad you're still here. I don't want to lose you. And the next time you go off like that, I will find you and I will kill you — myself." She sniffled and wiped her eyes as she turned away.

"I'm glad I'm still here too. And I'm so grateful I have friends like you two and Don. I don't know what I'd do without you." I was getting all sentimental and teary-eyed myself. I swung my legs over the edge of the bed. I still felt hot and dehydrated, but at least the body tremors had completely stopped.

Cheryl left to work on our dinner and Gale waited while I showered and dressed. The nurse came in with a wheelchair and I signed a pile of forms for the hospital. Gale followed us down the corridor. When we reached the front entrance, she left me in the nurse's care while she went to the parking garage to retrieve her car. When she pulled up to the carriage area, I left the wheelchair behind and, lugging a plastic bag labeled *Patient's Belongings,* climbed into her Mercedes.

Much later that day, after dinner, the three of us settled in on Gale's sofa with a bottle of wine. A floor-to-ceiling Christmas tree covered with tiny lights took up the corner of the room. Gale dimmed the lamps and poured each of us a glass of wine. The sky was crystal clear and the city sparkled below us. The new moon was here — a time for beginnings. I filled Cheryl and Gale in on the details of everything that had transpired, including the séance where Evandra was convinced Lily had sent her a warning message.

The *Chronicle* had also run a story about Dorothy's death and the attempted arson at the Gamble house. There was no hint that Dorothy was the guilty party or that she had been killed in self-defense. Under the caption was a stock photo of the Telegraph Hill house and a shot of a coroner's van next to a fire truck. That was all. The bigger story — of Reverend Roy and the Army of the Prophet — had forced this story to a back page. Either the police were being very tightlipped about the connection between Eunice's rescue and Dorothy's death or the media hadn't connected the events. I was relieved to see that my name wasn't mentioned this time.

"I'm curious, Julia," Cheryl asked. "You said that when you were lying on the grass outside the conservatory, you felt completely at peace. But you were trying to get help. Your life was at risk."

"I was in very bad shape, you're right. I was hallucinating. But I saw . . . I *felt* something brush lightly against my cheek. I could have sworn I smelled gardenias, but maybe I just imagined that."

"You can be sure gardenias aren't growing in San Francisco, especially in the winter," Gale offered. "And if you don't mind me reminding you, you were suffering from alkaloid poisoning."

I nodded. "True. But the most memorable thing was that I was filled with that sense of ease, the most deliciously safe feeling I've ever had in my life. As if everything would turn out all right."

Cheryl lifted a wine glass. "I'd like to propose a toast. To Lily."

Gale and I lifted our glasses in unison. "To Lily."

ABOUT THE AUTHOR

Connie di Marco (Los Angeles, CA) is the bestselling author of the Soup Lover's Mysteries (Penguin), which she published under the name Connie Archer. She has always been fascinated by astrology and is excited to combine her love of the stars with her love of writing mysteries. Visit her at conniedimarco.com, on Facebook at Connie di Marco (Author), or on Twitter: @askzodia.